Praise for Taft

"In *Taft,* modern variations are played on old-fashioned Shake-spearean romance: tragedy and comedy intertwine; broken families are mended; the dead are brought back to life; and what is lost is found again."

—*NEW YORK TIMES BOOK REVIEW*

"In her picture of Nickel, Patchett combines a rare sensitivity to issues of race with the unswerving knowledge that deeper than skin color is the essential soul of a good man who wants to repair the damage he has done."

—*NEW ORLEANS TIMES-PICAYUNE*

"This compassionate and deeply moving second novel by the author of *The Patron Saint of Liars* deals swiftly and intelligently with the mystery of human behavior."

—*BOOKLIST*

"*Taft* is a moving, dangerous book about love and despair and hope. Ann Patchett gives us fantastic yet believable characters that will stay alive long after the last page is turned. She is a wonderful, intelligent writer."

—JAMES WELCH, author of *Fools Crow*

BOOKS BY ANN PATCHETT

Taft

ANN PATCHETT

MARINER BOOKS
HOUGHTON MIFFLIN HARCOURT
Boston • New York

First Mariner Books edition 2011

The Library of Congress has catalogued the previous edition as follows:
Patchett, Ann.
Taft / by Ann Patchett. — 1st Perennial ed.
p.   cm.
ISBN 0-06-054076-1
1. African American musicians — Fiction. 2. Fathers and sons — Fiction.
3. Memphis (Tenn.) — Fiction. 4. Race relations — Fiction. I. Title.
PS3566.A7756 T3 2003
813'.54 — dc21   2002038738

ISBN 978-0-547-52189-3

Book design by Melissa Lotfy

Printed in the United States of America

DOC 20 19 18 17 16 15 14 13 12 11
4500800644

For Ann and Jerry Wilson
of Carthage, Tennessee

Home seemed a heaven and that we were cast out . . .

—HENRY GREEN

A GIRL WALKED into the bar. I was hunched over, trying to open a box of Dewar's without my knife. I'd bent the blade the day before prying loose an old metal ice cube tray that had frozen solid to the side of the freezer. The box was sealed up tight with strapping tape. She waited there quietly, not asking for anything, not leaning on the bar. She held her purse with two hands and stood still. I could see her sort of upside down from where I was. She was on the small side, pale and average-looking, with a big puffy winter jacket on over her dress. I watched her look around at the stuff up on the walls, black-and-white pictures of Muddy Waters and Howlin' Wolf in cracked frames, a knocked-off street sign from Elvis Presley Boulevard, the mounted head of a skinny deer. She pretended to be interested in things so she didn't have to look at anybody. Not that there was much of anybody to look at. It was February, Wednesday, four in the afternoon. The dead time of the deadest season, which is why I wasn't in any rush. The tape was making me crazy.

Before I even got the box open, Cyndi walked out of the

kitchen and headed right for her. "What can I get you?" Cyndi said. Then I straightened up because the girl in the puffy coat wasn't of a drinking age. She was eighteen, nineteen. Could've been younger. When you'd spent as much of your life in a bar as I had, you recognized those things right away. Cyndi, she knew nothing about bars other than getting drunk in them. She was just a girl herself, and girls were no judge of girls.

"Get her a Coke," I said, and headed over to them. But the girl put up her hand and I stopped walking just like that. It was a funny thing.

"I'm here about a job," she said.

Well, then I could see it. The way she was overdressed. The way she didn't seem to be meeting anybody but didn't seem like she was there to pick anybody up either. We got plenty of girls through there. We got the college girls looking to make money to pay the bills who wound up trying to read their books by the little light next to the cash register when things were slow, and then we got the other kind, older ones who liked the music and liked to pour themselves shots behind the bar. Those were the ones who walked out in the middle of their shift with some strange customer on a Friday night when the place was packed and then showed up three days later, asking could they have their job back. Those were the ones the regulars always took to.

"You over at the college?" I said, and Cyndi looked at her hard because she didn't like the college girls.

The girl nodded. A piece of her straight hair slipped out from behind her ear and she tucked it back into place.

"How old are you?" I said.

"Twenty," she said, so quickly that I figured she'd practiced saying it in front of a mirror. Twenty. Twenty. Twenty. She didn't look twenty, but I would bet money that her ID was fake.

It didn't so much matter in Tennessee. Seventeen could serve a drink as long as they kept it clear of their mouths.

"Any restaurant experience?" I looked at her hard, trying to tell her age from her face. "Ever work in a bar?" I was out of those employment forms. I made a mental note to order a box.

She nodded again. Quiet girl. "Not around here, though. I'm not from around here."

Cyndi and I stood there on the other side of the bar, waiting for her to say where she was from but she didn't. "Where?" Cyndi said.

"East," the girl said, even though that could mean anywhere from Nashville to China. East was the world if you went with it far enough. I didn't think she was trying to be difficult on purpose. The way she stood so straight and kept her voice low and respectful, it was plain that she needed the job. I liked her, though I didn't have a reason. Even when I just saw her standing there, when she put up her hand and for a second it felt like something personal. I liked this girl.

"What's your name?" I asked.

"Fay Taft," she said.

"Like the president?"

"What?"

"William Howard Taft."

"Oh, no," she said. "My father tried to trace that back once, but he didn't come up with anything. I don't think our Tafts ever met their Tafts."

"Only president ever to be chief justice on the Supreme Court." I had no idea why I knew this. Some facts stick with you for no reason.

"He was fat," she said in a sorry voice, like there could be nothing sadder than fat. "I always felt kind of bad for him."

Not very many people who come into bars can talk to you about dead presidents. I told her she had a job.

Cyndi turned on her heel as soon as I'd said it. Cyndi wanted two shifts a day, seven days a week. She wanted every tip from every table in the place. She saw no need in the world for a waitress other than herself.

"Come back tomorrow," I told Fay, not looking over my shoulder at Cyndi, who she was straining to see. "Come in before lunch. We'll get you started."

She wasn't saying a word. She looked too scared to take a deep breath.

"That okay?" I asked.

"School," she said softly, like the very word would be the end of it. No bar, no job.

"So come after class. Just be here before happy hour. That starts at five. Things get busy then."

She smiled, her face wide open with relief. For a second that little white face reminded me of Marion, even though Marion's black. This was Marion from way back, when I could read every thought that passed through her like it was typed up on her forehead. Young Fay Taft nodded, made like she might say something and then didn't. She just stood there.

"Okay, then?"

"Okay," she said, nodded again, and headed out the door. I watched her through the window as she went down the sidewalk. She took a stocking cap out of her pocket and pulled it down over her ears. The cap was striped blue and yellow and had one of those fluffy pom-pom things on the top. In it she looked so young I thought I must have made a mistake. One thing's for sure, she never would have gotten a job wearing that hat. It was gray outside and spitting a little bit of snow that wouldn't amount to anything. The girl, Fay, stopped at the corner and looked out carefully at the traffic, trying to decide when to cross. I watched too, watched until she crossed and headed up the hill and I lost sight of her skinny legs trailing out of that big jacket.

"Like we need another waitress," Cyndi called down loudly from the end of the bar.

But Cyndi hadn't been around long enough. She didn't understand about the spring, how waitresses take off for the gulf on the first warm day and leave you with nobody trained. Best to stock a few girls up when it's still cold outside, ones who look reliable enough to last you past seventy degrees.

"I'll tend to my job and you tend to yours," I said, going back to the Dewar's. Cyndi had a hell of a mouth on her. Maybe that's the way they teach girls over in Hawaii where she came from. "I'm the one that hires people."

Cyndi took up a couple of clean glasses and went back to the kitchen to wash them again, just to let me know it wasn't right.

If it was or it wasn't, I had no one to account to. It was my job. I hired people and got the boxes of scotch open. I counted up the money at two o'clock in the morning and took it to the night deposit box, every night waiting to see if somebody was hopped up enough to crack me over the head for it. I plunged the toilets when they backed up. I used to throw people out when they got drunk and started beating one another with the pool cues, but then that got to be a full-time job so I hired a bouncer, a former Memphis State linebacker named Wallace whose knees had gone bad. He worked the door on Friday and Saturday because no matter how drunk people got on a weeknight they just about never took to beating on one another. This is one of the great mysteries of the world. I was putting Wallace on behind the bar more and more during the week. He made a good mixed drink. The tourists liked him because he was coal black and huge and the sight of him scared them and thrilled them. When he wasn't

5

busy doing his job he was posing for pictures with strangers. One tourist snaps the camera while the other tourist stands next to Wallace. It tickled them to no end to have their picture taken with someone they thought looked so dangerous.

The bar I managed is called Muddy's and is on the water side of Beale down past the Orpheum Theater. It's owned by a doctor in town who holds more deeds in Memphis than anyone knows. He bought it back in the late seventies from Guy Chalfont, a bluesman we all admired. Chalfont swore the bar wasn't named for Muddy Waters or the Mississippi River, but for his dog, a filthy short-haired cur called Muddy that followed him with the kind of devotion that only a dog could muster. It seemed like all the old bluesboys sold out in the late seventies with some sad notion about going to Florida, They thought it would be better to die down there, sitting on lounge chairs near the ocean, wearing sunglasses and big Panama hats. They sold just before the real estate market broke open, a couple of years before their little clubs turned out to be worth a fortune.

The main thing I had to do to keep the job was book the bands and make sure they showed up and didn't plug all their amps into the same socket. In the winter it wasn't so hard because it was pretty much a local thing, the same people playing up and down the street on different nights. But the truth was that good blues were nearly impossible to find. Real music had packed off to Florida with the old boys. I had about decided the problem was that people didn't suffer the way they used to. I was an advocate of greater suffering for anyone who came through my club. Bands these days were always hoping to be what they called crossovers, which meant that white college kids would start buying their records, thinking they'd really tapped into something. People watered themselves down before they even got started.

They thought if their blues were too blue there'd be nobody to buy them since nobody, they figured, was interested in being that sad.

When I took this job everybody said I'd be the right man for it. I was a musician so I'd know, run the kind of club a musician would like to be in. But when I started managing I stopped playing. I forgot what all of that was about and people around town forgot I ever was a drummer. I was running a club just like everybody else who was running a club. I was the guy who passed out the money at the end of the night.

I took the job managing Muddy's at a time when things with Marion had come all the way around, from her doing everything to please me to me doing everything to please her. I said I'd stop playing and take on a regular job to show how steady I could be. I thought it was just for a while, like you always think something bad is for just a while. I figured I'd get her settled down and then I could go back to the band. I didn't take into account that I might lose my nerve, all those nights in a bar when I was watching instead of the one up there playing. I didn't imagine how that could undermine a person. Once you thought about a beat instead of playing it you were as good as dead. Nothing came naturally anymore. I could play at home when I was by myself, but as soon as somebody else was there my hands started to sweat. Then I just ditched it altogether. After Marion and Franklin were gone, long past any hope I had of them coming home, I kept my regular job as manager. It was all I knew how to do.

When Marion took our boy to Miami last year she stopped calling him Franklin and started calling him Lin, like she was in a hurry and there was no time to say his whole name. Sometimes she called him Linny, like Lenny. It was her way of saying I didn't know him anymore, that anything that had come before was no good, even his name. Sometimes I called him Frank, but Marion didn't like that one bit. If I called down there and asked to speak to Frank she'd act like she didn't know who I was talking about. No Frank here, she'd say, and make like she was going to hang up.

That was when I'd want to tell her that Lin was a pretty name for a daughter but I'd called to talk to my son. I never said that. Marion had been known to hang up on me and when I called back she didn't answer. She had a million ways of keeping me from him that had nothing to do with me and Franklin and everything to do with me and her. Marion was pissed off at me for winding up how I did, which is to say, winding up like myself.

When I pressed too hard for visits or a school year back in Memphis, she'd say that maybe Franklin isn't my son. Nowhere on paper did it say he was mine, since she was mad at me the day she delivered and left the father slot on the birth certificate blank, like maybe so many people had been down that road there was just no way of knowing. Franklin was my son. Marion was eighteen when he was born and for all her tough talk nine years later, I knew who she was then. Her face was wide open. Marion used to wait around for me while I was playing. She'd smile at me and turn her eyes away and laugh when I looked at her for too long. She wasn't screwing around and I wasn't screwing around. We were good to each other back then.

She liked me because I played drums in a band. One of the many reasons she didn't like me later on. I wasn't a centerpiece, no Max Roach, no showy genius like Buddy Rich, but I was as solid a drummer as you were going to find and everybody wanted me. I made the other people look good. That's what a good drummer does. He keeps everybody steady and paced. He shines his light at just the right time. That was me.

I was born drumming. My parents admit to that even though they were never happy about it. I was asking to hold two spoons from the time I knew how to hold one. I heard beats in everything, not just music, but traffic and barking dogs and my mother washing dishes. I heard it. That was who I was, big arms and loose wrists. Getting a set of drums just made things easier. Getting a band made them easier still. Twelve years old, I was sitting in with a bunch of high school boys. I knew, right from the start.

The band I was in when I took up with Marion was called Break Neck, now one hundred percent scattered. We played mostly in Handy Park and when we couldn't get in there we played down by the water until the cops ran us off. It was all hat passing then, decent money if you were on your own but a joke once you carved it up in six directions. By the time we were getting real jobs with real covers, we were already falling apart, changing out the bass player one week, going through three singers in a year. I left before the whole thing evaporated. I got another band and then another one. As soon as I could outplay them I was gone.

If I had to narrow myself down to one mistake I've made in my life, it would be that I didn't marry Marion as soon as I found out she was pregnant. She was eighteen and I was twenty-five. She was still pretty much under the impression that I had hung the moon. She'd gone down to the drugstore and bought herself one of those kits that tell you yes or no. You didn't have to wait around very long, not like the old days of girls going down to the doctor's office. Back then when the test came back yes, everybody would go around saying the rabbit died. But someone told me a long time later that all the rabbits died. Killing them was how they did the test. I imagine a lot of rabbit farmers went out of business when the at-home tests came on the scene.

Marion didn't say one word to me about it before she knew for sure. She was brave like that. There are a lot of things you have to give Marion credit for. When she told me, she was happy. Her face was always very pretty when she was happy. She has a high forehead that slopes back. She has big eyes and wide, flat cheeks, and a mouth that always looked like it was about a second from telling you everything but it didn't have to since it was all right there. We were sitting on the back steps of her parents' house, splitting a Coke because there was only one left. She was wearing cutoffs and a yellow halter top and she looked as good as any girl I'd ever seen. She hadn't gotten all dressed up or taken me away some place secret to tell me. There was nothing to be ashamed about. Marion's face didn't have a worry on it. It said, I love you and you love me and all of this is going to be fine.

And that was the thing that made me turn on her.

It wasn't the news itself. It was something about the way she looked at me, like she knew I would never disappoint her, that made me want to disappoint her badly. This is called being stupid and cruel. This is being twenty-five and a drummer in a band when there are plenty of pretty girls who aren't pregnant asking for your time. I had been faithful to Marion because she was right, I loved her. But I didn't need her. It was her need of me that made me turn cruel.

So what would have happened if I had acted like the people on television? Picked her up and kissed her. Set her down in an old lawn chair all nervous and put a pillow up under her feet. What if I had rested the side of my face against the yellow halter top that barely covered her stomach and just held it there for a minute. Where would we be now? Marion and I keep no secret store of love for each other, I will promise you that. Everything that was kind between us we killed with years of dedication and hard work. When I hang up the phone with her now it's hard to imagine that one tender word has ever passed between us. I find myself thinking that we must have been drunk or stoned during any minute we were happy together.

She tried to stay close to me when she was pregnant. She didn't know what else to do. I guess she wanted to be there in case I wised up. Some days I was good to her and some days I wasn't. I picked up a few other girls on the side. I started taking myself seriously, talking big. I gave her money, but I made her ask for it. I never said one word about marrying her. She was my own fat shadow, getting bigger and bigger as she trailed along behind me. Every time I made her crazy and she wanted to light into me, she bit down hard and kept quiet about it. She was trying to hold on to her old sweet self. Marion had a clear idea about what kind of girl she wanted to be, no trouble, not one who complained no matter how badly she was treated. I can see her clear as day, coming to the bar in the hot late afternoons while the new band practiced. She'd sit at a table drinking ice water with her legs stretched over two chairs. She never looked like she was listening, never said anything about the music one way or the other. She was just making the effort to put herself in front of me. She had to leave her parents' cool house after working all day and ride a crowded bus downtown, not to talk to me or be with me, but just to sit in front of me in an empty bar so I wouldn't forget she was going to have my baby.

Franklin came sooner than anyone thought he would. I was playing at the Rum Boogie. When the manager told me at break that it was Marion on the phone I didn't take the call. She didn't tell him she was having the baby and I didn't think of it, a whole month early. Later, it came out that she was standing at a pay phone in the hospital lobby, having contractions and waiting on the line because no one went back to tell her I wasn't coming. She stood there listening, waiting for me to pick up until her legs just gave out on her. That pretty much explains my name not being featured on the birth certificate.

A visit to the nursery may not be Paul's road to Damascus: I was a bad man before I saw and a good man after, but it's something like that. Children get right to the point. I've known solid men to take off straight away in the face of their sons. I've known men you'd think were bad, hustlers and junkies, who smoothed over, found something in themselves that turned them decent because now they have a baby to look after.

How did this work? When Marion, a good girl, came to me and said she was going to have my child, I said I'd call her when there was time. But when my boy Franklin came I was so crazy for him I wanted to marry her a million times over just to keep them close to me. And the second I told her so, everything changed. Now I wanted her. She could relax, collect herself and take a look around. It was then that Marion had the luxury of discovering just how completely she hated me.

Marion Woodmoore took our son and went to live with her parents after she left the hospital. Right away I began my campaign that they should come live with me. Her parents didn't want that, no surprise.

"Can't believe you're even standing in my living room," her mother said to me. "I'm going to have to vacuum for an hour just to get your smell off the carpet."

Her father stood in front of the couch with his arms crossed to make sure I didn't try to get comfortable.

"Let me talk to him a minute," Marion said to them, calling off the dogs.

"We'll be right in the kitchen if you need anything," her father said, looking at me but talking to her.

"Don't let him hold that baby," her mother said.

Once they were gone I told her to come live with me.

"Hah!" I heard from the kitchen,

"My parents hate you," Marion said. She put her little finger in the baby's mouth and let him suck on it.

"Make up your own mind," I said to her. "You're a grown woman now. You've got your own family, me and Franklin. Families ought to be together."

"So you'd think," Marion said. She looked at the door to make sure no one was watching. "You can hold him for a minute." She handed me the tight bundle of my son, not even heavy enough to be a good-sized ham.

I was holding Franklin, who was named for her father, who was named for Roosevelt, his father's all-time favorite president. I told everyone I knew that I had named him for Aretha. "See that," I said, chugging him gently up and down.

"What?" Marion pulled back the blanket to look at the baby.

"See how he's looking right at me?" I said.

Marion relented and moved in with me when Franklin was six months old. Her parents stood at the door and cried. He was a good baby by any standard; none of that colic, laughing all the time. He only cried to let you know what he needed, a bottle or a nap. I liked to take him out with me. I liked for strangers to come up and say what a good-looking boy I had. I'd take him to the bars when I could do it without Marion finding out. All the waitresses would leave their tables and the cooks came out of the kitchen. Everyone in this town has known me forever. I wanted them to know my boy.

I tried my best to make things work with Marion, to make her settle down and stay. But no matter what kind of flowers I brought home or how many times I told her I was sorry, she couldn't let things go. She moved out just before Franklin turned two, and she took him with her. It was like she couldn't stand the sight of me. Every day I was nice to her she turned on me a little more.

"That day you were playing at Raymond's," she said as soon as I walked in the door. Three in the morning and I'd been playing since nine that night. I was nearly too tired to sleep.

"Don't," I said.

"I was sitting there at the table with you, seven months along, and here comes that girl. She sat on your lap. On top of you! She wasn't that big around." She made a circle between her thumb and forefinger to show me. "You didn't even push her off. You didn't ask her to sit in a chair."

I slid down the doorframe and sat on the floor. That's how tired I was. I didn't want to get any closer to her. "I was wrong," I told her. "My head wasn't in the right place back then."

"I should have put your head in the right place," Marion said quietly. She was tearing up a paper towel in tiny bits, which is what she did when she was mad. Newspapers, napkins, Kleenex, the mail, Marion shredded them like a pack of hamsters.

"Baby," I said from way over on the other side of the room. "Why don't you and me get married? That would make all this better. Franklin needs to have married parents. Then we'll be a real family. We'll get married and put the past in the past. What do you say about that?"

But she didn't say, because by then she was crying. Marion didn't like to cry in front of people. She scooped up all the paper shreds and took them into the bedroom with her and shut the door.

Six months after she moved out she came back again, saying she decided what she wanted was to go to nursing school and she figured I owed her that. Marion had been working as the cleaning girl at a Catholic school because the hours were right, but anyone could see she was a million times too smart for that and it was bound to make her crazy. The nuns were always getting on her about how she dusted the statues, had she wiped behind their feet? Cleaned their heads? Marion said the glass eyes on the Virgin Mary chilled her. I was all for seeing her go back to school, especially if it meant them coming home. Franklin was all over the place at that age, talking in sentences, picking up everything so fast I thought he must be way above average. I wanted to see him every day, not just on the weekends. I thought if they moved back we might be able to work things out, the three of us.

"I'm talking about lots of school here. I need to take classes just so I can start taking classes. That means time and money. Regular money," Marion said. "You're going to have to find yourself a salary job."

"Band's doing fine," I said, though I knew good and well what she was talking about.

"One good night, one good week, that's not going to cut it." We were sitting at a table at Muddy's at the time, having a couple of beers. She was twenty-one years old, but she was so steeled up inside nobody would have believed that. She still looked pretty, not the same kind of pretty she was when I met her, but maybe better. She wore her hair brushed back in a tight knot now instead of fixed up and she didn't bother with makeup. The fact that she didn't smile that much anymore made her look kind of mysterious. She was sexy now, even when I knew that sex, at least where I was concerned, was about the furthest thing from her mind. She was sexy in that way that pretty women who couldn't care less can be sexy.

"So if I get a regular job, you and Franklin'll come back?"

"You help me pay for school, take care of Franklin when I'm studying," she said, and took a sip off her beer. All cards out on the table, that was Marion.

I put my hands flat against my thighs. Whatever it was, it wasn't going to be forever. I was a drummer. That was all I'd ever been. Now I was a drummer and Franklin's father. I didn't see how those two things could cancel one another out.

Marion looked at her watch. "I told Mama I'd be home to help with supper," she said, and finished off the beer. "You let me know."

"I'll let you know now," I said. "You and Franklin come on home. I'll get a regular job."

"We'll come back when you've got the job," she said.

I walked up to the bar as soon as she was out the door and talked to a fellow named Danny King, long since disappeared from Memphis. I asked him, Did he know what was out there, what had he heard? The next thing I knew I had a job at Muddy's, first booking the music and running the floor at night, then six months later the manager quits to buy a dance club and I had the whole place to myself. Easy as falling down.

Of course, it wasn't what Marion had in mind. She wanted to see me out checking phone wires for South Central Bell or selling Subarus. Jobs that took place in the light of day. But she didn't press it too hard. She knew it was the first regular job I'd had in my life and that these things took some time.

Marion went to school during the day while I watched Franklin and then she came home and took him in time for me to go to work. We didn't sleep much and we didn't much sleep together.

I'd get into bed at four and she'd never so much as roll over. By the time I woke up, she was gone.

All that time we lived together she never forgave me anything and I got plenty sick of asking her. There was a long time when I would have gone along, married her, everything, had she been able to drop the subject of my bad behavior for one minute. Then even that opportunity passed. I'd see her studying at the kitchen table and just walk right by, not even thinking about her being a breathing person in the room. I couldn't picture her at eighteen the way I used to. That was a trick I had, a way of making myself feel warmly towards her.

"Hey," she said, and shook my shoulder. "Wake up and quiz me."

"Quiz you?" The room was dark and sweet smelling. I remembered for a second that Marion wore perfume called Ombre Rose.

"Here, take the book." She clicked on the light and it hit me square in the face. I pushed up on one elbow. "I've been studying all night," she said. "I know it. I just need somebody to quiz me."

I rolled away from her and pulled a pillow over my head. "Quiz yourself."

"I'm serious," she said.

"Don't you think I'm serious?"

What time I had in the day I gave to Franklin, who deserved it. He was a ball of fire, getting into things, tearing things apart. I often thought that if I were capable of so much movement I would have been the greatest drummer that ever lived. He liked to play something I called the Name Game, which was going up to everything and identifying it, right or wrong. Potato. Chair. Wall. Door. Daddy. Table. Tree. It was a long time before I could look at anything without stopping to think about what it was called.

When Marion graduated from Memphis State I took Franklin to see her get her diploma. We sat with the Woodmoores, who had softened on me since I'd sent their daughter through nursing school. I held Franklin up on my lap and pointed her out and he said "Mommy," but she was too far away to hear. Then the three of us went home and I waited. Waited while she took her boards and found a good job at Baptist. Waited while she got three paychecks stored up in the bank. She thought I'd be so surprised when she came home saying she'd found an apartment for the two of them closer to the hospital and she'd be out by the weekend, but I'd been watching it heading towards me for years.

What surprised me though, what made me want to wring her neck once and for all, came later when she announced they were moving to Miami for no good reason.

"Better jobs down there," she said.

"You need a better job than what you have?"

"Go back in your room for a minute," she said to Franklin. "Find your blue scarf. I can't find that scarf."

Franklin went back slowly, wanting to hear what we were saying since it was him that we were fighting over. He was eight years old by then, which I found impossible, so stretched and thin you would think he was never fed. He was still too young for any sort of trouble that counted, but I knew he was moving into that time when boys needed fathers around, someone to keep them in line. Marion had done a good job with him, no one was going to argue that, but it wasn't the time to be taking off.

"Miami's too rough," I said.

"Memphis is plenty rough." She was getting ready to go in for her shift. She was wearing her white uniform. Her little white cap was sitting on the table by the front door, wrapped in a plastic bag. The white always made her look fresh, like she'd had a good night's sleep. Just putting on that dress kept Marion young.

"You got a boyfriend? Somebody you know going to Miami. Is that it?"

"I wish that was it," she said in a nasty way, as if to tell me I'd spoiled that for her, too.

Franklin reappeared, the blue scarf hanging straight down over one shoulder like a flag. "Bingo," he said.

"We're going to talk about this some more," I told his mother, and held the door open for Franklin to go on ahead of me.

"Don't worry yourself," she said. "This isn't going to happen tomorrow."

But it happened, sooner than I would have thought. We had our share of fights over it, but they always came down to Marion saying my name did not appear on the birth certificate. For all those years I'd done nothing to see that Franklin was legally mine and she could take him out of the state just for the pleasure of doing it. Other times she was kinder. She said her parents were here and sure, they'd be back plenty. I could take Franklin on vacation in the summer and come down to see him if I gave her some notice. She said it wasn't like they were falling off the face of the earth.

I never did get the real reason she was going, but I could imagine Marion just wanted to give something else a try. There she was, a few years shy of thirty and what had happened except she'd had a baby way too young and spent her whole adult life mad at a man for not being good to her when he should have been. The year before there was a nurses' convention in Chicago. The head nurse got sick at the last minute and they sent Marion in her place. That was the first time she'd been on a plane. She'd taken things as far as they were ever going to go in Memphis. If something better was going to come to her, then she'd have to be willing to leave.

. . .

It wasn't like I was so used to coming home to my son at night, but when they left for Florida I found I didn't want to be in my apartment anymore. I didn't much want to be anywhere, so I stayed at work. I built new storage shelves for the kitchen so that the extra flour and canned tomatoes could be unpacked and put away. There had always been boxes all over the place. After that the whole kitchen seemed bigger. I reorganized the bar next, and once I started I could tell it should have been done years ago. I put the things you poured the most right up front, instead of it being alphabetical, the crazy way it was before, with Amaretto and applejack being the things you always wound up grabbing. I even started listening to the demo tapes that people sent in, something that nobody in their right mind would do. I got to where I would know in the first ten seconds whether a band was going to be any good. Most of the time you could tell by how they'd written their name on the box. Most of them were so bad it made me wonder how they could have thought it was a good idea to spend the money for blank tape. Finally, I found a little blues band called Tenement House from New Orleans, a town I am suspicious of musically since they were the ones that came up with that Dixie crap. I told them they could come and play, and it turned out they were good enough to keep all week. They were popular here and everybody talked about how I'd found them, how I had the ear. I wanted to say no, it was nothing as complicated as that.

I told everybody that I was working so much because I needed the money, or I told them I stayed at work because I didn't have the money to be going out. Money was the other thing. I told them Marion was soaking me. Any man will give another man sympathy for that. When Marion went to Miami she decided she'd need to have a set amount every month, an amount that she figured up to cover things. I won't say how much. It makes me uncomfortable to talk about money and it always has. Up until Miami we never had a problem with this. I gave her what she needed. I took Franklin out for clothes and in the fall we went to Woolworth's for school supplies. I bought him binders and pencils and other things, things he maybe didn't need but just wanted, like twelve-packs of Magic Markers that smelled like different kinds of fruit. I liked it this way. I got to spend my money on him. It never seemed like too much. If someone came around to the bar telling me they knew a good deal on hams, I'd go out and buy one for Marion. I never went to her place in the summer without peaches or a basket of sugar beets. I wrote out the checks for the visits to the dentist. I bought shoes, which aren't cheap and get tossed aside six months later when they're outgrown. I saw that they had plenty. I took good care. Franklin always knew who was looking out for him. But in Miami I couldn't take him shopping. Marion wanted X dollars on the first of every month, or the fifteenth if that was better, but the same money at the same time like clockwork. I didn't want any part of it.

"He's your son," she said.

"Funny how that works. Sometimes you think he is and sometimes you're not so sure."

But I knew Marion. She could find her way without my money and without me, so I paid. I worried about that payment all the time. I was always checking to make sure I had enough to cover it. When I put it in the envelope I'd write a note to go along. *This is for half the electric bill, for class trips, for a new pair of jeans.* Something along those lines.

When I got home from work the day I hired the girl in the puffy jacket and the striped stocking cap, it was nearly three in the morning. I'd stayed open late because there were a couple of guys still drinking at the bar and I figured there was no point in throwing them out. I was in no hurry. Two minutes after I walked in the door the phone started to ring. I could only think it was bad news. When it was Marion on the other end and she was crying, I knew it as fact.

"Franklin," I said to her. "Tell me."

She took a breath. "He's okay."

"Marion, why are you crying? Settle down, tell me what you're crying about."

"He fell," she said, then started up again. "Where were you till three o'clock? I've been trying all night."

"He fell how?" I said. There was no spit in my mouth and I sat down on the edge of the bed, which I hadn't made once since Marion left.

"Where were you?"

"Work," I said, trying not to be short with her. She wouldn't call me at the bar. Not if a life depended on it. "Fell how?"

"At the beach. He was running with some boys. They pushed him or he fell, I don't know. He fell on some glass, a piece of Coke bottle he says. It cut his face. The side of his face." She was crying. "It was by his eye, but it didn't cut his eye."

I looked at the carpet, a bad orange and brown shag left over from the seventies. I should have found a day job, something regular, found a nicer place to live. "Where is he now?" I said, thinking maybe in the hospital.

"Right here, asleep. He's fine now. It just scared me to death is all. Then you weren't home. When I got the call I thought he was dead at first."

"Stop that."

"Everything's fine, but I thought—I didn't want to call my parents. I didn't know who to call."

"You call me," I said. Was there a bandage around his head? Was it only taped up over the cut? Did the white from the tape

22

make his skin look warm and rested up the way his mother's uniform made her look?

"Don't fight me about this," she said, tired.

"Who were the boys? Who was he with?"

"Boys from around here. There're boys everywhere. He has friends from school. They play."

"Are they rough kids? Do you know them?" I wanted to blame her, but only because I felt too far away. I wanted to go into his room and see him sleep. Miami was drugs and guns and gangs, packs of half-starved refugees who'd kill a boy like mine for the sneakers he was wearing.

"Some of them," she said, "but there's no sense in wondering. It's nobody's fault, unless it's my fault."

"You shouldn't have taken him so far away," I said.

"I need some sleep," she said. "I have to work tomorrow."

I started to ask her if she'd heard me, but she hung up.

I sat there with the phone in my hands, not able to put it down in case I thought of another question. I didn't know what things were coming to, how things had gotten so far away from me. This wasn't terrible. A cut near the eye was not a lost eye. I lay back on the bed and closed my eyes, touching the side of my face where I imagined the cut would be. I hadn't asked her if it was on the left side or the right. I saw my son's head. It was oval-shaped. His hair was as short as it could be and still be hair, but it wasn't shaved off on the sides and the back. There were no lines shaved into this boy's head, no thin braid at the nape of his neck. His skin was darker than mine or Marion's. It was not an inky black, a blue black. It was a warm color, brown black. His eyes were lighter than his skin. I thought about the shape of his eyes. I thought about his mouth, which was wide and bright. I thought of every tooth that mouth contained, every one of them straight and hard and white as chalk the way new teeth are. The phone began to make that awful sound phones make when they're off the hook and no one is at the other end. It startled me, and then I hung it up.

I thought about Franklin's face so hard I gave myself a headache. I wanted to know what happened. I wanted to know all of it. I pictured the day hot, even for this time of year in Miami. From a distance I could make out some shapes and then make out that they were boys. They were coming from every direction. The boys gathered up together like some sort of dust storm moving down the street. Haitian boys, West Indian boys, lighter Latino boys with black silky hair. They wear red tank tops, T-shirts that say Batman or Desert Storm. They are barefoot, in tennis shoes and flip-flops as they run down the street laughing. Boys picking up boys like dogs packing together. Then all of a sudden Franklin is with them. He's not wearing a shirt. He's wearing some shorts that are so big they cover his knees. They are electric blue. He is hollering with the boys and I can't hear what he's saying. They're on their way to the beach, which isn't far. They cut through the traffic, not waiting for anything, cut across the parking lot, weaving in and out between the cars, trying to hide and scare one another. They make their way down to the sand and across the sand to the water. They run back and forth with the waves, trying to keep their feet dry, acting crazy. One boy gets in the water and pretends to drown. He cries for help in a foot of water and the pack goes in to save him, but he struggles because everybody knows a drowning man will fight off the person who is trying to save him. Franklin reaches down to him, but when he does the drowning boy slings out his arm and catches Franklin hard on the side of the face. Franklin, hit, falls back into the water. Now the game changes without anyone saying anything about it. It is to drown someone instead of to pretend you're drowning. All at once they reach out to catch Franklin's arms

24

and pull him under. Franklin gets the change in the program just as fast as they do. There are so many boys, eight counting Franklin, and they get all tangled up together. One boy pushes him under by the neck and he shuts his eyes tight against the salt water. The water fills up his nose and ears and blocks out the sound of the voices. Franklin is terrified, scared like an animal. He kicks up out of the water with everything he's got and his foot makes contact with something and for a second he is let go. He takes that second to make his break. In the water he is slick and he slips between them. He digs his heels in the wet sand and takes off running, twice as fast as before, and the boys run after, screaming. He's pretty far away, past the empty lifeguard chair, halfway to the parking lot, when he takes a look behind him for one quick second, loses his balance, and goes straight down into the hot, soft sand. The broken bottom of a 7UP bottle, a flat disk of green glass with a quarter inch of jagged edge, cuts a half circle on the side of his face near his left eye. When he raises his face out of the sand he doesn't know he's bleeding. The sight of the blood stops the wild boys dead and turns them all back into regular boys again. Just like that. They forget that things had gotten out of hand or that Franklin is the one they were chasing, and Franklin forgets too, as soon as he touches his hand to his face because there is something, not water, dripping into his eye.

I had such a wave of sickness come over me that I thought I was going to throw up, but by the time I walked into the bathroom it had calmed some and I poured myself a glass of water from the tap and went back to the bed. Four in the morning. I held my eyes open to keep from seeing the part where he was falling.

Then for no reason at all I thought of that girl Fay. I didn't know where she lived. I didn't have her phone number so I could call her and tell her that she couldn't have the job, if I was to decide not to give it to her. I couldn't call to find out if she was okay if I was to go in tomorrow and not find her. It wasn't that I wanted to think about her, but by seeing her face I could make myself not see Franklin's, so I thought about her. I could barely fix her in my mind, the thin skin on her temples, the red that the cold put on her cheeks. I couldn't remember the color of her eyes or if her straight hair that wasn't blond or brown was cut into bangs the way so many girls her age like to wear their hair these days. I wondered where in the east she came from. I wondered who was looking out for her. Who made her that ugly hat. I remembered how careful she was when it came time for her to cross the street and it made me feel comforted. Someone taught her what to watch for. But then, they didn't teach her well enough if she was wandering down to Beale looking for work in bars. There was no watching them every minute, Marion. We can't be everywhere. What are you going to do but teach them to look?

It was very much like a hangover, but the dry, luckless kind that didn't follow any wild night of drinking. It was a hangover from not sleeping, from worrying about a cut near the eye but not in the eye, which led to bigger worries I didn't have names for. I lay on top of the covers all night with my clothes on until the room got slowly lighter. I stayed in bed, watching the clock while people went to work and came home for lunch and the woman in the apartment next door turned her soap opera on, which was always my sign that it was time to get up. Before long I was thinking I should head back to the bar. I stood in front of the bathroom mirror and wondered if I should take a shower and change. It didn't much seem like a next day, but I decided to clean up all the same, more in hopes it would make me feel better than any notion about what I ought to do. By this time I was feeling doubly bad, bad about Franklin and bad about not having slept. It wasn't so many years before that I could stay up for nights on end and then fall into a dead sleep on some strange sofa in some strange living room. I would have stayed at home, let things at work take care of themselves, if I thought for a minute that I'd have any better luck sleeping.

Muddy's opened for business a little before noon every day, but I rarely saw the place then. The day manager was a man named Eugene, who went and got the money out of the bank and put it in the cash register. He took the chairs off the tabletops and put them on the floor and served lunch with his own set of waitresses. The deal was that we would switch off, nights and days, but it turned out Eugene didn't like staying up. When I started coming in earlier, he started leaving earlier, until we developed the fine art of always missing each other, until I stopped thinking about him altogether.

So when I came into the bar it was more or less running itself, which it seemed to do just fine. If you felt like you had a hangover to begin with, a bar was as good a place to be as any. The few people who were there at two o'clock looked about like me. They weren't making any noise. They were finally getting around to coffee and maybe a quiet shot beside it. They kept their eyes down, not because they were shamed that here it was, only Thursday but because they felt like keeping things private. I turned the music off, and then went to sit at the kitchen end of the bar, having a coffee myself, not pretending to read the newspaper in front of me. I was working hard to not think about anything.

Cyndi was no fool, or if she was she at least knew when to stay out of somebody's way. She swept up the floor without my having to tell her and when she filled my coffee cup she didn't look at me directly. She acted like she was a waitress and I was any customer who'd come through, and that made me think she knew how to do her job. Cyndi was in the bar more than anybody else except me. She started working off the clock, just for tips, when

I told her I wouldn't pay overtime. At first I thought she must need the money like crazy, but it had to be more than that. She was trying to keep busy. As I watched her wipe down the bar, it occurred to me that I saw more of Cyndi than I did any other person. I saw her more than any woman I ever slept with, more than my son, and what worried me was that maybe she saw me more than anybody too. On top of everything else I started worrying about Cyndi.

"The hell with this," I said, and pushed off of my stool.

"What?" Cyndi said.

"I'm going out."

"Sure," she said, nodding a little.

"You think you can manage things all right while I'm gone," I said, not as a question, more to be ugly since I was suddenly feeling sentimental.

"I expect so." She looked at me with a limited amount of patience, tapping a pencil against the bar. I took my jacket off the hook next to the door and hurried out into the cold before I said anything else.

What I wanted was a drink and one of the few rules I had in the world was not to drink in the bar you worked in. This came years ago, when I was still playing and the house was always more than willing to stand you a tab that would wind up coming out of your pay. After two sets it was perfectly possible for a man to have drunk up his split of the whole night's work without even knowing it; pretty girls coming up to the stage with trays of drinks, always Jack Daniel's or something other than well to make the money go faster. Some nights I just broke even. I knew plenty of guys who were handed a bill by the time it was all over. It was always best to take your business where they weren't naturally inclined to cheat you. I decided not to change my ways even when I was the one running things. It wasn't good to drink in front of the people who worked for you. It was no good coming to think of that long, lit-up bar as your personal liquor cabinet. Never pour yourself a drink from the working side of a bar, that was a safe rule of thumb.

There was not one kind word to be said about Memphis that day. The pavement was the color of the sky, which was the color of the grass, which was the color of the Mississippi. It was all the same, no matter which way you were looking. The wetness in the air that made it painful to breathe some days in August was still there in February, but it was bitter now and it got up underneath your shirt and froze next to your skin.

Up on the corner was a boy named Eddie who was doing flips even though there was nobody around. In the summer and on some winter weekends when it turned warm, Eddie could have the street so packed the cops had to move through and break things up for traffic. He must have been eight, nine even, though that's hard to believe. He was a little guy, small as Franklin was at six. He made his living and his father's living by doing back-flips and walkovers and all sorts of no-hand things that involved him tossing himself up in the air so fast and so often that I got sick to my stomach just watching him. There were plenty of little boys who tumbled to make money off of crowds, but none of them could stand with Eddie. He was something of a little genius when it came to making people hold their breath.

"Hey there, Eddie," I said as I walked up towards him. "What're you doing out here in the cold? Get yourself inside, son. There's nobody coming down here." I saw his father tucked just inside the doorway of a bank. He wasn't much older than me, but he looked hard hit. He was sitting in an aluminum lawn chair with strips of green fabric crisscrossed to make a seat and back. I nodded to him and he made a little movement with his head that didn't count for anything.

"Give me a buck and I'll go inside," Eddie said.

"You've got more money than God," I told him. "You've got enough to buy Vegas three times. I've seen what sort of hat you're passing."

Eddie smiled a little. At heart, there was something shy about him, despite his talk. I reached into my pocket and peeled off two dollars. He took the money and threw himself up and backwards and down. His feet went all the way over his head and then landed in the precise same spot he started from. It bothered me because I'd given him that money so he wouldn't jump, so I wouldn't have to worry about him missing his mark and cracking his head all over the sidewalk. The way I saw it there were two types of people who gave Eddie money: those who did it to make him start and those who did it to make him stop.

"Two o'clock in the afternoon," I said, and leaned in to show his father my watch. "That's when boys are in school."

His father stood up slowly and folded his chair. As soon as he was up Eddie moved on ahead of him and together, but not together, they headed up the hill in the general direction of the Peabody.

I got myself out of the cold and took my seat at the bar of the Rum Boogie Cafe. I was thinking about catching up with them and taking Eddie's father by the throat, stretching his head off his neck an extra inch or so and slamming him hard into something brick. Stupid bastard. I closed my eyes and savored the feeling of real violence. It was something I'd given up a long time ago. There were still plain fist-fights when I was young. Now everybody over the age of ten seemed to be in possession of a gun. You

31

couldn't hit a guy the way you used to because you never knew what he might have waiting for you in his back pocket. Not that those fistfights alone didn't kill plenty of people, but at least then there was a chance. You give somebody a gun and there isn't a whole lot of chance to it anymore. I thought about it until the subject started to turn my stomach. I was ready for a drink.

The bartender appeared from the other side of the world and was no one I knew. He was a college white boy. Big bulky arms and a square face, the kind that college girls liked. It was a mean kind of face. My never having seen him before could only mean he was new.

He put a cocktail napkin on the bar in front of me with a little bit of a slap and he just looked at me, not angry and not friendly. There was no wasting time with "What'll it be, buddy?" and maybe that was fine. He and I both knew why I'd come. What I couldn't figure was what he was in such a hurry about. The bar was dead. This one, the one I left, these bars were sleeping babies.

I ordered my drink with water on account of the hour. When he told me what it would be (and it was a quarter more than the same drink costs you down the street), I told the college boy I'd run a tab. That didn't suit him. He said they didn't run tabs. He made the mistake of thinking that just because he was new, I was new too. I reached into my wallet and paid him, even told him he could keep the healthy tip. I didn't give him the news, that I have a very long memory and one day he'd be looking for a job. The memory I inherited from Marion. You don't spend all those years with a woman without learning something.

"You slumming?" said a voice behind me. I turned around and there stood a woman I knew perfectly well. She came into Muddy's all the time. I'd shot pool with her. I'd stood her a drink when she was low. Goddamned if I could think of her name, I guess my memory didn't extend to the names of women.

"Man's got to get out of the house every now and then." I tilted my drink towards her some and she gave the smallest nod of her head. "Again," I said to college boy, who believed that all blacks in Memphis knew one another and now was just that much surer. She backed onto a barstool, leaving one high-heeled foot on the floor. It gave her an uncomfortable look, like she might be taking off any second. College boy put her drink down and had the good sense not to mention that I should pay for it right away.

"I didn't know you ever left Muddy's," she said. "I heard tell you had a cot set up in the back." She was all smiles, this one, shiny teeth, shiny lipstick. I wondered what she was so cheerful about in the middle of the day.

"Ugly rumors," I said. "And I thought you had some loyalty. I didn't know this was where my good customers went."

"Following you," she said. And right there I heard everything I needed to know. Her intentions were so clear that there hardly seemed to be any point in going through with the drinks, sitting there on our stools making bad conversation. It was as good as over. We'd had our drinks and left, done it and gotten up. I had driven her back to where her car was parked. It had to be around there somewhere. As much as I was pleased, I felt tired, the way you will when you've seen it through to the end the minute it starts.

I tried to think of something I could ask her that would stretch the time out a little. I couldn't ask her what she was doing in a bar in the middle of the day since I was there too. I couldn't ask her what she did for work, or God help me, what her name was, because there was no doubt she had told me before.

"That's a pretty ring," I said, pointing to a little band of diamonds and some blue stones around her finger. She had nice hands, nice nails. I liked that.

"Wedding ring," she said, and took a sip off the drink I'd bought her.

I nodded slowly and she put that same pretty hand on my thigh, just midway up, and left it there.

I paid off college boy and helped this woman on with her jacket. We walked out onto Beale Street not long after three o'clock on one of the uglier days in memory.

Of course there had been women. But truly, things had been screwed up on account of my spending so much time going after somebody I wound up not loving who wound up not loving me. I knew the same thing had happened to Marion. We were careful not to get too mixed up in anything else in case we got it all worked out. Or maybe we were tired. The kind of love I'd had in my life was very much the kind I was getting ready for that afternoon. She was quiet and didn't ask where we were going. She took a pale green box of cigarettes out of her purse and cracked the car window before she lit one, which was thoughtful even though I wouldn't have minded if she hadn't. I went Elvis Presley Boulevard instead of the interstate just to slow things down a little. I didn't live but about two miles past Graceland, but I took pride in the fact that I'd never been there.

"This is it," I said when we got inside. My apartment stayed clean because I was never there, so I didn't have to worry about bringing a guest home. Every time I walked in it reminded me of some motel room in some city years ago where I'd come with a band.

"You got a kid?" she said, picking up the picture of Franklin on top of the television. "I didn't know that. He looks like you."

I took the picture out of her hand and looked at it for a minute, trying to see if what she said was true. Then I put it back on the little strip of TV that wasn't dusty and I kissed her, as sweetly and kindly as I was able. I didn't feel like talking, especially about Franklin. I wanted to make her feel like I was too overwhelmed with her to say anything.

She was maybe skinnier than I would have liked. After it was done she just stayed on top of me, taking shallow little breaths, and I could see a dark shadow under each of her ribs. I brushed her back with the flat of my hand and she pressed her face into the side of my neck and I wondered why it was that such a thing could make a person feel lonely. You would think two people on top of each other couldn't feel this way for love or money.

"I like you," she said.

"Yeah?"

She nodded. I felt it against my neck. "I've always liked you."

She was good about getting dressed. She understood I had to get back to work and, clearly, she had someplace to be herself. I drove her back into town. She told me where her car was and I managed to get a spot right next to it. When I started to get out to open her door she put her hand on my sleeve and I thought, Here it comes.

"Don't worry about it," she said in a kind way. "I can get there just fine."

"You'll be coming back down to the bar," I said.

She nodded. "Sure, sure. Nothing changes."

I gave her a kiss. Nice woman, had her head together, kept things straight. She opened the door and had one foot out, but then she turned around and looked at me.

"What?" I said.

"Nothing," she said, but she didn't go anywhere.

Maybe for a half a second I was flustered, but then I caught myself. I leaned over and kissed her and she kissed me back.

"Okay," she said, and picked up her purse from the floor. She was hoping there was going to be something more, something better, and at that moment she'd figured out that she wasn't going to get it. "Okay."

I stayed and watched her get inside her car and drive away. It was all spoiled now. She was sad when she left and that ruins everything. I felt the weight of every name Marion had ever called me. I was that man.

I was going to head straight back to the bar, but I got out of the car instead and walked down the steep hill to the river. There was no point to it, but there hadn't been any point in anything I'd done so far. The Mississippi was better-looking on a day like this than it was in the summer. For one thing, the cold kept it from really smelling the way it will, and for another the general lack of light made the water look a nearly blue shade of gray instead of the regular brown. All along this stretch the paddleboats were docked, party boats made up to look like fancy cakes that take the tourists down to nowhere, turn around and bring them back. It was better in the winter. People didn't like to come down to the water when it was cold. They kept their power boats locked up in rented garages. It just looked like a river now, with plenty of room for working barges to get through. Marion didn't like me taking Franklin anywhere near the Mississippi. She thought it was nothing more than a flowing child killer. But Franklin liked it. I'd bring him here on the days we came down to the bar, so he was already swearing not to tell about all sorts of things anyway. Boys like rivers and bars. Boys always like the Mississippi. When he was little I used to tell him it was his river, the river Frank, and he believed me. Kids have no idea what it means to own something at that age. I would say that it was good of him, letting all those boats on his river, and he'd nod his head. Even later, when he'd caught on to things, he would still call it the river Frank.

I stayed long enough to get good and cold and half get the woman out of my mind. Then I headed back and drove my car into the alley behind the bar. Almost five o'clock and not a thing had been done all day.

Inside, the girl in the puffy jacket was sitting on a barstool drinking a Coke. She didn't have her hat on, but I could see the top of the pom-pom sticking out of her pocket. I had forgotten about her altogether, even though I'd spent half the night thinking of her. And even though it hadn't been what you'd call a redeeming day, it warmed me to see her sitting there. The way her face looked when she saw it was me, all bright and relieved, it warmed me.

"You're the new waitress," I said, like I wasn't sure.

"Fay," she said.

"Fay. Right. And you've been sitting here all this time waiting on me."

"You didn't say when I should come in. You just said before happy hour was all. I wasn't sure."

Her face wasn't exactly as I had fixed it in my mind. It was paler in real life and not quite as fine. I wanted to ask her again how old she was, now that I'd seen her in her stocking cap, but I didn't figure she'd tell me the truth.

"Did Cyndi show you around?"

The girl shook her head.

"Cyndi," I called down to the end of the bar. "Didn't you show her anything for Christ's sake?"

"Show who?" she said, not getting up from her barstool. She held my gaze dead on and then went back to reading a magazine.

"She's not from around here," I said to the girl in the jacket. "She just has an ugly mouth on her. She won't give you any trouble."

"I'm not from around here either," she said. "I behave just fine."

I nodded. She had a point if you thought about it that way. "You said yesterday you were from out of town." I didn't want to seem like I had too much time on my hands, that nobody around here worked, but like I said, it was our quiet time of the year. I sat down on the stool next to hers, which I meant to be the sign that I wanted to hear the rest of it, but she didn't catch that. "Where're you from?"

"East Tennessee," she said. "Coalfield, outside of Oak Ridge. Nobody would know Coalfield."

I could see it then. She had a kind of hillbilly look. The straight hair that was trying to be brown but wasn't really, the pale, pale skin that you could nearly see through. I shook my head. "Nope."

"That's why I say east. Nobody in Memphis has ever been to east Tennessee before."

I told her I had. Knoxville, Oak Ridge, Jefferson City. That was one ambitious band I had been in for a while. We thought touring was going to be our answer. It was a long time ago.

"Well," she said quietly, "you're the first one, then."

As a state, Tennessee was nearly as screwed up as Texas, in that a man's allegiance wasn't to the whole state, just that little part he came from. People got stuck in the mountains. But in Memphis there's a river running through the middle of things. It takes people out, brings other ones in. That's why mountain people keep to themselves and delta people make love in alleyways. That's why there were boys like Eddie doing flips out in the street. In Memphis people pay money to see Eddie, but if he tried it in Oak Ridge I imagine they'd bundle him up and take him inside. When Memphis people went east they were likely to be run out of town. They got loud drunk. They slept with women they didn't intend to marry. But you put somebody from the east down in Memphis, it wasn't likely that anyone would notice.

"So how'd you manage to come out here?" I said. I thought it was a fair question, seeing as how she so clearly would prefer to be home.

"Accident," she said, and then folded her lips into her mouth and bit them in a dreamy way.

I showed her around the place. I showed her whatever came to mind. I told her things she wouldn't have to know. I took her back behind the bar even though she'd probably never pour drinks. I showed her where the fuse box was, where we kept the bags of syrup for the Coke machine. I showed her the big cans of nuts and the five-gallon jars of maraschino cherries, which she seemed especially to like. I took the lid off and gave her a few and she chewed on them slowly while I talked. We went through the swinging doors into the kitchen.

"Bring the plates back here," I said. "Put the glasses in the rack. You run it through the washer yourself if there's nobody back here. Mr. Tipton washes dishes on weekends and during the week in the summer."

She nodded, listening, taking it in. It wasn't so much to remember. It was just that she seemed intent on not having to ask me anything. The more I watched her, the more I started to think this girl had never had a job before. But what were you going to do? Call the references, see where she's been? Leave that for the FBI. Besides, I didn't have any of those forms when she came in. I figured anybody who paid that much attention to what I was saying about where to stack dishes was going to be a good worker.

It was her face, though, more than the lack of jobs, that troubled me. It was a tricky face as far as age was concerned. One minute I thought she was twenty, but when I caught her from another angle she had high school written all over her. There's nothing illegal about it, as long as she's not drinking. I knew for sure she was at least seventeen.

I was showing her where the aprons were when the back door opened up and Rose came in. Rose was the cook, and for as long as she'd worked at Muddy's the only time I'd seen her go in or out the front door was the day I hired her. She went out back to the alley to smoke her cigarettes. Rose thought that nobody knew she smoked, though it didn't make any sense since nobody would have cared.

"Rose, this is Fay. Fay's going to be waiting tables."

Fay stuck out her hand. It was so little, short nails and no rings. Rose gave a bit of a start, but she shook and said hello.

"Rose is always trying to turn us into a real restaurant," I said to both of them. "She's always slipping something fancy on the menu."

Rose shrugged. Then the three of us sort of looked at each other and I thought what a nightmare it would be to serve out your life with two such quiet women.

"Well, I'll take her back out front," I said. "Let you work." But Rose had already wandered off towards the walk-in. I doubted she'd even heard me.

"She's not from around here either," I said to Fay when we were out of the kitchen, thinking that it might make her feel more at home. I didn't know where Rose was from. She told me she'd worked in a boarding school in the north, that she knew how to make a lot of things for a lot of people, but I never checked that one out either.

The crowd was picking up a little for happy hour and I needed to get behind the bar. I turned Fay over to Cyndi, who was none too pleased.

"Let her follow you around, watch you some."

Fay followed Cyndi at a careful distance, just close enough to hear what was being said over the music, which I had finally remembered to turn back on. Later, when Cyndi gave Fay a table of her own, it was two women together, the kiss of death for tips for sweet-faced girls.

"A beer," Fay said to me from the bar. "A strawberry margarita."

"What kind of beer?" I said, and off she went to ask. Most of the mistakes she only made once. She was fine.

When things settled down I told Cyndi to pour the drinks and I went back to the office, figuring Marion would be home from work by now. I wanted to see how Franklin was feeling, make sure there hadn't been any complications. My office used to be a storage closet, but it was deep and there was a little window, which seemed lucky to me. It was back through the kitchen and up three stairs, far enough away from the noise for me to sound almost like I was calling from home.

"Hello?" Franklin said.

"Franklin?" I said, and sat up, surprised by his voice. "Frank, it's me. Hey, how's your eye there, son? You were asleep already when I talked to your mother last night or else I would have had her put you on. Is it doing all right?"

"Fine, I guess," he said. "It's a little sore, but not really. Mom makes me take the aspirin whether I want to or not."

"That's good," I said. "Listen to her. She knows what she's talking about. Did you go to school?"

"Oh, sure. It's not so bad. I got seventeen stitches."

I thought about the needle and the eye. I thought about it seventeen times. "Did it hurt?"

"The shot hurt," he said, his voice getting excited, "but then you can't feel anything on the whole side of your head. You can see the needle coming down and you know it's going in and out but you can't feel it."

Jesus. "Was the doctor nice?"

"He's somebody mom works with. He's okay. He says the scar won't be too bad since he took so many stitches."

"You're not running around with rough boys, are you?"

"No, sir."

"You've got to look out for yourself, you hear me?"

He told me stories about two boys he knew, Kevin and Jamal. He told me they made good grades in school, and that Jamal had a dog and that they took the dog out for walks in the afternoon. He was trying to soothe me. I knew that. I was surprised how clearly he would know what I wanted to hear. He was trying to make me worry less by explaining that Miami was the city of good boys.

"You want to talk to Mom?"

I didn't. I'd talked to Marion plenty. "Not tonight."

"Oh," he said. I could hear a little disappointment in his voice. He always thought his mother and I were getting back together, which made sense, seeing how many times we had. I told him good night. I told him I loved him. When I hung up I noticed how loudly the light buzzed and I wondered if there wasn't some way to fix it.

I didn't like to talk to Franklin from the bar because after I never felt like going back down again. Sometimes I'd find ways to stay up there for hours, shuffling papers and filling out orders. There were things to do. Cyndi would be waiting for me when I came down. She'd say I was hiding. That was what I was doing. I opened up the desk drawer and tried to find the form to get more of those employment applications. That way I wouldn't have to worry in the future about how old my waitresses were. The desk had one huge drawer where everything seemed to wind up, deposit slips and the night deposit bags, pens and rubber bands and boxes of staples and a snub-nosed .38 revolver. The gun had come with the desk. It belonged to the doctor who owned the bar. Belonged to him in that he paid for it, not that I thought for a minute it was registered to him. It was his idea of installing a security system, to leave a gun in the manager's desk. All I did was move it from side to side like the scissors and the telephone book when I was trying to find something in the drawer. Sometimes, if a night seemed especially rough, I would take it out and set it on top of the desk while I counted up the money. Then it made me think of a dog, a big black dog who sat by the door and showed its teeth.

I spent a good half hour looking for things that weren't there and then I figured I should go back downstairs and make sure nobody'd set the place on fire.

"That girl looks too young to be working," Rose said to me when I was walking through the kitchen.

"Do you think?"

She nodded. Her apron was as clean as when she put it on in the afternoon. I wondered if she even bothered changing them each day.

"Well, I asked her. She said she was twenty."

"She's no twenty," Rose said. "She may not be sixteen, but she's no twenty."

"She's doing a good enough job for her first day. I guess I might as well give her a chance." I was counting on Rose to say I should let Fay go for her own good, but she didn't.

"She maybe needs the work," she said. She looked at me like she does when she's finished talking. Rose wasn't very good at getting in and out of conversations. She just seemed to start and stop whenever she felt like it. I never knew what I was supposed to say. I went all the way to the door thinking she was going to tell me something else, but she didn't.

In the winter we put out trays of hot snacks over Sterno cans to draw the customers in for happy hour, but that meant they all filled up on chicken wings for dinner and by the time seven o'clock rolled around and the drinks went back to full price, everybody cleared out, happy and well fed. The tables looked like chicken graveyards. Little bones everywhere. Cyndi was back at her magazine, looking up every now and then to see if any of the stragglers needed anything. Fay was at the bar, talking to a skinny boy who was leaning hard against a chair. The boy was stoned rather than drunk, you could tell that from his eyes. The way they were standing, bending towards each other, whispering, the way she reached in to turn the collar of his jacket out, I figured it was her boyfriend, though she didn't look like the kind of girl who would have him for a boyfriend. None of my business. It wasn't until I was all the way down near their edge of the bar that I saw how much they favored, the shape of their faces, their eyes. Fay looked up and gave me a pretty smile. "This is my brother," she said, and put her hand on his arm. "This is Carl."

I introduced myself and shook his hand, which was so cold to the touch that it gave me a start.

"Cold outside?" I said.

He looked a little embarrassed and made his hands into a cup, then blew inside. "Getting that way."

"Get your brother a cup of coffee," I said to Fay, but she didn't go anywhere. She just stared at me. I was beginning to see a pattern here. She just stared until you came up with the answer she was looking for. "Unless you'd rather go on home. There's nobody around. Go on home if you want."

"That would be okay?" she said.

I told them to go on and she said how glad she was for the job and thanked me for being nice to her. "I hope I didn't mess up too much," she said.

"You were fine."

"I can come back tomorrow then?"

She wasn't even sure she had a job. "Same time," I said.

Carl didn't look as good once he let go of the chair, so they linked arms on their way to the door, like sweethearts. Whether he was older or younger than her, I couldn't be sure. Kids were ageless to me. She waited until they were just outside the double glass doors to take her hat out of her pocket and pull it down tight over her ears. It made me look away, though I don't know why.

IF FRANKLIN came home, I'd take time off. I'd be off for as long as he could stay, since the way I saw it I had about a year built up in overtime. Cyndi could run things okay. I could check in, unless Franklin and I decided to go over to the Ozarks to go fishing. Not that I knew anything about fishing, but I didn't see how it could be so hard. The time was going to come when I would be away from the bar, simple as that. I'd been thinking about putting Wallace on more anyway, and Fay, it hadn't been a week and already she was getting things down. She was smart, that one, and all the customers liked her because she had a sweet way. Mr. Tipton, the dishwasher, called her Little House on the Prairie. "I want Little House on the Prairie to bring me my iced tea," he said to me. "She knows how to fix it. Not like that Cyndi. She always remembers how many sugars I like."

Of course, hiring Fay turned out to be more like hiring Fay and Carl. He showed up every night towards the end of her shift to pick her up and take her home, but it was no accident that he always got there too early. Not that anyone minded him. He took a little table near the kitchen that nobody ever sat at and did his best to keep to himself. If anyone had the time, Carl was always happy to spend it with them, but he never kept you there forever. He liked to make comments on the weather or the size of the crowd. He was always polite. He drank coffee that he paid for, even when I told him he didn't have to. He liked to make himself useful. When Cyndi dropped a glass he was right there with the dustpan and broom without anyone having to ask, and one night, a Thursday when we got busy for no reason, he went back and washed dishes for a couple of hours. He was tickled with the money I gave him. "I'd do it for free," he said. "I take up space here all the time." I put ten dollars in his shirt pocket and he went right back into the kitchen to tell Rose, who I guess he'd made friends with while he was washing. He got on with every-body. That's the kind of kid he was, no enemies. He liked to talk to me about music, not that I ever told him I played. He said that before Fay got the job, he'd never even heard of James Brown.

"Back where I come from," he said to me, "all they sing about is Jesus. You'd be amazed at all the different ways there are to sing about Jesus."

As far as the drugs were concerned, some nights Carl was messed up and some nights he wasn't. I could tell, having spent my life in bars, in Memphis, with musicians. I had plenty of rea-sons to know about these things. I appreciated the fact that he was careful not to make his condition known. Nights he wasn't straight he showed up later and sat quietly at his table, keeping his eyes down, waiting for Fay to get ready to go. As far as I could tell he was still playing the field, he didn't have a drug of choice. Some nights it was harder for him to keep quiet than others, but he did it. I used to watch him, trying to figure out what was mak-ing his heart beat. The more I saw of him, the more he reminded me of Fay, the way he sat, how he held his back straight, the way his voice went up towards the end of a sentence. Fay was hard-working, nervous, always looking to please. Carl moved slow, stayed quiet, was always looking to please.

"You don't mind him?" Fay asked me, her hands full of dirty glasses she was unloading on the bar.

"Carl? No, he's fine."

She looked relieved. At first I wondered if she'd caught on about his problems, but I didn't think so. Girls like Fay, such things never crossed their minds. "He doesn't know a lot of people. At the house" — she stopped and tried to find a way to put it — "he isn't so comfortable where we live. But he likes it here."

"Maybe he should find a job," I said, not meaning that he was a deadbeat, but that it might give him something to do.

"Oh, he's got a job," he said. "He works in our uncle's drugstore after school."

"High school?"

She looked uneasy then. She ran her finger around the edge of her tray. "Yeah," she said.

There were stupid people looking after these children. Whoever let this boy in a drugstore had no idea of his nature. Then Fay put her hand around my wrist, around the cuff of my shirt. She held it tight and what surprised me more than anything was my first thought, which was, I wish it wasn't winter here. "Tell me again that you don't mind him," she said.

"I don't."

She took her hand away and she smiled at me. "He's a real good kid," she said.

Carl and Fay were the brother and sister in the fairy stories, the pretty white babies holding hands in the forest. Everything in the world was waiting to eat them up. This was not the job I was meant for, looking after other people's children, not when mine was in Miami. I thought that there was maybe one more year that I'd be able to get to Franklin, and then he'd change so much and I'd be so far away we'd wind up not knowing each other at all. Then maybe he'd be coming into some bar at night where guys with time would treat him kindly. I shook my head, like that could shake a thought out. I wasn't going to think that way.

"Hey Carl." I went over to his table to check on him. Fay could see me going over there and see I liked him fine.

"Hey," he said. He kept his eyes down, steadying himself. He was trying to stop himself from tapping out a rhythm on the tabletop, but he couldn't.

"You having a good night?" I sat down over a chair turned backwards.

"I'm having a good night," he said. He looked at me and nodded and I nodded back at him. He was speeding just a little. I remember a guy named Jimmy who played the drums better than me because he knew how to speed this way, just a little bit, just enough to make him faster but not out of his mind. Jimmy's hands tapped out 4/4 time on everything they touched. Women went crazy for him. Jimmy's mouth was always dry and I went and got Carl a glass of water. This was not my responsibility.

"Thanks," Carl said, and took it down in one clean swallow. He touched his fingertips to his lips. "If you need me to do anything," he said.

"Everything's under control."

"I mean, I'm just sitting here." His feet were tapping and he stopped them. "I'd do anything, if you needed it."

"It's fine," I said. His hair was too long, not like long hair, just like hair that nobody'd bothered to cut. It fell into his eyes every now and then and he shook his head.

"Fay, you're real nice to Fay. I appreciate that," he said to me. "She works hard, you know."

"She does a good job."

Carl was looking away from me, over to the little stage in the far corner where nobody was. "She likes you. I wonder what my dad would have said about that." He turned back around to me. Fay passed by us, half smiled and disappeared into the kitchen. "I don't mean that disrespectful."

I didn't know what the hell he was talking about, but I put up my hand to show him no disrespect was taken.

"It's just something to think about," he said. "You never think your dad's gonna be wrong, but I know what he would have said, and he would have been wrong about this. He wasn't that kind of guy, you know, one of them. He had a pretty open mind. Lots of the guys he worked with at the plant were." He nodded his head towards me rather than say black. "He always treated them equal. Never even thought about it. It's just with Fay, well, when you've got a kid I guess it's always going to be different. I mean, hell, if I didn't know you myself maybe I would have thought the same way. You have any kids?"

I said I had a kid.

"Well then, you know what I'm talking about. I shouldn't have said it anyway. Now you're just going to think bad of my dad and you shouldn't. There's not a bad thing to say. I just need to shut up. Shut up shut up shut up." Carl looked at me and then at his hands, which he had to put between his knees to settle down. There was such a look of panic on his face you'd have thought I'd come over just to scare him.

"I think I'll see if she's ready," he said in a little voice. A rabbit voice. "Is that okay? She can go?"

"Sure," I said. I still wasn't exactly sure what Carl was talking about. All drug talk was babbling as far as I was concerned. There was no point in wasting your energy trying to make sense of it. One thing I was sure of, I was ready to see both of them go. They came out of the kitchen and Fay went to get their coats.

"You don't need anything else?" she said.

"Go on home," I said.

That night coming back to my apartment was the first time I realized there weren't enough places to go. I could have stayed at the bar or gone to another bar that would have been just the same. I could have gone home or to any motel room in the city that had a bed in it. I could have gone and seen Marion's parents, the Woodmoores, who thought of me as family by now, but I could only see them on Sundays after church and even then I gave a phone call for plenty of advance notice. My own parents in West Memphis over the river I didn't see much. There was my brother in Little Rock. Old friends were music friends and that was just sticking a knife in it, not that I didn't do it from time to time. Other people worked for me or I sold them drinks. I thought of the skinny woman with the pale green cigarette box. I thought of her pretty hands and how I would have kissed them just then.

The next night while I was up in my office filling out orders for booze, Cyndi was down in the bar drinking. I knew it even before I saw her because Elvis Presley was on the stereo when I came downstairs. She'd done it like this before. It was music I might have liked if I lived in another town where it only came on the radio every now and then, but in Memphis Elvis follows you from the minute you're born. All you can do is try your best to keep away from it. She'd put on the *Blue Hawaii* record, the one she said ruined her, and she sang in her own pretty voice. She didn't try to sing like Elvis, the way most people do when they'd been drinking and somebody puts one of his records on.

"Turn it off," I said. "You're going to scare the customers away."

"This is what people come to Memphis for," she said. "Not that whiny crap you listen to." She put one hand flat against her stomach and reached her other arm straight out to the side and stood there like she was waiting for somebody to ask her to dance.

"You not going to work tonight?"

"Good of you to ask, sensitive. Yes, I'm working."

It was seven o'clock on a Friday night, quiet now, but there was a band coming in that would fill the place solid enough to slice by ten P.M. I needed to know how many sober waitresses I was looking at. The customers who were there already were watching Cyndi hard, thinking maybe there would be a little show before the show. Fay kept her distance over by the bar with a weekend waitress named Arlene. Wallace left his stool by the door and went over to join them. It was too early for fights.

"Did you know," Cyndi said, "that I used to be one of three featured dancers at the Kaanapali Maui Sheraton's grand luau? All the roast pork and mai-tais you can eat for twenty-nine ninety-five." She was still standing there, one hand on her stomach and one hand out. A couple of the regulars clapped and Cyndi nodded at them. Elvis was still singing. Blue, blue, blue, he was saying. Then as slow as it was possible, she raised up one hip. It went farther up than any of us thought it could go and then she lowered it, waited one count and raised the other. She tapped her left foot out in front of her twice, brought it back, and started with the hip again. She was barely even moving, and still there was something almost obscene about it. None of us had ever seen a person move that way before. Both arms came slowly out in front of her and her hands unfolded and waved.

"Come on now," I said. I had to stop her. It was clear she was showing people more than she meant to, and that she'd regret it once she thought about it.

Her hands came down as slowly as they'd gone up, and she picked up a stranger's drink from a table and took a long sip. "Bad day," she said.

"What in the hell kind of bad day is this?"

"Elvis's birthday," she said absently.

"Shit, it's not his birthday. I even know when Elvis's birthday is. What's your problem?"

"Just a regular bad day, then," she said, her voice gone to ice. She finished the drink while the man who'd ordered and paid for it sat and watched her, then she headed off for the restroom. I went and changed the tapes. Maybe it didn't all seem as strange to me as it should have. People in this town had been doing insane things in relation to Elvis Presley for a long time. What bothered me was the thought that Cyndi might not be nailed down too tight. I might not be able to count on her the way I'd wanted to.

With things starting out the way they did, it didn't turn out to be such a friendly night. The place was busy and the band was more loud than good. Cyndi tied a knot in one side of her skirt, jacking it to the top of her thigh and then giving anybody who looked at her hell about it. I wasn't planning on mentioning it.

With everything so busy, I don't think anybody but Fay noticed that Carl never showed. The band outstayed their welcome, breaking down into a bunch of drunken half chords they'd written themselves towards the end of the night. By the time we got the place emptied out and straightened up, it was two-thirty and Fay was looking out the window, holding her puffy jacket in both arms. Cyndi walked right past her without saying a word and went on out into the night. She'd had enough time to sober up a little bit, and it wasn't helping her mood any. I said my good-nights and told Wallace to turn the lights out while I went up to do the night deposit, a job I never liked. I didn't want anybody breaking in and killing me over money that wasn't even mine. On Fridays I was always tired and made some sort of stupid mistake and had to count everything up again. Once I'd been so dead I'd taken the whole thing home in a paper sack, change and everything, and put it in the bed with me. I couldn't sleep, thinking that somebody would find out and say I'd stolen it. God knows, if I had any interest in stealing I could have done years of it there. I zipped it all up in the blue Third National bag and went down through the kitchen to double-check the locks. I saw her standing there in the dark and nearly had a heart attack.

"God, I'm sorry," Fay said, scared as me. "I thought you knew I was here still."

We stood across the room from each other, all the chairs turned upside down on the tables. The place always seemed so much bigger when it was empty. Nicer too. A nice bar.

"Why are you still here?"

"Carl didn't come," she said. Her voice was quiet, but I could hear it so clearly. All night I'd been screaming to make myself heard over the noise.

"So I'll take you home," I said.

"Then what if he comes here? What if I miss him?" She sounded so nervous, I wondered if she knew more than I was giving her credit for. "I could go home and then he would come here."

"So then he goes home. Carl knows that somebody'd take you." Carl knew that I would take you. "He wouldn't not come if he thought you were going to be standing around outside."

She nodded her head. I could see it. My eyes were adjusting to the dark. "That's true," she said.

Of course, there was almost no chance that Carl was going to be at home, wherever that turned out to be. If he was in a state in which he was still capable of remembering, he would have remembered Fay. "Come on," I said. "We need to go out the back. I've got all this money."

"Money?"

I held up the bag. "From the bar."

"I thought it always stayed in the cash register," she said, and pulled on her jacket.

A person would think I'd feel a lot more worried taking this girl to the bank with me, since now I was responsible for both her and the money, but the truth was I liked it better this way. I was thinking about her and not the roaming crackheads. She got out of the car and followed me right to the cash drawer. I took the key out of my pocket and opened it up.

"You have a key to the bank?" Fay said, impressed.

"Only to a very small part of it." Then I dropped the money in.

"Like mailing a letter," she said, watching the blue bag slide down the chute into someplace nobody could get at it.

I was thinking, Hell of a letter.

Fay didn't talk going over to her house. She just gave me directions and none of them in advance. She told me to get on Union and keep going. We went through downtown, past long stretches of sleeping auto body shops and used car lots, past Sun studios and the Baptist hospital, where Marion used to work. The only bright thing that time of night was the occasional Jim Dandy store, lit up in a firestorm of electric lights. "You want anything," I said, and pointed to one up ahead. "Soda or anything?" I don't know why I was asking.

"No, I'm fine, thanks." Fay kept a sharp eye out the window, looking for her brother in every direction. Union was getting nicer all the time, until finally we were out past the big houses on Landis and she started pointing to where I should turn, Poplar then Chickasaw. Out there the lawns all looked like parks

55

trimmed with mazes of dried-out winter hedges. Everybody seemed to have at least a half dozen columns. This was old money Memphis. This is what the people out in Germantown dreamed about.

"Up here," she said, and pointed. God knows, there wasn't a bus going from where we'd been to all the way out there. A cab would have cost her half of what she'd made that night. "It isn't our house," she said when I pulled into the driveway. "It's my aunt and uncle's."

"Nice," I said. Big and brick with a castle thing on the front. Everything trimmed and straight and squared away. It wasn't by any means the biggest place out there, but it still would have made a nice small hotel.

"It's not the kind of house I'd live in," Fay said, even though it was clear she lived there. Maybe she didn't want me to think she was a rich girl and didn't really need the job, or maybe she was apologizing for having nice things. "Well, thanks for bringing me. I know it's a haul, middle of the night and everything." She had her hand on the door, but she was just sitting there, looking at the house, which was dark except for a front porch light. "Can you find your way back all right?"

"I'll wait here," I told her. "You go in and check for Carl."

"Oh, no," she said. "Don't do that. You've got things to do. Carl's fine. He's just sleeping, I bet. I bet he just forgot."

"I'll wait here," I said. The longer we sat there, the more I was sure he wasn't inside.

Fay nodded at me and got out of the car. She tried to close the door quietly and wound up not getting it closed all the way. I shooed her off when she started to try again. She leaned over to unlock the front door of her house and then she went inside.

It was a whole lot quieter out there than it was where I lived. No traffic noise, no voices, no loud girls telling each other their business outside every window. I turned off the car and held my breath without thinking about it. I couldn't remember the last time I'd heard such quiet. I saw lights going on upstairs. On in one room then off, on in another. It wouldn't be a good thing if someone was to open their curtains and see me out there, a black man sitting in his green Chevy Nova. A black man sitting in such a white driveway, waiting on this white girl. Whether or not a person was doing something wrong very rarely figured into these things. Being there in the first place, that's trouble enough.

Fay was walking a lot quicker coming out of the door than she was going into it. She got in the car. "Not there," she said, looking at me.

I sighed. Whatever it meant, it wasn't going to be good. "Maybe he went out with some friends."

"Carl doesn't have any friends," she said.

"Did you tell your aunt and uncle?" I knew full well that she hadn't, that she hadn't been inside long enough, that she wouldn't have told them based on what she'd said about their house, that if she had told them she wouldn't be sitting in the car with me.

"I'm not going to wake anybody up," she said.

I drummed my fingers against the steering wheel and thought about it for a minute, all of it. "Then I guess you're going to have to go inside and wait. If he isn't home by the time it gets light, I'd say you should call the police." Not the advice I would have given anybody else I knew, but with Fay it was all I could come up with.

"I'm not going back in there," she said. "I'm not going to wait around and call the police. We'll just have to find him."

Five minutes ago she didn't want to impose on me to wait in the driveway. "Where do you suggest we look for him?" I said.

"I don't know. I thought maybe you'd have some ideas."

57

"I don't know Carl."

"You know where people go," Fay said.

Let's say we could be sure he wasn't in his bed, wasn't at my apartment, probably wasn't at Marion's parents' house. That would leave the rest of Memphis. Maybe I knew where people went, some people, people who were older, people who played music. Maybe I knew where they went a couple of years ago and what I remembered I didn't like: after-hours clubs that closed up and moved without any notice, around the zoo, in the trees where nobody can see you; a couple of bad apartments in bad buildings in bad neighborhoods where people bought their drugs and became so overwhelmed with the sweet smell that they did them right there in the hallway. I liked none of it. I didn't want to go looking for places like that. I didn't want to go there because those were the places where people shot you for fun. Those were places where people got picked up without anyone first checking on the crime. I couldn't take Fay in with me and I couldn't leave her in the car and I couldn't find out a thing by driving around. Nobody tells you anything. The trick is to see it, accidentally, all by yourself. Maybe Carl was worth saving, but I wasn't the person to do it. Fay was staring at me. She was planted so deep inside my car I doubt I could have cut her out.

"We'll drive around," I said. I reached over her and pushed down the button lock on her door. She looked satisfied with the way things were going. I would find some bad places that weren't so bad. Whatever I did, she wasn't going to know the difference.

We passed out of the good neighborhood, towards parts of town she'd know nothing about. I went north up to Jackson, Hollywood, Chelsea. I tried to stay on dark streets. I wasn't interested in showing this girl every late-night thing out crawling around.

"Slow down," she said, leaning in one direction and then the other, looking, looking. "Turn there." She pointed out an alley. It was nothing you'd want to drive down.

"Why?" I was starting to tense up the muscles in my legs the way I used to do when I was playing. When I was nervous I kept time in my legs.

"Just turn some more, go down some side streets. We're just staying on one road all the time. That's not going to find him."

I wove in and out between buildings, past parked cars that looked like they'd been half eaten by something and then set on fire. Every time there was a heap on the sidewalk, a person, a bundle of papers and rags, she wanted me to slow down. I wound my way back to Union, back to where things were a little bit quieter.

Then I drove past the bus depot.

"Pull over," she said. "I want to look in there."

"He's not leaving town."

"I know he's not leaving town, but he might have just gone in there to sit."

I pulled over to the curb and looked around. The street was quiet enough. The bums were asleep. A nest of black boys were hanging at the front door, smoking cigarettes. "You can't go in there with me," I said. I used my father's voice, the one I saved for Franklin when I didn't want an argument. It worked on her fine. "I'm taking the keys and I'm going to stand here and watch you lock the doors. Then you're going to sit here and do nothing until I get back. That means nothing. You don't look at anybody, you don't roll your window down. You understand me?"

"You'll look in the bathroom," she said.

I nodded and put the keys in my pocket. Never leave the keys. Then they'll try twice as hard to get in.

The fluorescent lights in the Memphis bus station were working overtime to light up every dirty corner of the floor. Just inside the door there was a howling bank of video games, clanging

59

and flashing all by themselves. There was just one boy, eleven or ten, beating on one that was over on the end. He was just pretending to play, there was nothing actually going on other than the patterns the games throw up to tempt people to drop their quarters in. I moved through a cloud of cigarette smoke thicker than any bar could generate. This place was worse than a bar because the people didn't have enough money for a drink. There was a hippie girl asleep over a couple of chairs, two dirty babies asleep on her and another one who looked like them wandering around near the ticket counter. Men who are the worst kind of trouble watched her sleep and I started thinking about Fay in the car. There was a group of little boy whores in the back of the room talking to each other and one of them looked up at me and smiled when I walked by. He had a thin chest and a girlish face with pimples along the line of his jaw. I didn't go look in the bathroom.

"Not there," I said to Fay. She was pretty pale when I opened the door and I wondered if somebody'd come by and banged on the window trying to scare her. She didn't ask if I'd looked hard enough.

"Where's his school?" I said.

"Why?"

"Kids'll go over to their school sometimes, looking for trouble." I wanted to get out of this neighborhood altogether. "I used to do that. We liked to pry open a window and walk around at night. Sometimes a bunch of kids'll get together and write things on the blackboards, turn over trash cans."

"Carl wouldn't do that."

"Well, chances are you'd say Carl wouldn't disappear in the middle of the night either, which leads me to wonder what in the hell we're doing driving around."

She dug her hands into her pockets and pushed herself down into the seat. "East," she said. "East High School."

It was a relief, driving back out towards Chickasaw Gardens. We were at the school by quarter of four, but there was no sign of his car, no lights on inside. I pulled over anyway. I was past being tired. Things were starting to get that blurry glow, the way they will when you stay up too long. Fay walked behind me, wrapping her arms around herself to try and keep from the cold. We went around the chain link fence, which had been stuffed full of leaves by either the wind or children. "Look in the windows," I said.

Fay walked over and cupped her hands around her eyes to peer inside. "There's nothing there," she said. "I told you he wouldn't come here. Carl hates this place."

"Every kid hates high school," I said. "That's just normal." I looked around a little to make her think the trip was worth the time. I knew he wouldn't be there as much as she did. After a while I turned back towards the car.

Fay wasn't following behind me. She was standing there, her back up against the low window. "Carl was good in school," she said. Her teeth were chattering lightly from the cold. "He was on the wrestling team. He was state-ranked. They don't even have wrestling here. Idiots."

"I don't know a thing about wrestling," I said. "It's cold. Come on back and get in the car."

"He did good in most of his classes. He was good in MATH," she said, saying the word math so loud it made me nervous somebody would hear her. "He was number three in the whole state in wrestling and he was good in MATH. Goddamnit. Goddamn all of it."

"Hey, Jesus, quiet yourself." I put my hands on her shoulders and steered her back towards the car. "You want to find him, don't you? This is how you're going to find him? You need to grab hold here. Stop it with this craziness."

Fay straightened up her back. She was breathing hard, like she was looking to fistfight with somebody. "I'm fine," she said.

"All right, then. Let's go."

She nodded her head. She was trying to settle herself back down. "Just drive around a little while more," she said. "I know I've been asking way too much, but if you can, for just a while."

"Sure," I said. "I can do that."

I had never in my life heard of somebody setting off to find a person in a city and then actually coming up with them, but we kept driving. At one point I made a wrong turn and wound up on the bridge over to Arkansas. That phrase, "transporting across state lines" came into my head. "This is Arkansas," I said, then turned around and came right back. Then we were downtown again, past the Ramada and the Peabody. I don't know if I meant to drive to Beale, or if I'd just been out so long I'd run out of places to go. But something did occur to me for the first time all night. Carl loved his sister, and as late as he might ever be, he wouldn't forget about her altogether. I parked on Union and got out. Fay got out without asking me anything. All the bicycle police had ridden off and the bums had settled in for the evening to sleep in the doorways. The one sleeping in the doorway to Muddy's was Carl.

Fay started to cry a little then, though from what combination of things it would have been hard to say. She got down and shook him hard. Maybe she wanted to see if he was dead.

Carl batted her hand away before he ever opened his eyes. "Hey," she said to him. "Jesus Carl, wake up."

He was about as white as a white person could have been. I do not believe that a black man can ever look as completely fucked up as a white man. Even his eyes didn't have color to them anymore. Still, he was probably better off now than he would have been if we'd found him right off the bat. "It's cold," Carl said.

I leaned over and tried to help him up, but I could see pretty quick that that wasn't going to work. Carl wasn't walking. The only way to do it was to actually pick him up. He was small, maybe just five foot eight and awfully, awfully thin, the way boys with a predilection for drugs will be. I put my hands up under his arms and felt the skinny joint where the bone went into the socket. This boy had no means of protection in the world. He was small and not especially sharp. He had a naturally sweet way about him, which would do him a lot more harm than good. The way I saw it, the only thing he had standing in front of his destruction was Fay, and she was not such a big person herself. I wanted to get him in the car as soon as possible. I was thinking like Fay by then, better to keep this quiet. I reached down and took his legs in my other arm and carried him to the car the way I used to carry Franklin when he fell asleep at his grandparents' house after supper. Fay pushed her brother's head up against my chest so it wasn't just wagging around out there. It isn't good for a man to be carried by another man, like he was a baby. I was sorry for having to do it, but I couldn't see any other way.

I put him in the back seat and Fay did her best to arrange him so that he looked comfortable. Then she got up front. "What do you suppose did it?"

I told her it was drugs.

"I know that much," she said, a little irritated.

"You're asking me what kind of drug?" I looked in the rearview mirror at the boy crumpled up in the back seat of my car. "You think I know things I don't know." It may have just been

63

Southern Comfort and a couple of Valium, things that make you stupid and then kill you in your sleep.

"You don't think he needs to go to the hospital," she said, watching him breathe.

"If he's not dead now, I doubt it's going to kill him."

"I should have stayed at the bar," she said. "He was just late was all. He could have frozen to death out there."

"It isn't that cold."

In late February the sun didn't rise until it was good and ready. I looked at my watch, thinking it must be getting on seven o'clock, but it was only four-thirty. Four-thirty in the morning and I was driving around with this waitress and her brother.

"Don't think too bad of him," Fay said, looking in the other direction so that I could barely hear her voice. "Carl's had a real hard time. This move's been tougher on him than anybody. You'd never believe this, but it used to be before things happened that I was the one everybody thought was wild. I mean, not wild like *wild*, but if somebody said one of the Taft kids was in trouble you could bet it was going to be me. Carl, he was like a dog, go where you tell him, stay where you tell him. Now we're here and it's gotten to where I can hardly talk to strangers and Carl's all over the place. He thought we should've stayed in Coalfield. I don't know, maybe we should have. I don't know how we would have done it. There was no money. I mean that. None. You wouldn't think that two people could work for all those years and come up with nothing, but that's the story."

I got back on Union one more time. I wondered why there were so many cars, where everybody could be going this time of the morning. "So something happened to your folks," I said.

"No, not my mother. She's here. This is the turn," she pointed to the left. "My father died is all."

I nodded my head and turned off.

My car had a good heater on it and Fay cranked it up to high in hopes of thawing Carl out some. But the warmth seemed to put him in a deeper sleep and when we came back to that driveway neither one of us could rouse him at all.

"Carl," Fay said. She slapped him a little, not as hard as she should have. "Come on now."

I rested my head against the frame of the car door. It was all going bad to worse.

"Wake up," she said. His mouth dropped open. I could see his pink tongue resting inside. "He's not waking up."

I reached past her into the car, grabbed the collar of his sweatshirt and shook him hard. His mouth clicked open, shut, open again. "Get up!"

"Don't break his neck," Fay said. When I let go he folded right back into his spot. I checked over my shoulder. I didn't like being outside there.

She was quiet for a while, looking at Carl and then the door and the length of the driveway. "You're going to have to carry him in," she said.

"No."

"There's no other way."

"I can't go inside," I said.

"Nobody's going to know."

She didn't understand. If she was wrong, just a little wrong, if only one person saw me that would be enough. I shouldn't have been in that neighborhood, parking my car on that asphalt. "No."

"Please," she whispered. I could hear the word after she stopped saying it.

Such quiet on that street, like they'd paid off every living thing to keep it that way. "You can't carry him, can you?"

"I'm sorry," she said, and she put her hand on my arm. She was

65

so sorry I could feel it through my jacket. "There's no other way."

Leave him outside. That's where he wanted to sleep. Leave him in the grass, in the forsythia beside the house. "Anybody awake in there?"

She shook her head. "They sleep like rocks. All of them."

Be right, I was thinking. My hands were sweating as I leaned into the back seat and pulled her brother out. I was good at this. I'd done it a million times. Had Franklin been this light? A boy of nine wasn't heavier than this. Though Franklin smelled better, not just because he hadn't been spending nights outside, sleeping in his clothes, but because he smelled healthy, like a boy. Carrying her brother in my arms, I followed Fay up the driveway, past the thick line of hedges. I didn't have to worry about the people on either side seeing me, only the ones across the street. I was worried about them. They wouldn't look long enough to see if I was carrying Carl into the house or away from it. They wouldn't look to see Fay. They would only see me while they were punching out 911 and calling to their wife to get the shotgun out from under the bed.

Fay reached inside her shirt and pulled out a house key on a chain around her neck. The chain was too short, and she had to lean down to the lock to open the door. She practically had to press her face against it. I shifted Carl's match-stick bones in my arms and tried to step out of the porch light. Fay looked at me and put a finger to her lips. Like I didn't know to be quiet. We went inside the dark house. I was inside somebody else's house, holding their son, following their daughter. My feet were sinking into somebody's thick carpet. I saw the dark outline of their things. Flowers on small tables, the backs of sofas and wing-backed chairs. I wanted to close my eyes. Everything I saw incriminated me, proved I was there. Panic came up in my throat and turned my mouth bitter. Fay ran her hand along the wall until she came to the thermostat box. A second later the heater came on with three clicks and a groan and then sound poured up from every vent to help cover us. She walked over to the staircase. Upstairs would be worse. Harder to get out from there, fewer places to go. She moved without noise, but I heard everything: the heaviness of Carl's stoned breathing, the sounds the stairs made under our feet, under my heavy feet. I tried to breathe. The house smelled too clean, a little bit perfumed even. It smelled like a woman. I was inside the house. All doors shut, windows locked. The last stair made a loud, animal sound when I took my foot away and I felt the sweat beading up at my hairline.

I followed Fay down the hallway, past what looked to be an endless row of closed doors that held beds and sleeping people. I didn't know who or how many. I was trying to count them as a way of steadying myself. Then I heard something from behind the second door. I stopped and held Carl tighter to my chest. A bedside drawer being pulled open? Someone rolling over, reaching into a drawer? There are no questions they would have to ask. Seeing me was reason enough to shoot me. It would be reason enough for the police who would come later to fill out the paperwork. All of the neighbors would buy better alarm systems. At parties they would tell the story again and again. They would take Fay's aunt by the arm and say, *It must have been so terrifying for you, I can't imagine.* Fay turned around, followed my eyes to the door and shook her head. She made a motion with her hand that I should keep going. I stayed behind her, keeping my eyes on her back, on her hair, which stopped in a razor straight line just past her shoulders. She opened the last door on the hallway and I followed her inside. Neither of us said a thing. She pulled back the blankets and I lay the boy down on blue striped sheets. She took off his shoes and covered him. He had been so light that I barely felt the difference when I stood up without him. In the bed he rolled over and took hold of a pillow with both his hands.

Fay took the same path out of the house. I wondered about my footprints showing in the carpet. Going out felt easier and it was all I could do to keep myself slow. I was relieved Fay saw me all the way out, that she didn't just wave at me from his bedside. My eyes had adjusted some to the dark and I could make out pictures on the walls now, though I couldn't make out the people in them. She came outside with me. When I heard the door close I vowed to never be stupid again. Never. The air smelled like it might rain. I put my hands against my thighs and leaned into it.

When we got to the car she went around to the other door and got in, like we still had a couple more stops to make on this never-ending ride. "I can't believe we got him inside," she said.

I just nodded.

"Tomorrow is Sunday. Carl always sleeps late on Sunday. He won't go to church with them. Nobody'll even think anything about it."

I sat there without a single thing left to say. It was done. What I couldn't understand was why Fay kept sitting there. She was looking at the house.

"I'd like to go with you," she said finally.

"Where?" Could there really be someplace left to go?

She didn't answer me right away. She was still staring. "I'd like to go home with you."

Well then I understood. In that neighborhood where quiet was invented it would be hard to miss it. My whole body heard her. It said okay. Take her up, it said, fold that jacket in your arms, press that face to your face, put your mouth to the soft skin next to her eye. It said to take what was offered.

I should have asked Marion to marry me, the second she told me she was pregnant. That was the mistake.

"Go on," I said.

"I mean it."

"Get out of the car now. I've done enough."

She put her hand on my neck. It was small and cold. I thought, delicate.

"I'm telling you to go," I said.

It seemed like the hand stayed there a long time, but then I heard her door open and close and I saw the shape of her walking up the driveway to the house and still I felt that hand there and I put my hand on my neck to cover the place where she had been.

EVERYTHING HINGED on the dead father. That's what I was thinking. Something had turned them inside out, made them do things they'd barely heard of before. You could tell, Carl wasn't a boy to go licking up everything in the medicine cabinet for the pure pleasure of the high. And Fay. What had happened to her that she would be putting her hand on my neck? Over and over again I saw her sitting in the car, her head resting on the window when she was tired. She was tired. She had been worried for her brother, thought maybe he was dead. Those thoughts shake a person as deep as they go, I know that. You want a little comfort. She had reached out in the wrong direction was all, gone to touch something at the end of a long night and touched me.

What was surprising was how that minute put such a knot in me. At first I thought I'd just been made stupid by spending all night hunting Carl, but it was there while I slept and there in the morning waking up. It stayed with me all the way to Muddy's. I had felt a thrill. That's the only word for it. I recognized it easy enough. I had been thrilled before in my life. Mostly it came from music, times I had seen Muddy Waters play slide guitar with a broken-off bottle neck around his finger, again when I saw Son House in Chicago. A few times I had been thrilled when I was playing myself and everything had come together just so. My boy thrilled me, even Marion, though I hated to admit that, back at the very first. The sight of her face had thrilled me.

So when it happened with Fay, it was something I knew and I was grateful for it, even though it was probably nothing she'd intended. Even if it was all about something else, a father who was dead and a brother who was strung out and sleeping in doorways, and her hand had only touched my neck because they weren't there, I was pleased. It was a long time since I'd felt such a thing.

I already knew plenty about the brother, and it didn't take much for me to imagine the dead father. He looked like Carl, not quite tall enough but a good face that balanced things out. He was better looking than his son. Age had made him better. Carl always had the jitters. His eyes darted around from place to place. In my mind, Taft had none of that. It was easy to see him. It was easy to see his house, because it was like every other working-class hillbilly house in east Tennessee. One had a carport instead of a garage. Another one had a box hedge under the picture window. But it was all the same house. Taft would look back at it when he went to the end of the short driveway in the morning to get the paper. He was proud. He would have said I was wrong. He would have pointed out all the ways his house was different. The shutters were green. They had that nice screen door with a cursive letter T shaped from bent metal in the lower half. But the key to the difference was that his house contained his family, his children. He prided himself on being the sort of man who knew exactly what a good thing he had. He was in love with Carl and Fay. Every day of his life since they were born, he was crazy for them.

· · ·

"Look at you," Taft says. "All dressed up."

"I've got a date."

"Anybody I know?"

Fay stops at the door and smiles. This smile always shuts him right up. It is the smile of a girl who couldn't do anything wrong. "I don't think so," she says, and then thinking he might ask her not to go, she adds, "I won't be gone long." She stops to look at herself in the mirror in the hallway, runs her little finger over her lipstick.

It's a Saturday afternoon, bright summer. There's no point in asking where she's going or when she'll be back. Nothing ever happens on a Saturday, during summer, in the middle of the day.

"You have a good time then," he says. Next minute she's gone. Taft stands at the window to watch her. The way she looks makes him nervous. Too good, too grown up.

He heads out back to see if Carl's there. He wants Carl to drive over to the lumberyard with him. Taft's been thinking about putting a deck on the back of the house where they could all sit in the evening. He's been doing things lately that might make the place attractive to the kids. He wants to keep them home more. They're at that age now, running around all the time with their friends. That's the way it is, but he wants it to be different. It won't be long until they're gone for good. They'll get married, have babies and jobs. They'll stay in Coalfield or maybe go to Oak Ridge, but it won't be the same as having them home. This is the last chance he has to keep them all to himself, his family, the four of them together. He's spending too much money, his wife told him that. He bought a VCR last month and now he's talking about this deck.

"You seen Carl?" Taft asks his wife.

"Out in the garage, I think." She doesn't look up from her

work. She has the sewing machine out on the dining room table and is busy putting together a dress. Fabric with flowers the size of fists is spread out everywhere. He doesn't know if it's for her or Fay.

"Carl?"

"Sir," Carl calls back from the garage.

Taft follows his voice, goes through the small laundry room off the kitchen and down two cement steps. Carl has his weights out there. He's lying down on his bench, doing lateral raises, twenty pounds in each hand. Every time the weights come up to the top, his breath shoots out like somebody's hitting him in the stomach. Carl looks good. His color is good. His hair is slicked back with sweat and his face is a healthy red. There is real concentration on his face. He brings the two weights up even and slow, all the way to the top. He doesn't let them drop fast. He's small, but he has some real muscle on him. He wrestles at 126. He's ranked first in the Tennessee eastern division, third in the state for high school boys.

"Come on and go to the lumberyard with me," Taft says.

Carl doesn't say anything until he goes five more reps, and then he puts the weights against his hips and rolls up. "When do you want to go?"

"Let's go now," Taft says. Carl is easier than Fay, just eleven months younger in age but still a boy. Fay has a mind of her own now. She has friends, boyfriends, who Taft doesn't even know. Carl is still interested in going along for the ride. Taft wants to show him how to buy wood. Carl knows a lot about wrestling and not much about other things. Taft thinks this deck is something they can work on together. Hammering nails and all of that, he thinks it's the sort of thing a boy needs to know.

Carl pulls his T-shirt over his head and then uses it to wipe the sweat off his chest and arms. "Hang on a minute," he says. "I just want to get another shirt." Carl's been changing his clothes a lot lately.

Taft starts to get in the car and then changes his mind, goes and gets in on the passenger side. Wouldn't hurt to let Carl drive.

I was behind the bar when Rose stuck her head out from the kitchen and asked if I could come in the back for a minute. She said she had a message for me.

"Fay called."

I was half expecting this. She'd call before I came in to say she was going out of town or some such thing. "Okay," I said.

Rose stood there, giving me a minute to make a fool of myself. "You don't want to know what she said."

"Sure I do."

"She wants you to pick her up, on the corner before you get to her house, three o'clock. She says you don't need to call her back."

"What's she talking about, she wants me to pick her up?" But even as I was saying it, I felt the thrill again.

"I have no idea," Rose said. She went right back to the potato she was peeling. She didn't stare at me like any woman would after telling a man that a girl had called and asked to be picked up a block away from her house.

"Why'd she give the message to you?" I said. "You don't ever answer the phone. Why didn't she give it to Cyndi?"

"She's not going to tell Cyndi where she's meeting you."

"And she'll tell you?"

Rose shrugged. "It looks that way."

I kept standing there, waiting for her to say what must have been on her mind. I didn't like the idea of her having anything

74

on me. Rose was an odd woman. I hadn't even meant to hire her. It just happened that she came in looking for a job the day after James Whitlow's period of parole was up and he was free to leave the state, which he did in short order. James was from Detroit and was visiting a cousin down here when he got messed up in some bad business. Prison and then parole, he'd had enough of Tennessee. Rose said she'd work the first shift for free and then I could decide whether I wanted to keep her, and since I never got around to deciding, she stayed.

"This isn't about anything," I said. "She must just need a ride in is all."

"Good," Rose said. She dried her hands on her apron and then went into the storeroom, which I took to be her way of saying it was nothing she wanted to talk about.

I went back to the bar and poured a couple of beers for people who'd been waiting on me. It had been something, her hand. I appreciated that. But it would take a hell of a lot more than a hand on my neck to make me forget the fact that these were children and not my children. Fay and Carl. I was having a hard time separating the two. It felt like both of them were calling, saying, Come over to our house and we'll tell you what's next. There was always the chance that none of it was bad, that all they wanted to say was thank you or good-bye. I thought about not going at all because that would make it clear where I stood on things. But then I saw Fay out there on the corner in her nice neighborhood, waiting, knowing full well that I'd show and for reasons I can't explain I didn't feel like disappointing her.

"So I guess you're fairly hacked off at me," Cyndi said. She startled me. She was standing right in front of me and I hadn't even seen her. She had a tin of some sort of stiff paste in one hand and was working a cloth into it with the other.

"I don't know what my problem was yesterday," she said. "I'd just been drinking too much. That was it, really." She started spreading the paste over the guardrail at the front of the bar.

"What in the hell are you doing?"

"It's brass polish," she said, holding up the tin so I could see the word Brasso on the front. "I found it in the back. I don't think this thing has ever been cleaned. It might look nice, you know, if somebody worked on it." The paste was turning the rail a kind of grayish green color, but when I leaned over I could see something yellow down underneath. She was pushing into it with everything she had.

"You don't have to do that," I said.

"I kind of want to," she said. "I just feel like doing something."

Cyndi had tied back her hair with a piece of dishtowel, but it kept falling in her face as she worked the rag back and forth across the railing. It was hard to imagine her all done up in flowers and a grass skirt. She didn't seem like the kind of girl who'd put up with a lot of nonsense. "I didn't know about you being a dancer," I said.

"That's because you didn't read my application. It was on there: last job held."

"So you didn't like it there?" I had never thought to ask before.

"Didn't like Hawaii?" She looked at me like she must not have heard right. "Everybody loves Hawaii. Everybody loves the dancing. I mean, maybe the luau was shit, some crackerjack Sheraton, but it was really cool to be able to dance every night and get paid for it. All these couples who just got married come up afterwards and want to have their picture taken with you like you're some sort of good luck goddess or something. Hell no, there was nothing wrong with that."

"So why are you here cleaning a bar rail?"

Cyndi got down on her knees to check how corroded things were underneath. "You can bet it had something to do with a guy," she said. Suddenly she turned suspicious. "Why are we talking about this? Since when do you want to know?"

I put my hands up. "Just making conversation."

"I think we could find better things to talk about." She took another cloth out of the waistband of her skirt and started polishing. It was brass all right. Bright as day.

Maybe Cyndi wasn't crazy, maybe she just liked to drink. Everybody in Muddy's liked to drink. "Look," I said, leaning over the bar. "If I was to be gone for a while, you could take care of things, couldn't you? If I was to start getting away some more?"

"More money?" Cyndi said.

I thought about it; no one around here ever kept a job long enough to ask for a raise except for Rose, and she never asked. "Sure," I said. "I'll look at the books and come up with something."

"Okay," she said, looking pretty pleased about the whole thing. "I came in today thinking you were probably going to fire me."

"Yeah, well, you never know."

Before we had a chance to work out any of the details, a tour group came through saying they wanted a drink in a real Memphis bar. Usually whatever groups you got were on Friday nights when things were packed anyway. I couldn't tell where these people were from or why they were together, but they all seemed sick of one another. The women rifled through their purses, pretending to be looking for something, while the men picked the cashews out of the bowls of nut mix. They weren't a talking group, just drinkers. Cyndi left off her polishing and washed up. The bar rail stayed like that, half tarnished and half bright. I figured over time enough people would hold on to it that things would even out again.

I remembered how to get to Fay's, but it was different going there in the daylight. The houses were bigger and whiter now. There were a few warm days last week and it had been enough to bring the forsythia to bud. I kept catching little bits of yellow out of the corner of my eye. Every now and then I passed a maid standing out on the street. They were waiting on the one city bus that went through this neighborhood at three o'clock for the sole purpose of collecting maids. In their white uniforms they made me think of Marion. One of them waved to me, and I waved back.

From all the way at the end of the street I could see her standing there. She had been watching, but as soon as she saw me she stared at the ground. She looked small. It was more than the way everybody looks small from a distance. I pulled up alongside of her and leaned over to open the door. "Lost your brother again?" I said.

She got in quick. "You mind driving around?"

"That's what I do."

We just rode for a while, longer than I thought we would without saying anything. The way I saw it, she had called me. I could keep quiet all day. I was just making random turns again, going nowhere. It was fine, really, having her in the car. Simple. I thought there was a chance that this could amount to nothing. "How's Carl feeling?"

"Lousy, I guess. I don't think there's anything wrong with him. He's pretty much been asleep all day. He said to thank you though, for driving him home and everything."

I nodded, thinking it was funny how in memory it would be a ride home.

"I was wondering if maybe we could go somewhere." Her voice was hesitant, like she wasn't so sure she wanted to ask me. "I don't know how you're set for time or anything."

Something in me wanted to be sharp with her: Listen up, my days aren't for driving you around. But then there was the smell of her in my car, the way she sat with one foot up on the seat. The hand that had touched my neck was flat out beside me on the green vinyl. It shook the words up in my head. "Where do you want to go?"

She looked out the window. "That's the question," she said. "Where do people go? I mean, when they really want to be someplace else." She turned around and faced me. "What I'd like is to get out of Memphis. You ever feel like getting out of town?"

"Sure," I said. I knew all about that. The city seemed to boil down to two marks on the map, where I worked and where I slept. A hundred times I had thought there had to be someplace else, a third place it would make sense to go to. There were other places, back before Franklin and Marion left, but once they were gone everything tightened up.

"We could go to Shiloh," Fay said. "It's a ways, but I always wanted to go there. My dad went once. His dad took him. He was a big Civil War buff, my grandfather."

"Shiloh? Do you know where that is?" That was craziness. That was leaving, people looking for you, or at least people looking for her.

She glanced around, like maybe she could spot it from the car. "It's south and east," she said. She kneeled on the seat and pointed towards my left shoulder. "Is that east?"

I told her it was.

She readjusted her pointing a little. "Then it's that way."

"I've got a job, you know. That bar doesn't run itself."

"The bar does fine."

"I'm going to take you home," I said. "We're just out here wasting gas."

"I'm serious," she said, sitting back down again. "Why can't we go? What in the world difference would it make if we just went for a drive?" She was quiet for a while, but she could see which way I was heading. The streets ticked by. Every one was the name of an Indian tribe, Sioux, Tishomingo, Iroquois, Cherokee, Catawba, Arawata. Home in no time. "Last night when we were looking for Carl I was thinking, wouldn't it be nice if we were just in the car, just like we are now except we were there because we felt like it." She kept her voice down. Had we been farther away, had I driven like she wanted me to, she never would have said it. "I wondered if you would have gone anyplace with me if there wasn't a reason to go, if there wasn't someone to look for. Part of the time last night I wasn't even thinking about Carl."

I could feel it rising up in me again, something like a thrill. I was wondering what it was in her that could make me feel like I did. I was wondering if I stayed with her for the afternoon if I could figure it out. "You've got too much on your mind," I said. "You don't know what you're talking about."

"Come on and go to Shiloh with me."

"You interested in the Civil War?" I said.

"I'm interested in driving there," she said. "The rest of it we'll just have to see about."

I hadn't been there myself, but I knew where it was. When I was a kid in school my class had gone but something happened, I'd been sick or something, I don't remember. That was a long time ago. "We won't have a long time." All I had to say was that and it was over. The second I started entertaining the idea I was as good as lost. "By the time we get there it's almost going to be dark."

"But we'll be able to say we've been." You could hear it in her voice. She'd latched onto the little opening I'd given her. It was done, sunk, over.

"Sure," I said. "Why not. I don't see where going to Shiloh's going to hurt anything."

"Really?" she said, so pleased. "That would be great. Just going. Bang. Nobody knows where you are. That would be heaven."

I turned the car around and headed out to 40 East.

I don't know that Tennessee is prettier than other places. Sometimes I think that the pretty you like is just the pretty you know. There are a lot of places I hear are beautiful, out in the west where there are nothing but open spaces, and I think I'd like to go there to see. All the traveling in my life has been to play or to see somebody play. I've gone as far north as Chicago and south to New Orleans, but I never seem to make it more than a few hours away from the Mississippi on either side. Driving through west Tennessee to Shiloh, I thought I hadn't missed so much. Even in the late winter, which isn't our best time, the hills and trees and flat fields of broken corn stalks look fine, in as much as they look like home. The quickest way there is a two-lane blacktop with no shoulders that snakes its way through nowhere. It is such an empty road that Fay said the only reason it was built was to take us to Shiloh. In an hour we only passed three cars. She counted them.

"Four," she said when a blue Ford pickup went by.

She made comments on every animal we passed, too. Sometimes it was nothing more than her looking out the window and saying "Cows" when we were passing cows. She liked the horses best. I slowed down to give her a better look.

"I used to go riding some when I was a kid," she said. "For a while my parents talked about getting me a horse, but they couldn't do something like that. It's expensive, you know, once you board them and all."

I was sure I didn't know the first thing about it.

Neither one of us said anything about what we were doing, probably because we didn't know. It was better that way. While we were driving we were having a good time, not saying much. When we got to Shiloh it was nearly dark and the big sign at the front of the park said it all closed down at nightfall, but we'd come too far to just turn around. Right away I thought about Franklin, how I'd bring him here as soon as he came back. He'd like the cannon-balls that were stacked into pyramids all over the fields. It's easy to see how pretty it would be once it was really spring. Just being a little farther south the trees had budded out already. There was a ranger locking up the tourist center when we pulled in and he went back inside to get us a couple of bro-chures.

"Just don't stay too long," he said. "It gets hard to find your way out of here after dark."

"Late start," I said.

I saw him looking at Fay, trying to catch her eye, maybe to see if she was going to signal him that she had been kidnapped or something, but she was already wandering off towards the first marker. He gave me a wave as he got in his truck and I figured his mind was at ease about the whole thing.

"You coming?" she called from across the parking lot. "There isn't a lot of time."

The air was cool and it smelled sweet, or maybe it just didn't smell like Memphis anymore. I zipped up my jacket as I walked towards the path where Fay had gone.

It was a sight, her standing there with her back to me and on either side of her as far as you could see were tombstones, white stones not much bigger than school books sticking up. It looked like they grew there rather than were put there. So many of them that it was hard to think that each one meant a person. Fay crouched down to get a closer look at one. She ran her hand over the top where there were numbers chiseled in. Every stone had a number and some had names and dates besides. It was the ones that just had numbers that you felt for. Nobody even able to figure out who you were before they buried you. Fay was moving on to the next one and then the next in the row.

"We should have come sooner," she said. The way she said it, she made it sound like maybe we could have done something to prevent all this. "I didn't know there was going to be a cemetery. This would take all day by itself."

"What would?"

"Reading the tombstones." All the time she was talking she was moving from one to the other. "You've got to read as many of them as you can. My grandmother used to tell me that. That's what makes the dead feel better, having their tombstones read."

"That's crazy."

"You shouldn't just visit with the dead people you know," she said, like she was telling me some fact of science. "You've got to pay attention to all of them. It helps them rest. Living people remembering them is what they like."

"There are more than ten thousand dead people in this park," I said, and I took her arm to help her up off the grass. "Dead people from all over. There's no way you're going to be visiting with all of them."

Fay brushed off the knees of her pants and then shaded her eyes against the late, slanting sun so she could get a good look at all the graves. "I don't expect that any of their families come."

"No," I said. "I wouldn't think so."

We walked up the hill a little way until it crested and we could see the Tennessee River winding past the bottom of the red cliffs.

Spending your whole life on the Mississippi can make a person think of other rivers as incidental. But the Tennessee from such a height at that particular time of day looked fine.

"I don't think there's a thing in the world worth dying over," Fay said, looking down at the water.

I didn't tell her different, but I could think of half a dozen things without even trying.

We drove the car from one battlefield to the next, getting out and reading the markers until it was so dark we could barely see the words. You could imagine what it must have been like for them in the dark, stopping the fighting long enough to get a little rest. All those boys, holding on to the trees beside them, wanting to sleep and being too afraid.

"Stop here," Fay said.

I pulled the car over to the side of the road and tried to make out what she was seeing. It was a statue of some kind out in the middle of the field. It was tall as a two-story house.

"I want to go see that," she said.

I started to tell her no, that it was too late, and then I thought that one more statue wouldn't make any difference. We'd done something senseless in going there. When we got home was just splitting hairs. She got out and I pulled the car halfway into the field so that the headlights spread over the grass and gave everything the overbright quality of a nighttime baseball game. Then Fay stepped in front of me and lit up like a Christmas tree. I could see everything, every part of her was bright, the blue cloth of her shirt that showed at the neck where her jacket was open, her hands, her mouth, her bright eyes. The light made her beautiful in a way that she wasn't really. She smiled at me and waved.

I followed her out into the field, half dizzy from the sight of her. We crossed the dried-out grass to the tall piece of marble where a woman made out of bronze was laying a wreath.

"It's from Iowa," Fay said. "They put this here for all the boys from Iowa who died. Way out here in the middle of nowhere." She climbed up the base of the thing to spread her hands out on the marble. "It's beautiful," she said. "It's so cold. Come feel how cold it is."

But when I went to touch the statue it was Fay I touched, her hair. I put my hands on either side of her head and felt its small shape. I could almost get my hands completely around her head. My thumbs were resting on her eyebrows and I brought her head to my chest and I held her there against me. Her hair was fine and soft and I put my hand against her neck and wrapped my other arm across her back and she held me, like I was the tree and she was the soldier asleep. The headlights weren't so bright because we were far away from them, but they showed us to anyone who could have been passing by. When we walked back to the car she held on to my arm like it was all she wanted. Like this was the most natural thing in the world.

"We moved out here after my father died. Not right after. We stayed home for almost three months before it was just sort of clear that we couldn't do it. It wasn't like he'd been sick or anything. It was his heart. There hadn't been any time to think about what we might do later. My mother worked in my high school. She was the secretary, but that was only part-time and after my father died she didn't go back to work anymore. They kept her job open for her but she just couldn't go back. She wanted a big funeral. She said they didn't have any sort of a wedding because there hadn't been any money so at least she was going to have a good funeral. It was, I guess. I mean, who can tell the difference? After that there was nothing left. No insurance. Nothing. People were real nice and everything, everybody was willing to float us along, but you know that's got to come to an end sooner or later. We were just kind of hanging out, eating what people came by with and what the grocery sent over. I think sometimes if we'd been living in a city like Memphis there wouldn't even have been that. I didn't think about the money right at first. You don't think about it when you're at home and your parents have always taken care of things. I figured my mother was handling it. But she just sort of melted. She spent all her time outside. Even when it got cold she'd get all bundled up and sit out back in a folding chair. My father had been building a deck on the back of the house right before he died. It wasn't quite finished. It was like she felt closer to him, sitting out on that deck."

"You said he was building a deck?"

She nodded. "It was nice. Even unfinished it was nice. My mother sat out there all the time. She didn't like to be in the house any more than she had to be."

"What about Carl?"

"Carl got a job at the lumberyard after school. My dad had friends down there who were looking out for us. I already had a job at the Dairy Queen and they gave me more hours. Carl and I got so worried about money that we didn't even feel as bad as we should have. I mean, we felt horrible, but it was almost like there wasn't time. My mother was sitting outside all day. I'd always have to go tell her it was time to come in, time to have something to eat. She was always stalling, a few more minutes, another half hour. I think she would have slept out there if I'd let her. She didn't even know the power had been cut off until Carl got home from work. She'd been putting all the mail in a paper sack underneath the sink. We owed money to everybody in the world, people I'd never heard of. Even after I found all those bills, I still thought I was going to be able to pull it out of the fire. I didn't think there was any other choice, we'd just figure it out somehow, make it work. I never even thought about moving to Memphis until Carl started to slip. Maybe I should have done it right away. It was clear enough my mother was having problems. But it wasn't until Carl that I figured there wasn't any chance of working it out in Coalfield. It was too much for him, trying to keep up in school and working all the time. He stopped going to school and then he stopped going to work. They even paid him for a few weeks when he wasn't showing up. Those people at the lumberyard were good to us." Fay was quiet for a little while, rolling a piece of hair between her fingers. "I should have looked after him more, thought about his feelings. I thought we would all pull through because there wasn't any choice but to pull through. But there is a choice, there're lots of them. You can choose to just lay down. That's what my mother did."

"And that's what Carl did?"

"No," she said. "Carl didn't lay down exactly. Carl just started looking for things to make himself feel better. I don't figure that's such a crime."

I told her it probably wasn't.

"Well, that's when I called my aunt and uncle and told them we'd move to Memphis. They'd offered a couple of times. There wasn't any other way. We were backed up at the bank like crazy, not paying the mortgage, credit cards. I'm hoping when they settle it all out there'll be something left, but I'm not holding my breath."

"Did you tell your aunt and uncle about Carl?"

"Lord, no. They don't have any idea. They're not the kind of people who'd pick up on something like that. They don't have children. It's funny though, how once you see something you can't believe that everybody in the world doesn't see it too. They're mostly worried about my mother. She says she's not getting over it. Never. She loved my father, that's the thing. Everybody loved my father." Fay looked up at me like she'd just that minute noticed I was driving the car.

"I'm talking too much," she said. "I'm boring you. I'm starting to bore myself."

"You're not talking too much."

"I'm boring myself," she said again and turned on the radio. We were just coming into Memphis so the reception was good, but every station she landed on seemed to be commercials or weather reports. After a while she just left it on to a woman who was talking about soup. Fay seemed like she was really listening to it, like she was trying to remember everything the woman said. Every now and then she'd repeat something she'd heard, like "celery" or "stock."

I was worried about taking her back. I would have rather we stayed in Shiloh, found some motel where she could have slept and I could have kept an eye on her. Some people might say there's no point in fooling yourself, but I would have been all for it, at least for a night.

"You want me to drop you off in the same place?"

"I guess so," she said. We were in the city. The streetlights made everything bright. "I wish I could bring you over."

"Don't be thinking about things like that," I said.

"I'd like it if you could see them, my mother and Calvin and Lily. Then you'd know what I'm talking about."

"I know what you're talking about," I said. "I've been inside their house."

That made Fay laugh. "God, what would they have done if they'd seen that?"

"They would have shot me," I said.

The corner where Fay got out was Garden and Cherokee. It was smart. The house that was there sat so far back from the street that the people inside wouldn't have noticed the girl or the car or the color of the man driving it. "I'm coming to work tomorrow," Fay said. She looked for a second like she might say something else, but instead she smiled and blew me a kiss through the window and after she turned away I sat there because I was thinking about the day I'd hired her, and how young she looked wearing that stocking cap.

The bar closed early on Sunday nights, so I figured I'd go by for an hour and then do the money. I wondered if I could teach Cyndi how to make up the deposit, if I could trust her. It's not something you want to say about a person, but it occurred to me.

Everything was running fine without me. Wallace had come in to tend bar and Arlene was waiting tables with Cyndi. I was thinking I should put both of them on more.

"Wallace," I said, taking a spot at the bar. "Having a good night?"

"Good as the rest of them," he said. He asked me if I wanted a drink and I figured what the hell, I had been all the way to Shiloh and back. Wallace was a good bartender. He had a memory for what everyone drank. "That boy's been looking for you," he said. "He's been here since five o'clock."

"What boy?"

Wallace pointed over to the little table by the kitchen. "Carl," he said.

I picked up my drink and walked over to what I had come to think of as Carl's table. Cyndi was sitting there with him and they were whispering to one another. Their heads were bent so close they were almost touching. Carl looked up and saw me before I had a chance to say anything. They both sat up straight.

"I'm going to get back to work," Cyndi said, not especially to me or Carl, either one. She walked over to the table across from us and asked the people if they were interested in drinks.

"Where's Fay?" Carl said.

"I would think she was home."

"Wasn't home before," he said. "She said she was coming to work."

"She didn't work today."

"So where'd she go?"

"Carl," I said, "go call your sister if you want to talk to her." I wasn't quite in the mood for him just then. I'd had my fill the night before. He didn't look so bad, really. I don't think he was doing anything. He just seemed to have one of those all-day hangovers.

"It could be I just didn't understand what she was saying."

"That could have been it," I said. I started to head back to the bar to see if Wallace wanted me to cover the last hour for him.

"I appreciate you coming down to get me last night," Carl said.

"Sure."

"I just lost track of the time, was all. I shouldn't have been so late."

I turned around and looked at him. I was trying to figure out just how much of an idiot he was, or how much of an idiot he thought I was. "Listen," I said, leaning into him over the table. "I make a point of keeping out of other people's business, but I'm going to tell you something. You have a real problem, son. You need to see about getting your act together. I know you've had a hard time —"

"I'm not your son," Carl said.

"You know what I meant."

"I know what you meant," Carl said.

I started to say something else, but judging from the look on his face there was no real point in trying to talk. I nodded at him, stood up from the table and went about my business. I didn't hold it against him. It was the carrying. A man shouldn't be carried that way. There's nothing to do but resent the person who picks you up when you're sleeping on the street. No one picks you up, then a time comes you either die or you get up by yourself. At least that way you don't have to worry about feeling ashamed.

The news about Fay not being there didn't seem to bother him any. Carl stayed until we closed up. He was happy there. Every now and then somebody'd stop by his table and talk to him for a while. I thought that maybe I was giving Fay a little rest by watching him. If that's what it was, then I was glad to do it.

When it was time to go Carl stopped by the bar. He must have made a trip to the bathroom because his eyes had gone all watery again. "Good night, then," he said.

I told him Fay was working tomorrow. Both of us were trying to show there were no hard feelings.

"So I'll see you tomorrow," he said.

I locked the door behind him and took the cash drawer out of the register. Then I went upstairs and did the money. It was never very much on a Sunday night. People go to church and change their minds about drinking for the day.

"Stand still," Taft whispers.

"Do you see something?"

"Hush." It's hard to see in the dark. Maybe he hasn't seen anything, maybe he's heard it. His eyes are straining to open wider.

Carl isn't good at being quiet. His boots make a sound as he shifts his weight from side to side. He's young. He has too much energy to hold still. There was something, Taft's sure of that, but whatever it was it's gone now.

"Nothing," he says. "Come on."

"What was it?" Carl says.

"Doesn't matter," Taft says.

The sun is coming up fast. It'll be pitch dark and then a minute later, nearly day. Taft keeps his flashlight pointed down. All you need to see are your feet. There's nothing else to look at. Just watch your feet and concentrate. They had come in the day before and tracked to a good spot, a meadow at the bottom of a sloping hill, closed in by trees on all sides. Better to get your shot when they're out in the open. Deer are always on the alert. He tells this to Carl all the time. They're on the alert so you have to be on the alert. It's October and there's no walking through so many leaves without making some noise. When Taft was a boy he liked to read books about the Indians, the Cherokees and Chippewas who lived in east Tennessee and could walk through the leaves without crushing them beneath their feet. He had practiced, but he never could do it. He thought it must be something in the blood. He had given the books to Carl, but Carl wasn't so interested. Reading meant keeping still.

"Up here," Taft says.

Carl comes up next to his father and they make their way down the slope together, up to the front line of trees. The dogwoods there still have their leaves and the leaves, Taft can see in the first of the light, are blood red on the branches. There are a few white birches, pretty trees, he's always thought. Most of the other ones around are black walnuts. The last to get their leaves in the spring and the first to lose them in the fall. His wife sent a net bag with him, asking could they pick up some black walnuts on the way back if there was time. Taft doesn't know why she fools with walnuts. Once you line them up to dry, the squirrels make off with half and whatever's left is damn near impossible to get into. He feels for the bag in his pocket. It's still there.

"How long you think we'll have to wait?" Carl whispers.

"Depends on the deer." There are two types of hunters, the ones that run after the deer and the ones who stay still and wait for the deer to come to them. Taft says he's a lazy hunter because he waits. He's seen those fools, trailing after a herd, breaking their necks in the underbrush. Doesn't matter how well you know the woods. The deer know them better.

They stand there, looking. The light is coming up fast now. All around them things start to take shape, the trees and grass, tough jewelweed growing nearly waist high. It was good for poison ivy, something else he'd learned from his Indian books. Taft smells the air and wishes he were a Cherokee who could smell the deer a mile away.

"Hope some come soon," Carl says.

Taft sits down and takes a thermos of coffee out of his pack. "It's black," he says.

"That's all right," Carl says.

They each take a cup of coffee and enjoy holding it more than drinking it. "I'm going to shoot us a deer," Carl says, and he pulls up his Winchester and looks through the sight, through the meadow, and takes aim at a white birch on the other side. "Pow," he says softly.

"You've done real well shooting targets."

"I can knock off the cans," Carl says. Carl shoots better than Taft. He has a natural talent for it. He can hold himself steady, concentrate once he's looking down a gun. And it's not just cans he's good at. Taft bought him some paper targets and tacked them up to a piece of plywood. Carl shot in the three inside rings every time and usually he nailed the bull's eye. Taft couldn't understand how a boy who couldn't sit still for more than a minute could take such aim. He thought it must have something to do with the wrestling.

"Go ahead and load up," Taft says. Carl has an ammunition belt he bought for himself with money he made doing chores. Taft keeps a handful of loose shells in his pocket. He brought the soft-tipped Spitzers. That makes it easier. Makes a nice big hole going out. He'd given his old rifle to Carl, a Winchester .30–30 lever-action that he'd had ten years. It's a good gun for a boy. His wife doesn't like it, says Carl's too young to have a gun of his own, but Taft had his first gun when he was thirteen. Here Carl is, sixteen already. Besides, Taft wanted that new Remington .270.

They wait in the quiet. In the trees.

Half an hour goes by before Taft touches Carl's leg and points. It's a buck, maybe two years old, a hundred and fifty yards from where they're sitting. Not a huge deer, but a good deer, a nice four corn.

"Wait," Taft whispers. He wants the deer to come out a little so Carl can get a clean shot. The deer is grazing. There's plenty of time. Carl gets up on one knee, raises his gun.

"Wait," Taft says. He has been on hunting trips where the men sat in the same spot for hours. Sometimes they camped, went two or three days without catching sight of a deer. Now Carl's first time out, it's right there. It would give the boy the wrong idea about how things went. Waiting for them, that was most of the fun.

Carl looks through the sight. "Now," he says.

"Wait," Taft says.

But Carl can't wait. His hands are sweating. In another minute they won't be steady anymore. He will have thought about it too much. He looks in the scope. It's right there. He aims for the neck, not the heart the way his father had told him. You shoot them in the heart and miss, you can track them by the blood. A neck shot was better, but it was trickier. You had to nail it, snap the bone. If you missed in the neck the bullet went right through the muscle and the wound would heal up fast. Neck. He fires. Taft is up. The animal swings down the second the crack goes off. It falls on its right side and its legs kick out again and again like it's slipped and is trying to scramble to its feet. It kicks like this for a half a minute, maybe a second more, not because it's suffering but because the brain isn't there to tell the legs it's dead.

"Got it!" Carl says, and he drops his gun and runs past the trees and into the grass. Taft picks up the rifle and follows him out into the clearing just to make sure the animal doesn't need another shot to finish it off.

"It's dead," Carl says. "Did you see it?"

"I saw it," Taft says. He's a little angry. The boy should have waited, he shouldn't have gone for the neck, but he got the shot off clean. There's no sense taking away from that.

"It's a big deer," Carl says, and squats down to stroke the animal's pelt like it's a dog asleep. He stays clear of the rip in the neck. The fur is turning soggy with the blood. "Did you see it go down?"

Taft nods. "You did a good job," he says. "A good, clean shot."

Carl looks at his watch. "Seven forty-five and we've already got a deer."

They're going to have to carry it to the truck. The thing surely isn't going to walk there by itself. It's probably a hundred-and-forty-, hundred-and-fifty-pound deer. Taft takes his Gerber knife out of its casing and rolls the animal onto its back to gut it. The guts will save them forty pounds. "You want to do this?" he says. He holds the knife by the blade and turns the handle out to Carl. He is careful. He can feel the edge of the steel inside his hand.

Carl shakes his head. Taft's father would have made him do it: "You shot the thing, you're going to have to dress it." But there's plenty of time for that. No need to learn everything in one day. Taft pulls back the animal's tail and slips in the knife. Carl flinches as his father cuts around the rectum. Then Taft brings the blade up between the hind legs and pulls the knife towards him. It's as good a knife as is made. You barely have to saw it at all, just work it up and down a little, a little more once you get to the brisket. It's the smell that Taft never gets used to. It's always worse than he remembers. Hot and dead. Carl takes a step back.

"You have to take the throat out," he says as he cuts the neck. "That's where all the acid is. Leave the throat and the thing will turn gangrene before it's dark."

They turn it over together and pour the deer out of itself in a great wave of blood and entrails. Steam comes up from what's lying there, and the smell of all the dark, wet things inside. "Let it sit a minute," Taft says.

Taft wipes off his knife and his hands. He's done this enough to know how to keep himself clean. He turns away from the deer. Everywhere he looks there are black walnuts. On this side of the meadow the ground is covered with them, too many to ignore. He takes the mesh bag out of his pocket. "Let's go pick some of them up for your mother," he says.

"We don't need to bring home walnuts if we've got a deer," Carl says.

"She wanted some. It'll only take a minute."

Carl wraps his hand around one of the antlers. He lifts the

head up off the ground, just an inch or two to feel the weight and then he sets it down. "I want to stay here."

"It's dead, son. It's not going anywhere." Taft walks off in the direction of the trees and Carl watches him as he bends down again and again to pick up the nuts in their muddy black husks.

"Carl," Taft says.

I was still sitting in the office, still working on that drink Wallace had poured me two hours ago. I'd just been carrying it around from place to place and now the ice was gone. The water made the whiskey easier to take. I thought about calling Franklin, but it was late to begin with and an hour later there. I should have thought of it sooner.

IF ANYONE had told me a dozen years ago that I would be going over to have dinner with the Woodmoores in the middle of the week for no other reason than they asked me, I would have said you were thinking of the wrong man. But there I was, a Thursday night, stopping off to get some flowers and a pack of cigarettes. Mr. Woodmoore liked company that smoked. I quit back when Franklin was born. Marion said it wasn't good enough that I promised not to smoke around him, she said sooner or later I'd slip up. I had to quit altogether, she said. It was a matter of a good example. But her father was a man who liked to bum cigarettes. He would ask anybody down to the basement after dinner to see whatever little thing he was building. You weren't at the bottom of the stairs before he was asking you if you had a smoke. I don't remember him ever having any of his own. For a while he was asking the mailman to come downstairs, till finally the mailman quit smoking or started to lie about it. The first couple of times I went over there without cigarettes, Marion's father would get so angry he wouldn't speak to me for the rest of the night. This was back in the days when they all hated me to begin with. So I learned. He liked it best when I brought Pall Malls. He'd turn the little red pack over and over in his hands, taking pleasure in thinking about it before he lit up. I don't bring those anymore. His blood pressure is high. I buy him something light and mentholated. I tell him it's because nobody can smell it on you later. He breaks the filter off and taps the loose tobacco back in with his thumb.

In the beginning, Marion's parents didn't like me because I played in a band. Didn't like me because they suspected I was having sex with their daughter. Hated me once she turned up pregnant. Talked about having her brother, Buddy, shoot me (Marion told me this) when I didn't marry her.

It was a girlfriend of Marion's who told me about Franklin being born. When I showed up at the hospital, hung over and a full day late, Mrs. Woodmoore grabbed my throat. She caught me coming through the waiting room, jumped out of her chair and clamped her hand into my neck like some sort of rabid dog, digging in her nails till she drew blood. She didn't say a word to me, didn't even blink. I couldn't shake her and I wasn't going to hit her. She cut my air off for a good minute before some orderlies came by and tugged her loose by pulling on her from behind. It was a story she loved to tell. For a while she told it to remind me that she'd done it once and was perfectly able to do it again. Later, when she started to like me, she told it to company when I was around like it was a funny story. "Did I ever tell you about the time I tried to kill John Nickel here?" she'd say, and everybody would laugh. "Show them the scars where I choked you." If I just sat there she'd come over and pull down the collar of my shirt to show the two crescent shaped marks her nails had left. The other cuts healed up fine, but those two left pale, ropy scars. "Look at that," she said, and touched them with her finger. She liked to tell the story at Easter and Thanksgiving dinner especially. She didn't tell it on Christmas, thinking it was too soon after Thanksgiving. Telling it was her way of showing there were no hard feelings. It made her proud to remember herself as someone who'd try and kill a man for causing her child suffering. I could understand that, having a child of my own.

If all my good behavior had no effect on Marion, it did plenty to bring her parents around. They saw how much I loved my boy. They started to like my regular job and the money I was making. They were proud of me, taking care of Franklin and sending Marion through school. When we went over to their house, Marion's mother would ask her politely to come into the kitchen and help her with supper. After they'd been in there for a while, she'd start to holler at her. "You've made your point," Mrs. Woodmoore would say, loud enough to make the neighbors lean towards their windows. "Now you're just being contrary. The man wants to marry you."

Marion would start to argue back, telling her to keep her voice down, that the baby was asleep. About that time Mr. Woodmoore would put a finger up to his lips and point to the basement door. The two of us would slip downstairs to smoke.

"Boy ought to have his father's name," Mr. Woodmoore would say to me. "It's criminal what she's doing to that child." Then he'd take a deep pull on his cigarette and shake his head.

Marion never liked me any better after those visits. In truth, I think they helped her decide to go to Miami, which was the last thing in the world her parents wanted.

It was raining like crazy when I got to their house and I held the flowers upside down to keep their heads from getting knocked off.

"You're going to drown out there," Mrs. Woodmoore said to me. "Come on, get inside."

I shook off my coat best I could on the porch so I wouldn't flood their house. I gave her the flowers and kissed her.

"Ruth, look at this," she said. "Now why don't you bring home boys who give me flowers?"

"Nobody brought him home," she said.

I was surprised to see Ruth there. The last I'd heard she had some job up in Detroit. I'd always liked Ruth and she liked me, mainly because she didn't like her sister. "What are you doing in town?"

"Ruth's moved home," Mrs. Woodmoore said. "She had some hard times so she came back. All my children are always welcome at home."

Ruth looked anxious to get out of the room. "I'll get you a beer," she said. It would be hard on Ruth to come home. She was the wild one. Everybody thought Marion was wild, getting pregnant and then staying single, moving in and out of everyplace all the time. But Marion was staid at heart. She would have liked to get married and settle down if things had gone differently. It was just that her luck was bad. I wondered if some of that bad luck had come to Ruth.

"Business good?" Mr. Woodmoore said. He was always under the impression that I owned the bar no matter how many times I told him otherwise.

"Good enough," I said. "Yourself?"

"Boat's still running. I picked myself an industry that's never going to fold." Mr. Woodmoore ran a tugboat that brought the freighters into dock. "I figure when they retire me I'm going to get myself a job on one of those gambling boats. Then I'll be just like you, spending all day in a bar." He laughed at his joke and Ruth gave me a beer in a bottle.

"What're you doing now?" I asked Ruth.

"This and that," she said, meaning that it wasn't the time to talk about it. Ruth looked like Marion. She wore her hair different and she didn't have the same sort of style, but there was no mistaking the similarity. Being in that house always made me feel like I had gone back to another part of my life. Pictures of Franklin sat on every tabletop. There were her parents. Ruth was Marion. I drank my beer.

"Let's go ahead and eat," Mrs. Woodmoore said. "I know you have to get back to work. That's why we didn't ask you over for Saturday. I know how busy things get for you then."

Ruth stood up in a tired way, stretched a little and headed out to the kitchen to help her mother put out the food.

"Buddy okay?" I asked Mr. Woodmoore.

"Fine," he said. "Fine except he stays away too much. I don't see why they have to station him in Germany. Too hard to come home. Crazy how they keep those boys over there. Hell, fifty years later. It's too far away."

Mrs. Woodmoore stopped frying things when the doctor told her she was killing Mr. Woodmoore with kindness. "Feeding him to death," Marion used to say. She still put bacon in the green beans though and there was chicken gravy for the potatoes. "Take more," she said to me. "You probably never get any food at all. You didn't used to be thin like that."

I put another biscuit on my plate. Whatever people might say about me, it wasn't that I was thin.

"You hear from Marion much?"

"I talk to Franklin once a week. Sometimes I talk to Marion then."

"So you heard about him getting the stitches," Mrs. Woodmoore asked cautiously, like she wasn't sure I had heard.

"Marion called me right after it happened."

Mrs. Woodmoore smiled and nodded.

"It's dangerous for a boy down there," Mr. Woodmoore said, salting his corn. "He shouldn't be running loose that way."

There was nothing for me to say.

"You playing at all?" Ruth asked me. I looked up at her, surprised.

"We don't think Marion is happy," Mrs. Woodmoore said. "Last couple of months, every time I talk to her she starts crying about one thing or another. She says the hospital's not as good as the one here. She said the job she left was better than the one she has. They'd take her back, too. Baptist was always crazy about her."

Ruth put down her napkin and got up from the table. "I'm going to get another beer. You'll have another one, won't you?" She went to get it before I answered, though I would have said yes.

"I don't think Franklin is happy there either."

"He keeps telling me about his friends," I said. I'd be the first to list off all that Marion's done wrong in her life, but no good came from talking this way about a woman to her parents.

"I don't think he likes the school as much. Marion's said that. I think they both want to come back. She just doesn't know how to do it. You know how Marion is, prideful. She'd just as soon choke on her own pride than ask for help."

Ruth came back from the kitchen holding two bottles of beer. She was smiling at me, walking in a slow way. Her sweater had ridden up and was showing an inch of her stomach above her jeans. "Mama thinks that if you ask Marion to come back to you, she'd do it now." She set a beer down on the tip of my knife.

Mrs. Woodmoore looked at her younger daughter, not unlike the way she looked at me when she tried to pull my throat out.

"Marion wouldn't come back to me," I said. "We've tried that. Every way two people can try, Marion and I tried that."

Mrs. Woodmoore took a sip off her tea. Nobody at the table was eating any more except for Ruth. "But if it was true, if she was willing to come back, would you . . . ?"

I waited for her to finish her thought. Would I what? Have her? Marry her? Help her? I was at their dinner table. These people were good to me. I wasn't about to say I wanted no business with their daughter. "I want what's best for Franklin," I said. "I'd be a lot happier if he was home."

The Woodmoores seemed to take this as the right answer, in so much as they both started eating again.

After dinner there was coffee and chess pie. Mrs. Woodmoore never did forget what I liked. She brought out about a half a dozen photos and handed them to me. "These just came this morning," she said. "I thought maybe you hadn't seen them."

Franklin at the beach, wearing his electric blue shorts. It was hard to tell how much bigger he'd gotten until the one where he was standing with Marion. He came up to her shoulder nearly. She was wearing shorts and a T-shirt and big sunglasses. In the picture he was standing in front of her and she had her arms wrapped around him. They were both laughing. For a minute I hated her all over again.

"He's getting so tall," Mrs. Woodmoore said.

I nodded. "Looks good," I said, and handed them back to her. They must have been taken right before he fell. There was no scar. It wouldn't be any time soon that Marion would send us pictures showing that scar.

Mr. Woodmoore said he was working on something down in the basement that he wanted to show me. "I'm putting a ship in a bottle," he said. "Harder on my blood pressure than anything I'm eating."

I got the cigarettes out of my coat pocket and followed him downstairs.

"I can always count on you," he said, peeling back the foil.

"Sure you can."

He handed me the bottle. I could see the little wooden hull of a boat sitting in the bottom. "It's the damnedest thing," he said. "You put it all together inside with needles and tweezers. Buddy sent it to me from Germany for my birthday."

"More than my nerves could take," I said, and put it back in its stand.

"Everybody needs a little something to keep them occupied." He lit a cigarette and then handed one to me. "What about you? You seeing anybody?"

As soon as he said it I got a picture of Fay standing in front of my car at Shiloh. I didn't think Mr. Woodmoore would count a white girl whose head I'd held against my chest. I wasn't sure I counted it either. "Nothing to speak of."

He smiled at me and nodded. "But you're keeping busy. That's good, you should be. All I want from you is a little favor," he said, flicking off his ash into a coffee can. "It's nothing serious now. I just want you to call Marion. Tonight, tomorrow night, doesn't matter. You don't have to say anything in particular, just call and let her know you're thinking of her. The girl's having a hard time. No one would be more in their right than you to say no thanks, but it's like you said, you've got to think about the boy."

"Sure," I said. "I can do that." Maybe I was wrong to go along with him, but I figured if there was anything to be cleared up that was Marion's job to handle. I'd just as soon make the old man happy.

"Good," he said, and patted my arm. "That's good." Then we put out our cigarettes and headed upstairs.

All three of them walked me to the door.

"You still at Muddy's all the time?" Ruth asked me.

I felt sorry for her, a grown woman standing there with her mother and father on either side of her. I thought of her being up long after they went to sleep, sitting in the dark living room, watching television. I told her she should come by.

When Ruth was a kid she kissed me once. It was right before Marion got pregnant. It was August, and at five o'clock it was still 104 degrees. Marion called and asked if I'd take her to the public pool to cool off. The pool closed when it got dark and it didn't get dark in August until past nine. When I pulled up I could hear screaming coming from inside the house. The door flew open and out ran Ruth wearing a swimsuit top and a pair of cut-off shorts. She was skinny and wild looking, like a hot, hungry dog. Marion was right on her heels.

"Don't," Ruth screamed, and she ran and stood behind me. Marion stopped short.

"I can go with you, can't I?" Ruth said.

I always thought it was best to let Ruth come along when there wasn't any chance for me and Marion to be alone together. A public pool when it was 104 didn't hold out a lot of promise of privacy. "You going to be good?" I said.

"Perfect," Ruth said.

Marion rolled her eyes and raked her toes across the gravel on the driveway, but she wasn't going to make a scene about it. Marion had a habit of going along with anything I said back then. "I've got to go get my towel," she said, glaring at her sister.

Ruth hopped in the front seat, giving a little squeal when the hot vinyl hit the backs of her thighs. That's what you get for wearing shorts like that. She leaned out the window. "Get me one too!" she called.

I got in the car and turned the ignition on to listen to the radio.

"Too hot," Ruth said.

"That's August."

"Well, I don't like it."

I looked at her. She had her bare feet up on the dashboard and was trying to fan herself with her hand. When she saw me looking she leaned over and kissed me straight on the mouth, pressing her whole self up against me. It was the kiss of somebody who knew a couple of things about kissing.

"She's going to chop your head off," I said, pushing away from her.

"There wasn't a whole lot of time," she said, readjusting her swimsuit top, "or I would have done it better."

"Jesus," I said. "What are you thinking about?"

Marion opened the front door of the car and stood there holding a bunch of towels under her arm. "Get in the back," she said.

Ruth crawled over the top of the seat rather than go to the trouble of getting out and then in again. She made a real point of dragging one of her legs across my face as she slid over, but that was that.

I said my good-nights and Mrs. Woodmoore tried twice to give me her umbrella. "You should just stay in Buddy's room," she said to me. "Nobody should be going out in weather like this." When I finally got away I ran across the street for my car. From where they were standing, they would have thought I was running from the rain.

A bar can be a nice place to wind up on a night like that. Business was good. Wallace was pouring me a drink as I was walking in the door, and even though I'd been meaning to tell him about my policy against drinking where you work, I took it anyway.

Things always ran smoothly when Wallace was behind the

bar. That's because people liked him and were afraid of him at the same time. It occurred to me all of the sudden that he would be the man to hand the money over to. Nobody was going to bother Wallace at the night deposit box, unless they were planning on shooting him, in which case we all stood an equal chance.

"How'd you do in math?" I asked him.

"Better than I did at some other things," he said. "Is there going to be a test?"

"I was wondering how you'd like to learn to close the place. I can't keep doing it every night myself."

Wallace was a solid character. Football had made him tough. I'd seen him play when he was a star at Memphis State. If it hadn't been for those bad knees, I think he would have gone pro. "I could do that," he said.

"Good." I took a sip of my drink. "We'll get started on that then."

"Tonight?" He said it in such a way that made it clear that it wouldn't be the best time for him.

"Not tonight," I said. "There's no hurry."

This would work out better than Cyndi. She was smart, but she was a moody girl. There was always the chance she wouldn't do what you told her to.

When I went through the kitchen to go up to my office I found Fay and Rose staring in a pot. Fay was stirring.

"Hey," she said. "Look at this. Rose is teaching me how to cook."

"You're teaching her to cook?"

"She asked me," Rose said.

"I'm only coming in for short lessons, just on my breaks," Fay said. "You were so late, we'd about given up on you coming in altogether."

I didn't like the way she was looking at me, so clearly happy to see me when Rose was standing right there.

"Don't stay back here too long," I said. "I'm going up to the office."

I wasn't three steps past them when Fay told Rose she'd be right back and followed me. When we got upstairs she closed the door.

"Something wrong with you?" she said.

"I just don't think it's such a good idea, you coming up here with me when Rose is standing right there."

"She doesn't care."

That much was true. The rest of it I didn't feel like explaining. "Okay," I said. "Never mind."

"Where'd you go tonight?" she said, not like she was prying, more like she was shooting the breeze.

"I had dinner with some friends."

"Did you have a good time?" She was stalling, wanting to stay in the office with the door closed.

"Good enough."

"Carl told me last night that you have a kid."

Carl must have liked that. "I have a son."

"You never told me about him."

"Never came up."

"Do you have a wife to go with this son?"

"Awful lot of questions," I said.

"Are you married?"

"No."

She nodded her head and then sat down on the edge of my desk. Her legs were pale and bare and she had on white socks and black tennis shoes. I watched her leg swing back and forth. "I know you think there's nothing going on here, and probably you're right. But I'm glad you don't have a wife."

"Me too," I said.

"How old's this son?"

"Nine."

"What's his name?"

"Franklin."

"Franklin," she said. "I like that. I could see naming a boy Franklin. If I had a son, I'd name him Levon."

I never knew what it was about women that made them pick out names for children they didn't have.

"I should get back out on the floor," Fay said. "You don't mind Rose teaching me to cook, do you?"

"It's okay as long as she doesn't mind."

"My mother was always going to teach me," she said. Fay had a way of talking that made it seem like her mother was the one who was dead.

She hopped off the desk and stood in front of me. Neither one of us had any idea what was going on or what we were supposed to do about it. "I had a good time yesterday," she said. I nodded at her. She waited for me to say something, but I didn't. It was better that I didn't get started. "I guess I'll see you downstairs, then," she said.

There's no getting overtime in the factory where Taft works. He's lucky to still be full-time. Plenty of people with just a year or two less have been cut down to part-time and lost their benefits. There's been talk of getting a union in there for years. Back in the beginning, Taft was all for it, but he doesn't see that there's much point in it now. You can't get blood from a turnip, and Royal Hill Carpet didn't have enough orders to keep everybody on. It isn't like it used to be. Taft is lucky to have gotten the job as night watchman down at the lumberyard two nights a week. Sometimes he thinks it's wrong, him having two jobs when other people can't find one, but he needs the money. Friday and Saturday nights he's down there ten until five in the morning. Five dollars an hour to wear a uniform and walk around. Sometimes he sits in the office and watches part of "The Tonight Show," but he always winds up shutting it off. He thinks he hears things.

Taft walks between the stacks of lumber. There are floodlights outside that make it light as day in some areas. Then you turn a corner and it's dark again. Part of Taft's job is just to make himself seen, let anyone who may be driving by know that they spent the money to hire a night watchman. He whistles when he can think of a song he feels like hearing. He isn't looking for anybody, he's just trying to stay awake. He wonders what things are coming to when you need to hire somebody to guard wood. Nobody's going to steal anything, he tells himself. No one is coming.

To keep himself occupied he thinks about his family. He thinks about what kind of husband Fay will have. She has too many boyfriends now. Everybody likes Fay. He's hoping she waits at least until she's twenty. Girls get married too young. They fall in love and that's that. They don't see all this time they've got ahead of them. He thinks about Carl and his wrestling. He sees him winning the state championship next year, going on to the nationals. He is pinning boys from Texas and California, the referee circling them and counting. He wonders if Carl could get a wrestling scholarship and go to Iowa and work with Dan Gable. Taft has no idea what kind of grades a boy would have to have to get a wrestling scholarship. Then he remembers Carl's deer, how they hung it up for two weeks to age in the yard from the pole that held the clothesline because it was cold enough. Fay acted miserable about it the whole time. She'd only go in and out the front door and demanded they keep the curtains drawn in the back of the house so she wouldn't have to look at it. It costs money to shoot a deer. The license costs, the rifles, the ammunition, but when your freezer is full up with venison you can't help feeling like a rich man. Taft boned the whole thing, showing Carl how to cut around the bone. Then his wife came out with freezer bags and helped to cut the meat into steaks. She wrapped the roasts and ribs. She cooked the tenderloin for dinner that night.

Taft thinks about his wife the least because in a way she stays outside his thinking. She is a fact, as much as his own life is a fact. The things she does that used to annoy him he hardly ever notices now. The things she does that thrill him he has come to expect. They are together. They have been together since they married, the first Sunday after their high school graduation. They were together before that. It is so true that it's barely worth mentioning.

When Taft is too tired to think about his family he thinks about lumber. It is everywhere. Plywood sheets and two-by-fours. Four-by-sixes and pressboard. Stacks of fir and knotty pine in a separate section near the office. Boxes of trim and quarter-inch dowels. Whenever he lets his mind wander, it goes to the wood. This is how he decides to build the deck.

When Taft gets home it's still dark. He doesn't know if he should eat something or go right to bed. Everything in the house is quiet. He wonders if someone were to break in while he was gone if anyone would even hear it. Taft takes his clothes off in the kitchen. He puts his shoes and socks underneath the chair and lays his pants and shirt on top. He walks down the hallway, past Carl's room and Fay's. The carpet makes everything quiet. He won it for his wife in a production contest that went on for six months. The fastest man on the line. It's a thick shag, an inch of solid blue pile sitting on a quarter-inch padding of quilted foam. Top of the line, plenty of wool, he should know.

"Levon?" his wife says. "You home?"

"Shh. Go back to sleep."

She raises up on one elbow. "Was your night okay?"

"Sleep," he says quietly. He can't see her. He follows her voice into bed.

"I'm up," she whispers.

"It was fine. Quiet. Nothing happened."

"I always worry about you down there by yourself."

"Don't worry."

"You're going to have to talk to Fay," she says as he slides into bed beside her. "She was out until one. Nothing I say makes any difference to that girl. She thinks when you work nights the rules don't apply."

"I'll talk to her."

"Are you hungry?"

"Hm?"

"Let me fix you some eggs," she says, and reaches down to the foot of the bed for her robe. The second she moves away from him, he wants her back, wants her more than he wants the eggs. He wraps an arm around her waist and holds her there next to him.

"Stay put," he says.

"Let me make you something," she says. "I don't mind. I'm going to be getting up soon anyway." When she starts to pull away again he puts his other arm around her and smells her hair. He kisses her neck at the top of her nightgown. Then she understands what he's talking about, and she rolls over to face him.

The next morning Taft puts the foundation down for the deck.

Even coming in at five A.M., he still wakes up before Carl. The

113

sleeping a child can do at that age is almost inconceivable. Fay is up by ten. She brings Taft a cup of coffee that her mother has sent her out with.

"Morning, Daddy."

"Heard you stayed out late last night," Taft says.

It catches her off her guard. Fay looks at her feet. She makes a line in the dirt with her toe. "I didn't know what time it was," she says.

"You know what time you're supposed to be in, don't you?"

"Yessir."

"I'm telling you, Fay, you have to mind your mother. Just because I'm out for the night doesn't give you the license to go living it up and making her worry. Do you understand me?"

"Yessir."

"We can make that curfew earlier if you want to, if you think that would make it easier for you to remember when to come home."

"Dad," she says.

"Okay, that's enough then. You'll remember from now on. Don't make things hard on her, Fay. There's no call for it. Hand me that can of nails over there."

Fay picks up the can full of tenpenny nails and brings them to her father. "Go see if you can't raise your brother from the dead," he tells her.

She goes into the house, looking relieved about the whole thing. Taft wonders if he didn't let her off too easy. Fay's problem, as he sees it, is that she likes men over women. She likes her father and her brother. She likes the boys in school. But she never has special girlfriends. She has girlfriends, but they don't count with her the way boys do. Taft knows women who can't go anywhere unless they're in a whole pack of other women. The time they spend with men only seems to be for collecting stories that they can go back and tell to their girlfriends later on. But that's not Fay. Fay thinks women are boring, silly. Fay never minds her mother. Sometimes, Taft even thinks Fay looks down on her some. All she's interested in is what the boys are doing. That kind of business only gets girls into trouble.

A half hour later Carl appears, his hair working in several directions. He's had his cereal already. Carl doesn't do anything before he eats in the morning. "Thought we were going to work on this deck," Taft says.

"I slept too long," Carl says.

"I want to carry some of the lumber over from the garage. You up for that?"

Carl nods and yawns. He seems so exhausted by his own sleep that it makes Taft tired just looking at him.

It's a fine day to be working outside. One of those great April days when everything is up and blooming and the weather isn't hot or cold. The bank of iris bulbs Taft put out for his wife last September came up so thick you would have thought they'd been there twenty years. Work is easier on days like this. The two of them start bringing the two-by-fours out of the garage. Taft could have done it himself, but he thinks it's important that the boy helps. If Carl is in on every step then when it's all over he can take some pride in the deck, know that he built it too. They carry five boards each trip, laying them in stacks on a sheet of plastic drop cloth Taft has put next to the house. Carl is going faster. That's what Taft is thinking. So much younger and faster than me. He wonders if Carl is showing off. Taft is going slower and slower. There is a good April breeze that blows over the smell of the iris and Taft is chilled from his sweat. Something, the sweat or the smell of the flowers, is making him sick. The boards aren't so heavy, but they are getting heavier. He tries to catch his breath and can't and can't until he has to stop. There's a pain in his left arm so sudden and sickening that he looks down to see if he hasn't run something through it. The pain shoots all the way up into his jaw. There is a straight line of pain from his fingertips to his molars. A pressure comes from someplace outside him and begins to crush him as he stands there. Everything starts to drop away. The boards slip one at a time and hit against each other with a terrible crashing sound and then he is falling, down on his knees. He is sitting down next to the boards, holding the bad arm in the good, trying to breathe.

"Dad," Carl says. His voice is loud. He runs and sits beside him. Taft is dead white. Carl puts his hands on his shoulders.

Then just the way it came, everything starts to move backwards. The pain recedes. He inhales slowly, his chest making small, cautious movements in the face of air. "I'm fine," Taft says.

"Stay there," Carl says. "I'm going to get Mom."

Taft takes his son's hand. "Sit," he says, "I'm fine." He looks back over at the house. There's nobody at the window. No one saw. "I didn't get enough sleep last night," he says. "I should be more like you."

He is still sitting on his knees. Still holding the bad arm, though now it is only a dull ache. "I think you're sick," Carl says.

Taft loves him. At that moment he loves his son more than he has ever loved anything in his life. Carl is sitting beside him and Taft puts his hand on his son's leg, thinks, I made this.

"Listen," Taft says. "Don't tell about this. Don't tell Fay or your mother. Once they start worrying it won't ever end and all I did was drop some wood. I was up till five this morning. I have a right to be tired."

"You sure?"

Taft nods, smiles. They stand up together. It would have been hard to tell from a distance who was pulling up who. "You put this lumber back?"

"No problem."

"I think I'll go in and take a nap." The nausea is still there. It would be good to lie down. "By this afternoon we should be right back at it."

Taft starts to go towards the house and Carl stays right with him. "Go get the wood," Taft says.

"I will in a minute," Carl says. Carl walks Taft all the way back to the bedroom and turns down the bed and undoes his shoes. Carl pulls the curtains closed until the room is dark again. "Get some rest," he says, and then he kisses him.

I don't know how long I stayed in my office, an hour or two, but when I came down to the bar Carl had taken up his rightful spot. There was somebody I didn't know sitting at his table and they were talking. Carl nodded at me when I walked by.

"Your brother's getting popular," I said to Fay.

"Thank God," she said. "He hadn't made any friends in Memphis till he started coming over here. Carl's a social kid at heart. He likes being around people."

Wallace put three bottles of beer, two bourbons and a gin and tonic out on the bar and Fay loaded them onto her tray. "See you," she said, lifting it all up with one hand. She had good balance.

"You watch that brother's sociability," Wallace said to me once she was gone.

"What's that supposed to mean?"

"It doesn't mean anything other than you should be keeping an eye on him." Arlene came to the bar and gave Wallace a long order and he started to work again. Wallace was a young man. Figuring when I'd seen him play ball, I put him at about twenty-three or -four now. It was his size, maybe, that made everything he said seem so credible, either that or his voice. Wallace's voice was quiet and low and he didn't talk fast. You had to almost lean in to hear him. It made you pay attention to what he said.

I looked over and saw that whoever Carl had been talking to had left his table and left the bar. I picked up my drink and went over to see him myself.

"How you doing there, Carl?"

"Hey," he said, pulling out a chair for me. "I'd wanted to talk to you before. Some guy was lonely, you know, just parked himself here."

I sat down. Carl looked a whole lot better than he usually did. His eyes were clear and he wasn't sweating. Drugs made Carl sweat, I'd seen it before. As far as I could tell, he was all there.

"I wanted to tell you I felt bad about last night," Carl said. "I didn't mean to be such a jerk. I was just mad at myself was all. When you and Fay found me down here the other night — " He stopped for a minute and opened up his hands. There wasn't a good way for him to say it. "I was doing things I shouldn't have been doing. I was messed up. I was sorry you even knew about it. I mean, I guess it was a good thing you did. If you hadn't picked me up somebody else would have."

It had a bad sound the way he said it, somebody else. "That problem you were having that night, how much of a problem is it?"

"No problem," Carl said, taking a sip of his Coke. "Everything's under control now."

"That's good," I said. I didn't believe him, but there was really no point in telling him so. A boy in Carl's place has to figure out some hard things. You can tell them what they should do until you don't have any breath left, but the thing that stops them, the thing that scares them bad enough to stop, is something they have to come to by themselves.

"Can I buy you a drink or anything?" Carl said. "I'd like to do something and I can't think of what."

"I don't pay for my drinks," I said. "You don't have to do anything for me. You just worry about taking care of yourself. That's what's going to be best for everybody."

"Best for Fay," Carl said, looking over at his sister carrying beers to a table. "She's had a bad time. I shouldn't be worrying her so much."

We got everybody out by eleven-thirty. Rose was gone after the kitchen closed at ten. Carl and Fay walked out with Arlene. It was just me and Wallace there when I opened up the cash register.

"We'll start on Sunday," I said, lifting the whole thing out. I liked to count the money upstairs, where I wasn't in front of the windows.

"You think it's a good idea, trusting me with all that?" Wallace said.

"I don't think there'll be any problems."

I was just heading back when the door opened and Fay and Carl came in. "I left my jacket," Fay said. "It was so nice I just walked right out and forgot it."

Wallace looked under the bar and came up with Fay's puffy jacket. "Thanks," she said.

"I'll come out with you," Wallace said. "Lock the door behind me."

I put the register tray down on the bar and followed the three of them to the door. Carl was just standing there quietly, waiting on his sister.

"Night," Fay said.

When I got up to the office I started thinking about calling Marion. It was late, but she worked all sorts of crazy shifts. There was always the chance I was going to wake her up no matter what time it was.

"Marion," I said. "It's me. Were you sleeping?"

"I wish I was," she said. "I just got in a little while ago. Franklin's asleep."

"I figured that. I was calling to talk to you."

She yawned. "Did you get the pictures I sent?"

"No, but I saw them. I was over at your parents' house for dinner."

"I never will understand why they like you so much all of the sudden," she said, but she said it nice enough. I was glad I'd called. I'd caught her in a good mood.

"They were telling me that I should call you. They said you're having all sorts of problems down there."

"They shouldn't be talking about me."

"You having problems?"

She was quiet for a minute. "It hasn't been so good lately. I don't know, Franklin getting stitches and all, that really threw me. Now I'm worrying about everything."

I hadn't figured her parents might be right about her not being happy. All Marion ever told me was that the world had been going her way since she hit Miami. "So do you want to come home?"

"What do you mean?"

"Come back to Memphis," I said. "What do you think I mean?"

"Nothing," she said. She was quiet again. "I was thinking we might drive up for Franklin's spring break next week. I haven't taken any time off since I've been here. Franklin misses you," she said. "I think it might do him good to see you for a while."

I sat up in my chair. "Come home then," I said. Her just saying that made me miss him so strongly it felt like it was the day they left.

"Maybe we will," she said.

"You know Ruth's home." Franklin liked Ruth, even if Marion didn't get on with her so well.

"I know. She lost her job or something. She doesn't really say what happened. Seems like whenever things get bad the whole world packs up and goes back to Memphis."

"It wouldn't be like that for you. You have a good job. You could get back on at Baptist in a minute." I was letting my mind run away with me. Franklin would come back. I could take care of him. He could come and live with me for a while. I'd see that I got a lawyer, that it was legal that I was his father and he was mine. Nothing like this could ever happen again. "Marion," I said.

"What?"

"We've known each other a long time. A long time. If you came back we could manage fine, better than we used to. We wouldn't have to be fighting about things. We'd take care of Franklin. You don't have to worry that I'm going to make any sort of trouble for you. If I'm the reason you're thinking about not coming back, I'm just telling you, don't worry about it."

"No," she said. "You're not keeping me away."

By the time we got off the phone she had all but said that she was going to bring Franklin up for his vacation. That was promise enough for me. If they were happy back here for a week, then why not a month, or a year? Why not move back altogether? I had a son. I was the one to look after him. I was starting to think that the world was a dangerous place for boys.

MIDDLE OF the day and Cyndi was flying. She had a stupid grin plastered on her face I'd never seen before. While she was standing at the bar waiting on her drinks she started slapping out a beat on the half-polished guardrail. Four light slaps and two hard, two light, two hard. It could have been the base for any one of about two thousand songs.

"What did you have for lunch?" I said.

"Not a thing." Cyndi wasn't a grinner. It was all I could do to keep from staring.

Quick as I poured the drinks she was buzzing them off to a table. She was walking so fast her skirt was twitching. I knew that walk. I knew those eyes. I was tired of it.

"Cyndi," I said.

Back she came, like her feet weren't even touching the floor. She was smiling at me, laughing. I was looking at her and the more I looked the more she laughed until she was just cracking herself up. Her pink eyes started to tear she was laughing so hard. She made me realize just how good Carl was at holding himself together when he was stoned. "What?" she said.

"I'll fire you," I said. "Just watch me."

She tried to straighten up. She was still giggling. She was on a roll. She couldn't stop herself, even though she was trying hard. "Don't," she said.

"No second chance," I said. "Understand that? No more of this shit."

She breathed in deep, hiccupped and nodded. I turned my back on her, busied myself at the bar. I was goddamned tired of these kids.

Fay came in looking like a soaked cat from the rain. Everywhere she went she left a little dripping trail of herself. The first thing she said to me was that she had to leave in a couple of hours. "I called Arlene," she said. "She's coming in at six to cover for me. It's my uncle's birthday. They want everybody to be home for the party."

"As long as you're covered," I said, even though I'd been thinking about calling Arlene myself to see if she couldn't come take Cyndi's place.

"Believe me," she said, lifting herself onto a barstool. "I'd rather stay here and make some money."

I handed her a stack of cocktail napkins. "See if you can't dry your hair some."

She wadded them up and dabbed at her forehead. "It's pouring," she said, as if to tell me she couldn't help it. Outside the water was coming down in sheets, making a wild river next to the sidewalk. The whirlpools over the sewers looked strong enough to suck up a child.

Fay was still blotting herself when the door opened up and Ruth walked in wearing a raincoat. She shook out her umbrella and hung it on a peg beside the door, then walked up to the bar without a drop of water on her. Ruth had a way of looking good no matter what was going on around her. Her hair was always fixed and I'd never seen her when she wasn't wearing lipstick. "The surest sign a woman doesn't have a child," Marion used to say.

"You look like somebody held you under," she said to Fay.

Fay looked up and tried to think of what to say. She didn't come up with anything.

"What're you doing out in this rain?" I said to Ruth.

She leaned over the bar and gave me a kiss on the cheek. She smelled like lilies. Ruth was smooth. Everything she did came off looking natural. Fay was staring at her.

"I just thought I'd come down and see how business was."

"I ought to get to work," Fay said quietly.

"Work?" Ruth said. "You're hiring children?"

"Best waitress I've got." I could say that, now that Cyndi was too stoned to stand up.

Fay smiled a little, pleased for the compliment but not so happy about anything else. "See you," she said.

"She's a baby," Ruth said, watching Fay walk into the kitchen. "I mean it. You'd think there'd be some kind of law against that."

"She's fine."

"Well," Ruth said, bringing her elbows up on the bar. "I'm glad to hear it."

"You want a drink?"

"Give me a beer," she said. "Whatever you like."

I reached in the cooler and got her a Rolling Rock. "I was surprised to see you last night. I thought that once you went over the state line that would be the last we'd ever hear from you."

"Yeah, well, things have a funny way of working out."

"What didn't work?"

"One thing and another," she said. "The job went bad. The man went bad. You name it. Things were getting a little tight was all. But I'll tell you one thing, being home isn't the answer.

Adults aren't meant to live in their parents' house. Sleeping in those little beds again." She shivered. "I wake up in the morning and look at those awful frilly curtains and think any minute somebody's going to be rapping on the door and telling me to get ready for school. Mama's going to make me sit on the floor between her legs and plait my hair so tight it makes my eyes pull back. You laugh, I'm serious. I've seen her looking at my hair."

"She never wanted to let you move out in the first place."

"Now that I'm back I've inspired her to bring all the chickens home," she said. "She's trying to get her hands on Marion and Franklin. I guess you figured that one out. The next thing you know she'll be asking the president to ship Buddy back."

"You think Marion's coming back?"

She was taking a sip of her beer, but the minute I said that she put the bottle down and looked at me hard. "Jesus Christ, you're not still waiting around on her?"

"Hell, no."

"It's just too much, her jerking you around all those years, then Mama and Daddy sitting there at dinner saying you should ask her to come home like everything's forgotten. You asked her so many times I thought you were going to have it tattooed on your chest."

"Marion doesn't have any interest in me," I said. "We're pretty square on that one."

"Don't you be so sure." She shook her head. Her dangling coral earrings swung back and forth. "She's been alone for a while now. It's a lot easier to say no when somebody's asking you all the time. Nobody's asked Marion lately."

"What ax are you grinding with Marion?" I said.

"She's a fool," Ruth said. "You know how the saying goes, 'I don't suffer them lightly.'"

"She's had her share of trouble."

"And she made every bit of it herself."

"Not all of it," I said. "I helped her out some."

Ruth waved her hand like she was brushing me off. "People don't have to pay and pay and pay for something that happened a lifetime ago."

"I'm not paying anything," I said. "That's all done."

"The hell it is." Ruth pushed her beer aside and leaned towards me. "I'll tell you what I know," she said. "I know something that every other person in my family forgot. I know something your own son never even saw, and that's that you were the best drummer in this town."

"You're thinking about somebody else," I said, half laughing. I was watching Cyndi. She was walking slower now, pulling herself together.

"Don't you remember anything?" Ruth said. "I remember when I was fifteen years old and you'd bring me and Marion down to Handy Park when you played in the summer. God, she hated it when you let me come along. She used to tear my hair out when we got home, but it was worth it. You were so good. I'd do anything to get to watch you play. You were the one that everybody came to see. You'd come over at breaks and buy me and Marion Cokes. Every girl there wanted to be me, wanted to be her. They would have done anything just to get you to look at them and it was all because of the way you played."

"You're crazy."

"I wasn't the crazy one," she said. She was looking at me hard. "You had something nobody else had. The closest we ever got to being famous was being able to watch you. Marion took that away."

"Nobody takes that," I said. I didn't like to talk about this. I made a point not to talk about this. "You give it up."

"You gave it up because she said if you did, you'd get Franklin.

Then she took him, too. She made you eat your own heart and you're not even smart enough to blame her. Look around this place and tell me what you've got now."

Fay came up to the bar. "Bud, Bud Light, Bud Dry," she said.

When I reached into the cooler my hands were shaking. As long as my back was turned, Ruth kept quiet. I crouched down and pretended to have a hard time finding the Light. The cold air felt good. The bottles felt good in my hands.

"Got it," I said, and I took off the caps.

"Your hair's all dried," Ruth said to her.

"It dries pretty fast," Fay said, touching her hair lightly. As soon as I handed her the beers, she was gone.

"I think she's scared of me," Ruth said. "Wonder why that is."

"You're fucking scary is why that is." I turned my back to her and made myself busy with some glasses.

"You don't get it at all," Ruth said. Her voice was tired, like she'd spent her whole life trying to explain it to me. "Remember when I was fifteen? Remember when you were first getting work in bands? Remember how you used to buy me lemon ice in those little paper cups and how you used to say to Marion when I was standing right there, 'She's going to be the heartbreaker.' Middle of the day, we'd all get so bored. You used to say you didn't know what to do with yourself when it was light outside. We'd all go riding over to Arkansas just to be crazy, and I'd sit in the window of the car with my hands up on the roof. Don't you remember anything?"

"I don't think about that."

"Furry heard you play," she said. "I remember. He nodded at you and everybody saw it. Everybody was saying, Did you see Furry nod at him?"

"Stop talking like this," I said, keeping my voice low and even. "You don't go bringing these things up. Why don't you know that?" She looked like Marion. Fifteen and seventeen, the two of them walked down the street with me, one on each side. People called out, "He's got a pair of them. A big one and a little one." Marion would shoot them a dirty look and Ruth would just hold her head up and smile.

"I don't think it's ever too late for a man to come to his senses," she said. "Maybe if you had somebody around to remind you what you are then you'd go back and start playing again."

"We're through talking about this," I said.

Ruth picked up her purse and got off the stool.

"Come on back," I said, shaking my head at her. "I'm not telling you to leave. Listen, Ruth, you're family. Sit down and have another beer. There's got to be something better we can talk about than your sister and what I didn't make of myself."

"I'm not family," she said. She went to the door and pulled her raincoat on. The weather hadn't slowed for two straight days. "Come over to the house and see me if you have the time." She opened her umbrella while she was still inside and then she was gone.

There are women who like men better than other women. If that woman is your sister, if that man used to be your sister's lover, it still isn't going to make any difference.

Ruth did me a favor once, right after Franklin was born. She stayed in my corner. She took pictures when nobody would let me in to see him. She came over to my apartment at night and told me how much he weighed and how long he was and how he was eating. She was the one who said I was the father no matter what and sooner or later they'd have to relent. She went at them again and again until finally on the fourth day I got to hold him and Marion talked to me a little when her parents were out of sight. Ruth did that for me.

Ruth was three months away from finishing high school

when she took off to New Orleans, stayed gone six months, and then turned up again. After a few more years in Memphis she took up with a slide guitarist I knew to be trouble, but there was no making Ruth listen. She went with him to Chicago and then came back. The last time it was Detroit, but it had been Detroit for long enough that I thought she might have settled down.

"Who was that?" Fay said. She looked around, thinking that wherever she was she might be back in a minute.

"That was Ruth," I said. "I've known her for a long time, since she was a kid."

"Hard to imagine her being a kid," Fay said.

It was raining so hard that by four o'clock it looked dark and by five o'clock it was. The night before, the weather had forced everyone who was caught outside to come into the bar and have a drink, but tonight people had gotten wise to things and just stayed home.

"I'm sleepy," Cyndi said, sitting on a barstool braiding her hair. I poured her a cup of coffee.

Fay was standing at the window, watching the flood on Beale. "I hate to have Carl drive all the way out here in weather like this," she said, making conversation with her own reflection in the glass.

I didn't much like the idea of Carl driving in any circumstance. The bar was quiet, except for the sounds of the rain. There were three old men drinking beers in the back of the room, but there was no noise coming out of them. "I'll take you home," I said.

Fay and Cyndi both looked up at me.

"Nothing better to do around here," I said. "I'd just as soon get out. Arlene's going to be coming in any minute."

"I'll see if I can catch Carl," Fay said. She ran over to the phone behind the bar. She went too fast.

"Is Carl there?" she said.

"What the hell is going on?" Cyndi said.

But I wasn't worried about what Cyndi was going to think, not after the shape she'd been in at lunch. "Go back in your cave," I said to her.

"He said it wasn't any problem." Fay held the phone with both hands. "It would save you the trip. Go on now, and I'll just meet you at home. Really. No. It's easier." She hung up. "It's fine," she said.

"That's great," Cyndi said. "The two of you just go on."

"I'm coming right back," I told her.

"My uncle owns Martin-Quick Pharmacy. Their last name is Martin," Fay said to me in the car.

Martin-Quick. Old money. Everybody has an account. You don't even have to say your name. They hand you a bag and it just winds up on your bill. I went in once to buy Franklin a soda. I can't remember what we were doing over there now, but I can promise you they didn't offer us credit. The woman behind the counter kept a close eye on Franklin while he was looking at the candy. "Don't pick that up unless you plan to buy it," she said to him.

"Carl's been working there after school and on weekends. Me and Carl are used to working. When we came to town my aunt and uncle said no more jobs. They thought we should have the time to get settled in and go to school and be depressed. Whatever. They said they'd give us an allowance. It made us crazy, not working, not making money. When things were going so bad after my dad died we started thinking that money was the answer to everything. I know it's not, but I'll tell you, it's a lot. Finally I asked my mother. She pretty much says yes to whatever anybody asks her these days, so Calvin and Lily had to let us get jobs. They said the deal was that one of us had to work in the pharmacy. If we were looking for work and Calvin had some, then we should be able to work for him. I was all ready to do it, but then Carl took the job. It was really good of him, Carl hates Calvin, but we figured I'd probably be able to make more money since I'm older."

"And they don't mind you working in a bar?"

Fay was squinting, trying to see out the window. "They don't know about that."

"Where do you say you are?"

"I told them I waitress at a twenty-four-hour Friendly's. Fast, friendly, family-style. Believe me, they're never going to check."

I was driving slow because of the rain. There is no rain like the rain in Tennessee. At times the road just disappeared, and then the yellow line would wash back into the headlights. I had the windshield wipers on high. I didn't like windshield wipers. The beat was too regular. It got on my nerves.

"Wouldn't it be easier to work someplace you wouldn't have to lie about?"

"I can make better money at Muddy's. Me and Carl figure once we make enough money we can go back to Coalfield. Everything we make, we save."

I knew for a fact that Carl was spending money, or maybe all his pleasures came from the back of Martin-Quick, Valium and Dexedrine. Maybe he was walking off with Dilaudid and a handful of those individually wrapped, disposable needles they sold to diabetics. Drugstores are where the suffering go to lessen their suffering. Carl put their purchases into bags and wrote down the price in the account book.

"Memphis hasn't been so bad for me since I've been working," Fay said. "But it's hard on Carl. There're too many ways for him to get in trouble here."

"There's a lot to be said for staying with your family."

Fay shook her head. "Family's more complicated than that. It can be more place than people."

I thought of Taft, waiting for his daughter to come back and read his tombstone.

"Used to be I never thought I'd miss this place," she said. "I always thought as soon as I had the money I'd be out of here." We were in her neighborhood. You could tell by the pillars. "But it's different now. It's starting to be different."

I pulled over at the corner a block from Fay's house and turned off the car. The rain was coming down so hard you could barely hear yourself think. "What do you want to do?" I said, wondering if she wanted me to drive her all the way to her house tonight. It was just a ride. That's all it was. There was no reason for her to walk anywhere in this weather.

"I want to stay here with you," she said. She moved over next to me on the seat. Her shoulder was pressing against my shoulder and I could feel myself starting to sweat.

"You've got to be home," I said. "They're waiting on you."

"Walk over with me."

"I'll drive you over."

She put her head on my shoulder. I felt it all the way down my arm. "It wouldn't be so bad if we were together," she said quietly.

"Stop that," I said. Two words and I could hardly get them out of my mouth. I was wondering if she'd ever been with anybody before. I was wondering what she knew. I was thinking what she would look like in my bed, her flat stomach and little hips twisted up in my sheets. I could feel the blood moving through my body and I thought I would be safer out of the car. I opened the door and stepped out in a rain strong enough to drown you if you put your head back. It was beating through my jacket. Thirty seconds and my shirt was wet. I held out my hand for her and she took it and followed me out into the weather. Then we were up against the car and all I could feel was her, not even the water. She had her arms around my neck and I was pulling her towards me and I kissed her. I was kissing her eyes and the line of her jaw and I felt her mouth on my face. The rain confused everything. It turned a lip into a forehead and a hand into hair. I couldn't tell where I was on her body because the rain melted everything together. Then my mouth would find her mouth and that was something different, because I felt how it was warm inside of her. I pressed her against the car and felt her outline like she was traced into me. I felt her bones, her shoulders and hips. I felt how small they were and I stepped back. She was holding onto both my hands.

"You need to get home," I said, though there was no telling if she could hear me for the noise of the rain. I pulled her away from the car and up the street towards the house where she lived.

It was dark in every direction. The only light came blurred out of windows from houses that were set back far from the street. No cars passed us. The rain kept everybody tight indoors. There was so much rain it was hard to get a good breath. It didn't seem like I was pulling Fay anymore. She had started pulling me, and I was walking behind her up the driveway. My shoes were heavy with water and they squished and pulled against my feet.

"Go on in," I said.

"You're here," Fay said, holding on to my hand tighter in case I decided to make a run for it. "You've got to see something."

We went off the driveway and into the mud. Mud was the least of our problems. I stayed with her. I thought of the night I was inside that house and thought that this wasn't so different. Inside or just a little outside was all the same. It made me nervous. Men didn't walk girls between houses in the rain in the dark. We came around to the side. We were walking through bushes and the loose branches of some trees. We were practically at the window when she stopped me. It was like watching a movie, the screen divided up by windowpanes. It was so bright inside that they never could have seen us, even if they had been looking. The water on the glass was steady enough that it was almost clear. I remembered a sugar Easter egg my grandmother brought me when I was a child and when you looked inside you saw the world was full of rabbits and chickens made out of a hard, bright frosting. They were in the dining room. I saw Carl. He looked sullen, standing near the table in his T-shirt and jeans, his toothpick arms crossed in front of his chest. There were two women, one was blond with her hair piled up on top of her head, the other had hair that was short and no color in particular. A man walked into the room and the blond woman started to make over him. You could see their mouths move but the rain kept them quiet.

"You know Carl," Fay said, pointing. "The woman next to him, that's Virginia, that's my mother. The one with the lipstick is Lily, she's my mother's sister, and the man is my uncle, Calvin, They're all wondering where the hell I am right about now. They're ready to start dinner. They don't like it when things run late. Hey," she whispered. "Idiots. Right here." She started to wave, but I took her hand and held it down.

It was like I was hungry to look at them, because I couldn't make myself stop. The wallpaper was striped blue and white and there was some sort of pattern I couldn't make out in the blue. There was a brass chandelier with the lights shaped to look like candles in glass globes. The aunt was putting silverware on the table and the light caught on her rings like she was a mirrored ball in a dance hall. The uncle was talking to Carl, who wasn't listening. I could tell that from the bushes, but the uncle didn't seem to know. Virginia just sat quietly at the table, less in the room than me or Fay. She hadn't dressed up like her sister. She had forgotten it was a birthday party.

"I don't look a thing like my mother, do I?" Fay said, her mouth close up to my ear. "Carl and me look like Daddy. Carl looks so much like him it's spooky. First thing everybody used to say when they met him, Do you know how much you look like your father?"

I broke myself away from the movie and turned to Fay. She looked like Taft. She was so wet it was like she was underwater. She started kissing me. Little kisses, ten, twenty, thirty, on my lips. I knelt down beside the house, in the deep mud of what would be a flower bed a few weeks from now. The little green tips of the jonquils were up already and I crushed them with my knees. I felt too sick to stand. I didn't even have to think about what it would be like to make love to her there. I could see it like it was happening in front of me. "Go inside," I said.

"No."

"They're waiting on you."

She put her hands inside the collar of my shirt. It was so wet she had to work them down, as if she was separating skin from skin. My face pressed into the front of her shirt and I felt the shape of her breast with my cheek. It was all the water that was drowning me. She kissed me.

"Fay," I said. I was trying to pull up through the water. I took her shoulders in my hands. I was six inches from the brick of her house. "Tell me how old you are. Tell me the truth."

"Eighteen," she said. "Eighteen next week."

I knew it was something like that. I'd always known, but I asked because hearing it would stop me. Seventeen meant high school, never coming to work before three in the afternoon, reading from textbooks on breaks. I stood up. My legs were stiff and clumsy as we walked away from the house. I rubbed her bare knees until the mud came off in my hands. Other than that, there was no way to fix her up. "I'm going now," I said, and this time it was true. The people in the dining room were eating little snacks on crackers, trying not to spoil their supper while they waited.

"You can't," she said. Was she crying? There was no way in the world to know.

"You go on and get yourself something to eat." I took a step away from her and she stuck herself to me. She was so light, lighter than Carl even.

"I'm lonely," she said in my ear. She said it like she might have said I'm tired or I'm hungry. It made me crazy. It made me want to promise her things, to cover her up. It took a lot to get her off, but when I finally did she just stood there, watching me. Even when I was at the end of the driveway she was still standing there.

I walked back to my car in the rain.

I knew the way to her house and back from her house in my sleep. Any street in town could get you there or take you farther away. It wasn't like driving. I was just going along. What I was doing I could do nothing about. There was a Jim Dandy just before the Fowler Expressway. From a distance I could see they had one of those pay phones you could drive up to. I knew Marion's number by heart.

"Hey Mrs. Woodmoore," I said. "It's John."

"What a treat to talk to you two days in a row," she said.

"Well, I wanted to thank you for supper." The rain was beating on the piece of metal that hung over the phone, making such a racket I could barely hear her.

"Are you outside?"

"It's just noisy in here," I said. "I'm calling from work."

"I don't know how you stand it."

"It's not so bad, really." The rain was blowing in through the open car window, making a lake in the front seat. What the hell difference did it make? "Hey Mrs. Woodmoore, I was calling to see if Ruth wanted to come down. There's a band playing tonight, some old friends of hers. I thought she might like to get out."

"You've always been thoughtful of Ruth," she said. "I think it's hard on her being home. Would you like to ask her yourself? She's right here."

"That would be good."

Fay had left her purse in the car. I picked it up and kneaded the leather in my free hand.

"Hello?" It was Ruth.

"I'm about ten minutes from home right now. I'm calling from a pay phone. If we both leave now we can get to my apartment at the same time."

There was a pause, but I never thought she wouldn't do it. "All right."

"You have to leave right now," I said. "Do you understand me? Don't put on lipstick, don't brush your hair." I pulled the purse into my lap. "Just put down the phone, get your car keys, and walk out the door. I've already told your mother where you're going."

"That sounds like fun," she said. Mrs. Woodmoore would be standing there, smiling, as close as I was to the windshield. "I'll see you then." She hung up the phone.

When I was driving I tried not to think about anything. I didn't think about the people inside the window or Taft or Ruth. I kept my eyes on the road. It took a lot of concentration, driving in weather like that. I didn't even want to think about Fay. At first I saw her pulling her wet sweater over her head but then I stopped it. I didn't want things to go further yet. I didn't want anything to change. That moment, the car and the night and the rain, the way I could almost feel her, I wanted to hold everything exactly like that for as long as I could. Cars drove by spraying walls of water into each other. All of the sudden you were blind. Two times the wheels lost contact with the road and for a split second I felt myself slipping, but I got it back. I tried going slower.

I pulled into the parking lot behind my apartment building and made a run for it. Marion was standing inside the alcove in front of the door. She was leaning against the wall like she'd been there all night, like she had nothing but time.

"I thought you said come right away." Ruth. I could tell the difference in their voices. It was Ruth.

She didn't have a drop of water on her, just like she didn't before, but she wouldn't have thought there was anything wrong with me being soaked. Just look at the night. No one would blame me for looking the way I did. I didn't say anything. I closed my eyes and put my hand behind her neck and brought her to me. There wasn't a lot of time. Not while everything was still clear in my mind. I kissed her there at the door. I kissed her neck and her ears. I kissed her hard on the mouth and she kissed me back, pulling her dry arms around me. Once I could feel the pressure of her against my chest I could think again. Then I could smell her and see the people in the sugar egg. I could pull her down to me the way I wanted. I reached under her coat and lifted up her shirt, ran my hands across her back and down to the sides of her hips. I touched the slick material of her underpants with my fingers. She kept kissing me. She was pulling on my belt. My clothes were so wet she had to struggle with them. I felt her tongue against the side of my face. It was the same rain making the same noise. The noise kept everything else quiet. Her raincoat slipped off of her and suddenly she was everywhere. I could feel her in back of me and in front of me at the same time. She was against the door and still I felt the door on my back. I wanted her. I told myself so over and over again in my mind. This is how I made love to all of them, equally.

Taft doesn't like going to Memphis. He doesn't like his wife's sister or her husband. He doesn't like the thought of their family being anything more than the four of them. Lily is always talking about family, family this and that. "We should do more things together as a family," she says, and Taft wonders what the hell she's talking about. He doesn't see any way that their two families link up. Lily has her eye on his kids. That's what it's all about. Never had any of her own and now she wants to get a hold of his. She's always asking Fay and Carl to come up for holidays or spend the summer with them. Virginia told him her sister couldn't have children. Or maybe it was Calvin. There was something wrong with one of them and it showed. Whenever Taft walks through their house he thinks, You can't have carpet this pale and expect to raise a family on it. Of course, it wouldn't be bad having that kind of money. He doesn't like looking at Lily's jewelry all the time. He thinks she could wear a little less when they're around, or give a piece of it to her sister. One sister raises two children on next to nothing, keeps a job and a clean house and is lucky to get a nice sweater for Christmas. The other one goes out to lunch at the country club while somebody else gets bused in to do her vacuuming and she gets something called a tennis bracelet for Christmas which she never takes off. She doesn't play tennis, either.

When Virginia and Taft were first going out Lily used to drive to Knoxville to study in the medical library because she'd read in a magazine that that was the best way to catch yourself a doctor. She didn't know the pharmacology students studied there too.

But this one had a family business, four generations of Martin-Quick pharmacists. And he was from Memphis, which was far enough away from Coalfield to forget about it altogether. There went Lily. It wasn't until Fay and Carl were born and there were no babies for Lily and Calvin that they even started hearing from them regularly.

Taft and Virginia and Fay and Carl are all going to Memphis. Carl is going to wrestle in the state championship. Virginia says it's killing two birds with one stone. Taft usually manages to get out of the trips to see her sister, but he would go anywhere his son was wrestling, even to Memphis.

Taft doesn't like going to Memphis. He doesn't like the look of the place. It's too flat. The river is dirty. He's been sitting in the shadow of the Smoky Mountains since the day he was born. The mountains, he thinks, are beautiful. He doesn't like the weather, which never seems to cool off. Every breeze is choked with humidity. It's like trying to walk through water. The people are too rough, too forward, everybody knowing how much money everyone else has and where the money came from. In Memphis, money is worth more if you didn't have to earn it. The old money lives in special neighborhoods. They have picnics and parties together where they feel especially clever because they don't have to work, although a few of them do, just to pass time.

It's a long drive. It is Tennessee end to end, mountains to delta, with the dip of Nashville and the valley in the middle to break things up. Fay can read in the car without making herself sick. Carl is staring out the window, concentrating. He's been training like crazy, running up and down the school bleachers holding bricks over his head. His weight is exactly right. He measures out the water he drinks and wraps himself in Hefty bags and sweats in the sun. He knows there are two boys ranked higher than him, and another half a dozen beneath him who could take his spot.

Taft looks at him in the rearview mirror while he drives. He worries for his worrying.

As for himself, Taft has stopped worrying. The pain in his chest did not come back. By the time he woke up from his nap on the day he and Carl were working on the deck he was already beginning to forget about it. A cramp, a spasm, indigestion, exhaustion, strain, none of those things were important. Doctors are for sick people and Taft isn't sick. Once they start looking it opens up a whole can of worms. They find things wrong, one thing and then another until you're dead. That's the way it went with his father. He went in to see about a simple cough and came back with cancer. The more those doctors looked, the more they found. They said his father was shot through with it. They said they needed to explore. The exploring took them deeper down the mine shaft, into veins stuffed with cancer. They said he wouldn't live six months, and so he didn't. Taft believes people are like wells, clear water with some sediment on the bottom. As long as you don't disturb them, they're going to be fine.

This is the way he likes it, his family in the car, everybody together.

Taft gets off the interstate and drives through downtown. His wife has forgotten to buy a gift for her sister. She wants to bring her something, a box of candy or a shaker of bath powder. Never go to someone's house empty-handed, she says.

"I'll wait in the car," Taft says.

Carl and Fay want to go with their mother. They're restless from sitting for so long. They like the shops in Memphis. There is nothing like them in Coalfield.

"We won't be twenty minutes," his wife says.

Taft turns off the engine and rolls down the window and sits and waits. He's watching the people. And while he is sitting and waiting and watching, Taft thinks about the reason he doesn't like Memphis: too many blacks. In Coalfield this has never been a problem for him. There are plenty of blacks at the carpet factory and he likes them fine. He doesn't make jokes behind their backs. He doesn't think they shouldn't get the same breaks at work as everybody else. Plenty of people at the factory are this way and Taft isn't one of them. When Tommy Lawson lost two fingers in the cutting blade Taft chipped in more than any white guy on the line. Whenever there's an accident like that the guys put some money in the card. Taft likes Tommy. They ate together in the lunchroom sometimes. Tommy knows a lot about basketball and once they'd even talked about driving down to Knoxville together to see a Vols game, but they never did. Sitting in the car, Taft knows he doesn't have any problem with blacks. Tommy Lawson is proof of that.

But in Memphis, it's different. In Memphis, downtown in the middle of the day, he feels funny being a white man, there are so few of them around. When he decides to count every black person who walks by his car, he can't. He has to count the white ones instead. Things aren't the way they're supposed to be. That's the problem with Memphis.

"I got some pretty little hand soaps," Virginia says as she gets into the front seat and Carl and Fay slide into the back. "Look at these. They look like shells." He wishes he could ask them if they've noticed, but he never would.

Lily makes a crown rib roast for dinner and then takes offense that Carl will only eat salad without dressing. "I made it for you," she says. "For luck tomorrow."

"It's his weight," Taft tells her. "If he doesn't make weight tomorrow he can't wrestle."

"Well, everybody eats dinner," Lily says.

They move their food around on their plates. There's something about the room. The sound of the knives and forks tapping against each other seems magnified a thousand times. Taft can hear people chew. The room is too fancy to really enjoy the meal. If he could choose, he would take their breakfast nook any day. The table is only big enough for four, and anything you want you can reach, or somebody can pass it to you without it being any bother. They use placemats instead of a tablecloth. They use paper napkins. Who in their right mind would want to fool with cloth napkins?

Taft can't think of anything to talk about. Will he say to his brother-in-law, How's the drug business? He finds himself staring out the window that is half covered up by bushes and low tree branches. If it was him, he'd cut all that back so a person could see out.

Calvin comes to the wrestling match with them, but Lily doesn't. She says that gymnasiums make her claustrophobic, all those people crammed together on bleachers, sweating.

The waiting goes on forever. There are a dozen pairs that go before Carl. Taft watches every boy carefully. He looks to see if they are better or not as good. He watches for moves, any little trick he can tell Carl about later.

"Look at that one," Fay says. "He's cute."

When Carl comes on, he's focused. The look on his face is the same as it was the morning he shot the deer. He isn't jittery the way the other boys are. He's all warmed up, but doesn't shake his hands and jump around. He stands at the edge of the mat in his red singlet and stares at the boy from Jackson, who he then pins in eighty-five seconds.

"Fish!" Taft shouts from the bleachers. "Go Carl!"

Carl pins two more boys, one of them the number-four-ranked 126 from Nashville. Then he is up against the number-two boy who is from Memphis. A black boy from Memphis.

There are a lot more white kids at the meet than black. Taft knows Carl doesn't see it. All he is thinking about is size and shape, weight and speed. Color doesn't make a difference when you're trying to put a boy's arm behind his back. But Taft sees it. Sees it as they circle each other on the mat. Sees it as they lunge, miss, lock. They are twisted together, leg to arm, head to torso. The black boy goes behind. He passes Carl over his back and wins three points. Carl tries for a double leg tackle, but he can't hold him. The boys are slick with sweat. The black boy sweats more than Carl. He is number two in the state. By the end of the day he might have a championship. Taft can see that Carl is going to lose and what he wants him to do is roll over. Save his energy, take the pin. He wants his son out of that tangle. There is something about seeing those arms around Carl's chest that makes him want to go down into the ring and put a stop to it. The boy has Carl on his stomach. He has one of his legs pulled back, his head is down. The boy has his knee in Carl's back. Taft has seen this hold before. It's the position you use to brand a calf. Then the boy flips Carl, both shoulders firmly on the floor. It should be over, but it isn't. The referee is circling them on his hands and knees, counting like it was a boxing match, counting, higher numbers than they've counted for any other boys, 54, 55, 98, 212. It isn't fair that he should be pinned like that, that he should have to suffer so long. It is all Taft can do to watch.

I HAD FALLEN asleep. I looked at the clock and it said ten. I had to think for a minute, ten o'clock at night. Outside I could hear the rain going same as ever.

"You up?" Ruth said.

There wasn't anyplace to go in a situation like this. Nothing to do but roll over and kiss her, and even knowing that I closed my eyes and lay there for another minute. Above the rain I could hear a light and steady sawing sound. Ruth was doing her nails.

Neither one of us had been drinking, but there was something distinctly drunk about what had happened. We'd done it before talking, before coming inside, and once we got the door unlocked it all started up again.

"I know you're awake," Ruth said.

"I'm awake."

The sawing stopped and I felt her coming towards me in the bed on her hands and knees. After that time Ruth had kissed me when she was fourteen I had never liked being alone with her. It made me nervous.

"I always knew my sister was a fool, but I never knew how much of a fool until now." She ran a rough nail up my side.

I asked her if she would get me a drink. Ruth was family. She'd been in my apartment a hundred times. She knew where everything was.

She got up and walked naked through the room and out into the kitchen. I'd never thought about it before, but she had a body like Marion's too, small in the waist, big through the hips, pretty legs. I was sure that would be the last thing she'd want to hear.

"I knew you were listening to what I was saying this afternoon. I didn't think you'd call me so quick, but I knew you'd be thinking about it." She sat down on the edge of the bed and handed me some bourbon in a Mickey Mouse jelly glass that had been Franklin's. As much as I wanted Ruth to be any place in the world other than my bedroom, I have to say I felt some admiration for her, the way she sat there so casually, like she'd forgotten she was naked.

"What were you saying this afternoon?"

"In the bar," she said, slapping my shoulder in a friendly way. She took the jelly glass from my hand and had a drink.

Then I remembered. I hadn't been thinking about what she had said. Drumming didn't seem like such a pressing issue, not with everything else that was going on. "I wasn't calling you about that. I just thought we could get together, have a drink or something."

"Well then, let's have a drink." She lifted the glass.

I lay back in the bed, thinking that maybe if I closed my eyes she'd just be gone. "You have to understand. I had a bad night was all. There's just a lot of stuff on my mind." Hey Ruth, I couldn't with Fay, not six inches from her uncle's house. Not with her thinking about her father. There is some shit even I won't get into in this world. Seventeen.

"This is a bad night?"

"Listen, I shouldn't have called you. I just don't think it's right, you being Marion's sister and all."

"What the fuck does Marion have to do with this?" She was on her feet now, standing straight up. There was no way not to notice how good looking she was.

"Nothing. Not a thing. I wasn't thinking about Marion."

She looked at me and for a second I thought she was going to smile. "Then who were you thinking about?"

"I was thinking about you."

"Jesus," she said. "You're not even good at this." She started looking around for her underpants. She had to leave the room to find them.

I got up and pulled the sheet around myself and walked out into the living room. There was a lot of damage out there. Wet clothes slung all over the place, a lamp knocked off a table. Ruth was untangling her shirt from mine where they were holding on to one another in a corner. "I don't know what kind of girls you've been doing," she said. "But they must be a pretty simple lot if you've been getting away with this." She leaned over and hooked her bra behind her. "It's different for me. The sex was good, and I've liked you for a long time." She stopped for a minute, her blouse half on and half off. She wanted to be sure she meant every word she said. "But the next time I'll kill you."

Ruth was her mother's daughter. I had a crazy kind of fondness for her all of the sudden. I wanted to ask her to sleep in my bed for the night and have it not mean anything. Ruth was wild and if it hadn't been for everything else this all could have meant something to me.

She found her shoe and slipped it on. She had to open the door to find her purse and raincoat and umbrella. She was lucky they were still there. The neighborhood wasn't that good.

"I can walk you out," I said.

"The hell you can." She slipped on the other green high-heeled shoe and was gone.

I had just laid back on the bed with my jelly glass, thinking about how many things I could screw up when the phone rang. It was Cyndi.

"Are you dead or what?"

"Sidetracked," I said.

"You used to call," she said.

I waited for a minute, tapping the receiver on my forehead. I couldn't think of anything to say to her, so I just hung up.

At Muddy's, a mysterious crowd had formed out of the rain. I'd just get to where I knew everybody that came in the place and then all of the sudden there'd be a new flock of strangers. Maybe I hadn't been paying enough attention to things lately. Maybe the tourist season was early. Everybody looked like they were having a good time. B. B. King was on the stereo, singing "Nobody Loves Me but My Mother." Cyndi was behind the bar and Arlene and Carl were waiting tables.

"Carl?"

He was in a hurry to get someplace, but he stopped. His hair fell into his eyes. "I was here and Cyndi needed help," he said. He had a white apron tied around his waist. I knew the T-shirt he was wearing. It said Coalfield Wrestling. I'd already seen it once that night. "Is it all right?"

"You don't have a card to serve liquor," I said.

"Fay's been working here all this time and she still hasn't gone down to get hers."

I never did remember to check those damn things. "Did you bring Fay?" I would have seen her if she was there. She would have come and said something to me.

"Fay's at home. I'm not here with her. I just felt like getting out was all." Carl glanced over nervously at his tables to make sure nobody needed anything. "She got really drenched after you dropped her off," he said. "She looked like she'd walked clear from the bar. My mother sent her up to bed after dinner. You carried her home?"

"Sure I did."

"I don't know what's wrong with her." A man at a back table waved his hand. "I gotta go," Carl said.

I guess Carl had been watching people wait tables long enough to get the hang of it himself.

"Never thought anybody would be in tonight," I said to Cyndi.

"Busy man like yourself has too much on his mind to think about a little bar," she said, pouring some Absolut over ice. "You've got your livery service to run, too. I know that cuts into your time."

I walked back behind the bar and poured myself a drink. Hard rules are broken in hard times. "Why don't you see if you can't go scare some of those people," I said to her.

"All right," she said. "But leave Carl out on the floor. He's doing a good job."

"Money out of your pocket, not mine," I told her, but she wasn't listening to me anymore. She took a hard look at all the people and then eased out onto the floor like a car pulling into traffic.

I stood at the bar watching Carl, thinking about how close I'd come to making love to his sister while he was five feet away. I don't know what seemed more unbelievable to me, that I'd started up with her in the first place or that I'd left her there. I wondered how long she stood outside after I'd gone. A minute, ten minutes, an hour? Was she watching me walk back towards my car or did she keep her eyes on the window? Was she cold? All that rain and I never got cold. When she finally went inside, did she go upstairs and take off her wet clothes, wrap a towel around her head before coming down to the dining room where her family was waiting on her? Did she sit down at the dinner table with them, in front of the blue wallpaper and under the brass light fixture, sing "Happy Birthday," and watch while her uncle blew out the candles on his cake?

"Miller two times," Carl said.

"You're good at this." I reached into the case and got his beers. He looked happy. Compared to how I'd seen him through the window, he looked like he was on top of the world.

"Runs in the family," he said. He smiled and headed off to his table. I didn't like it, how much he looked like her.

There were only two hours between my coming in and closing the bar, but by the time we shooed the last customer out I felt I'd been there for a month straight. I would have just as soon thrown a match in the cash register than counted up the money. Cyndi and Arlene were walking in their sleep, turning chairs onto tabletops and trying to push brooms, but Carl was everywhere. Maybe he'd been to the bathroom for a perk, but at least this time there was someplace for all that energy to go.

"We'll have this done in no time," he said to the room.

I went upstairs and did the money, thinking how much better life was going to be once I taught Wallace how to do it. When I came back down, the place was quiet and everybody was gone but Carl. He'd taken a chair off a table and was just sitting there, staring at nothing. The whole room was dark except for the streetlights coming in through the front window. All the other chairs were turned upside down.

"The girls went home," he said. "I didn't know if you liked somebody to wait around or not."

"You don't need to stay," I said. "Appreciate all your help tonight."

"I've never been in here when nobody else is around. I like it, so quiet. You wouldn't think a bar could get this quiet."

I nodded. I had wanted to hurry him up, get him out of there, but all of the sudden I felt so tired I didn't want to do anything but sit for a minute. I tossed the blue bag down on the table and pulled off a chair for myself. I was thinking about Ruth and Fay. I was too tired to stand.

"I used to like to go to the gym when nobody was there," Carl said. "It was the same sort of thing."

"You were a wrestler."

"Fay told you that?"

I pointed at his chest. "Your shirt," I said.

Carl looked down and seemed surprised to see it there. He nodded. "Had a hell of a year last year," he said. He ran the flat of his hand across the letters. "You ever wrestle?"

I shook my head. "Boxed some when I was a kid. Mostly street stuff."

"Boxing," he said. "I was always interested in that. They don't have a lot of high school boxing. They think it's all right for kids to pin each other's heads to the floor, but they don't want you hitting."

"I'm not saying I took boxing lessons. We were mostly just interested in punching one another out. There wasn't a lot of sweet science to it."

"Wrestling is a great sport," Carl said. "All about concentration and strategy. All up here." He tapped his head with two fingers.

"We used to say the same thing about boxing, but it was just a bunch of us whaling on each other. It doesn't sound so appealing to me now."

"I couldn't wrestle anymore," he said. "Even if it's about using your brain, you've got to be in a certain kind of shape. Discipline, mind and body, that's what the coach used to say. I'm too far off my weight now. I didn't work out all winter."

"So maybe you should pick it up again."

Carl waved his hand, like I had suggested he should become an astronaut. "It's too late for that."

"Too late? What are you, old man, sixteen?"

"Seventeen," Carl said, like that should make it all clear to me.

I leaned into the table, feeling a little less tired all of the sudden. "But Fay's seventeen."

Carl nodded. "We both are right now. Eleven months apart. In February we're both the same age. My father used to say that for a month a year we were twins. It took us a while to figure that one out. My father used to say it was his favorite time of year, two birthday parties, two cakes."

"So your Dad's in high cotton now." I did not know what possessed me to say it. I hadn't forgotten about Taft, even for a minute.

Carl looked at me, so surprised. "He's gone," he said.

"Left?"

"Dead," Carl said.

We were both quiet. I told him I was sorry to hear that.

Carl nodded. He looked at his T-shirt for a while, thinking things over. "Let me have a drink."

"Can't do that. Not right after you told me you were seventeen."

"Be a friend," Carl said quietly. He was asking, not expecting it. He was just putting his request out there and hoping. "Nobody here but us chickens."

It made me laugh to hear that come out of his mouth. "You've been listening," I said.

"I'm listening all the time."

"What do you drink, Carl?"

"Southern Comfort."

"Jesus Christ." I shook my head. "You're never going to get anywhere in this world drinking that." I got up and went behind the bar. I put some ice in some glasses and picked up the Southern Comfort and a bottle of Maker's Mark. "You give this a try," I said. "If it doesn't suit you, you can go back to where you came from." Cough syrup. A man ought not die before his son learns to drink something other than Southern Comfort.

Carl poured himself a healthy dose of Maker's Mark. "I appreciate this," he said, getting down to the business of drinking.

"Just don't go telling anybody about it."

"My father let me have a beer with him every now and then. He said he'd rather I do it where he could keep an eye on me."

"Your dad been gone long?"

"Last June," he said. "Early."

"That's no time."

"It changes. Sometimes he's been dead for years and other times it was yesterday or this morning or ten minutes ago. It just depends on how things are going. There's no counting on it." Carl put his finger in his drink and spun it around. He was trying to make the ice melt faster. "Sometimes I think he's going to walk in that door." He licked off his finger and pointed to the front door of the bar. "He's going to say, Carl, what in the hell happened to you? Then I start to get all worried, you know, trying to think of what I'm going to tell him. I start trying to make up some sort of lie. I'm thinking, Tell him you have a really bad flu. The flu's been making you run a fever. Tell him you've been working nights and it's fine but you haven't slept. Insane, bullshit stuff. Really insane, because right in the middle of getting all worked up I remember he's dead." He tilted his head back and sucked down the rest of his drink. Then he took a mouthful of ice and started crunching on it. "I like this," he said, picking up the bottle of Maker's Mark.

"I'm afraid that's it for tonight," I said, taking back the bottle. I knew where this was going and I didn't want to be driving another Taft across town.

"You in a hurry to get someplace?" Carl said. "There's no place to go this time of night. No place nice."

"I meant to be asleep an hour ago." I cleared off the table and turned my chair upside down. Then I started to wonder about something. "When do you sleep, Carl? You and Fay both are here seems like every night. When do you get your schoolwork done?"

"We're not here all the time," he said, like he genuinely had no idea what I was talking about. "I feel like I'm never here, I'm always waiting to get here. And sleep, I can sleep anywhere. In the morning, I sleep in the car, in the parking lot at school. I miss a few classes every now and then. I'm not so interested in school."

"What about Fay?"

"Fay does okay in school, I guess. Better than me. She does her homework after work. She just doesn't sleep. I don't think the light is ever off under her door."

"Maybe she sleeps with the lights on."

Carl thought about it for a minute, like it had never occurred to him before. "Maybe so," he said.

"I'll walk you out."

Carl pulled on an old jean jacket, took a Winston out of the pocket and lit it. For some reason I thought how glad Mr. Wood-moore would be to make a new friend who smoked. "Maybe you'll show me how to box some time."

"Like I said, I didn't have the science of it. It was all just a bunch of hitting to me."

Carl put his cigarette down in an ashtray on the bar. We were ten feet from the door, but that's not the same as being out the door. "I don't know a thing about hitting somebody."

"Then you're better off."

"I'm serious," he said. It was clear enough that he was. "Show me."

"Jesus Carl." I didn't stay with boxing long. I was too worried about my hands, about jamming something in my wrist. When it comes to not getting punched, no group of people are more on their toes than musicians. The ones who liked to fight never lasted in the business long. Spending your nights in bars with too much booze and other men's women can be dangerous for your hands if you liked to fight. Hands were bread and butter. I put the blue bag down on the bar and took his hand. It was built like a peony, this hand. The same sort of white and pink colors, too. One strong blow would knock it all to hell. I rolled it over and looked at the other side. I remembered it then. I had held this hand already, when it was Fay's. "When you make a fist, you think about rolling your fingers in. You need to cut those finger-nails shorter if you don't want to slice yourself up." I curled the fingers in, just little finger bones slipcovered in skin. I felt almost like I was bandaging his hand. "This is going to protect them. You're going to put your thumb here, in the front, right under this knuckle." I moved his thumb over. He had torn down the cuticles on either side till they were bleeding. Carl watched his hand like it was television. "That's a fist," I said. "When you hit, you hit here, from the top joint to the knuckle." I slapped my hand against his to show him where. "Hit flush. Keep it just like that and chances are you won't break your hand when you go to punch somebody."

"How do you punch somebody?"

"Carl," I said.

"What am I going to do? Somebody's hitting me and I'm going to show them what a nice fist I can make?"

I nodded. "Okay. Keep your wrist locked, keep it straight. You punch somebody with your fist tilted down and you're going to break your hand off." I straightened out his wrist. "See that? I'm figuring you're stronger than you look with all that wrestling, but you're still going to want to get behind this as much as possible. Throw it out from the shoulder. Put your whole person behind it. Spread your feet apart, like that. You want to be steady. And take good aim. If you go to all this trouble and you don't make contact, then he's going to kill you."

"Got it."

"Okay now, hit my hand." I put up a flat hand. I had six inches and sixty, seventy pounds on the boy. I didn't need to put up my hand. He could have hit me anywhere he wanted for the rest of the night and it wouldn't have mattered to me. Carl punched my hand. "That's good," I said. "Keep that wrist straight. Do it again." Carl punched. He brought both fists up to his face in between blows like he was a boxer. He danced around a little bit. "That's good. That's right. Put some weight behind it." I moved my hand up and down, and Carl swung into it. You could see that he'd been an athlete. At that age, it takes a long time for a body to forget all the work it's done. Carl started coughing. He stopped for a minute and took a drag off his cigarette.

"Where do you hit them, if you want to get somebody good?"

I thought about the day I stopped fighting, when I lost to a boy named Jono. "Jab them in the face a little punch, and when their hands go up to their face you hit them in the throat. That'll stop just about anybody."

"In the throat," he said.

"You can't just think about the punch you're throwing now. You've got to think about the one that's coming next."

"Wrestling is like that."

"Now you know how to hit somebody," I said.

Carl nodded. "Thank you for that. You never know when you're going to need it."

"Try keeping out of trouble." Had I ever once tried to keep out of trouble when I was seventeen?

"You think you might be interested in wrestling at all?" Carl said, opening up the door for me. "I could show you some holds. Just if you were interested."

I couldn't see that happening.

As tired as I was, I got precious little sleep. My wet and muddy clothes were still lying on the floor of my apartment and the bed looked like some sort of animal had tried to make a nest in it. I could smell Ruth in the sheets when I lay down and all I was thinking about was Fay. I was thinking about everything she had on her plate, and now there was me, something else to worry about. She should be in Coalfield, riding around in pickup trucks with the hillbilly boys, or the cracker boys who'd come up all the way from Georgia just to see her. She should be thinking about what dress she's going to wear and who was going to ask to dance with her next. All those boys, tall and skinny with hair that won't lie down. White boys in twenty-five different shades of pale, lined up all the way down the street, packing themselves into Taft's yard, waiting to ask Fay what she wanted to do that day, where did she want to go? Would she like a Coke or something to eat? That's what Fay should have now. Instead she's got worries and losses, a brother she can't make stay inside. And she thinks the only bright thing she's got going, the only thing she wants for herself, is a man who runs a bar and is more than twice her age. A man who could have been her father had he started early enough.

The next day the rain finally broke, even though the sky stayed gray until midafternoon. Fay steered clear of me. She managed to spend an awful lot of time in the kitchen, hiding in Rose's skirts. Every few minutes she'd buzz onto the floor, check her tables and dart back through the swinging double doors.

"We were better off when her brother was waiting tables," Cyndi said. There was still no sign that things were warming up between Fay and Cyndi, but then Cyndi didn't warm to much of anybody.

I wanted to talk to her, see how she was doing, but she was moving too fast. She wouldn't catch my eye. I just saw the back of her yellow sweater as she was going by me from as far away as possible.

I followed her into the kitchen.

She and Rose were standing at the cutting board. Fay was talking low and I couldn't hear her. The girl would have to be pretty hard up if Rose was the one she was turning to for comfort.

"Fay," I said. "Can I talk to you for a minute?"

But it wasn't Fay who answered, it was Rose. She looked at me in a pleasant enough way, took her purse out of the bread drawer and went out the door into the alley to have a cigarette.

"Look," Fay said, and I waited but she didn't say anything else.

"I just wanted to make sure you were okay," I said. "Carl told me last night you'd gotten awfully chilled." Is that what Carl had said? I couldn't remember.

"I was out in the rain a long time," she said.

"Didn't you go inside?"

"With you," she said impatiently. "I was out in the rain a long time with you."

Her face was flushed and she was rubbing her hands together like they were cold. Little white hands like Carl's. "Fay, I'm sorry about what happened. I shouldn't have, you know? I wasn't thinking."

"Shouldn't have what?" Fay said.

I stood there while the kitchen got bigger and bigger. "Shouldn't have kissed you," I said, like that was what I'd done, kissed her.

She sighed and nodded her head. "See," she said, "I was going to say you shouldn't have left me there alone." She wiped off her hands on a dishtowel, even though they looked perfectly clean and dry. "I'm going to get back to work," she said, and she passed me, widely, so that she could get to the door.

I stood there for a while and then went back to the door that led out into the alley. Rose was sitting on the stoop, smoking. When she heard me her hand darted down beside her skirt to hide the cigarette. "We're done in here," I said. "You can come back in."

I went up to my office and shuffled papers just as a way of hiding. I found an application form underneath a pile of mail from a boy named Teddy who wanted a job as a waiter. The date on the thing was only a week old and I couldn't figure out how it had gotten up there or who had found the application forms and given him one. I picked up the phone and called him, told him he had a job. On paper he was qualified and over twenty-one. I thought I better start hiring some more people, more boys.

When I couldn't find anything else to do, I put my head down on the desk and went to sleep. I didn't dream about anything. That was the nicest part of it.

It was Fay who woke me up. "Hey," she said, staying over by the door. I pulled my head up and rubbed my face with my hands. "Somebody looking for you," she said. Then she turned around and left.

My first thought was that it would be Teddy, come to start work. I was confused. I went out into the bar in the haze of a midday nap and there stood Franklin and Marion.

Big, big, big, that's all I could think. Bigger than the pictures ever made him out to be.

"Bet you didn't think it was gonna be us," Franklin said, grinning, but he held his ground.

I went to him, picked him up (heavy, too), kissed him and squeezed him until he gave a little yelp. Oh, he smelled good, sweet and warm. I kissed his neck and put him down. I was so happy that I put my arms around his mother. "Hey there, girl," I said. "Aren't you a sight." Marion looked good. She'd gained a little weight since she'd gone to Florida and it suited her, softened her up some. She had on a thin black coat that made her look stylish. She patted my arm.

"We came early," she said.

"I see that."

"Franklin hadn't missed any school all year," she said, and she put her arm around him and drew him into her. He put an arm around her waist. Marion knew without even thinking, knew this would feel strange to him, and out went the arm and pulled him to her. "I got the days off work and we were talking and we said, Why not just go?"

"Just got in the car," Franklin said.

I put my hand on the side of his head and ran my thumb over his scar. It was a thin half moon, just the size of half the bottom of a bottle of Coke, sitting dangerously close to his right eye. It wouldn't have been so bad at all except it was pink.

"The doctor says it's healing up real well," Marion said. "You know, they all look that way for a while. It just takes some time. I rub vitamin E on it before he goes to bed at night, softens it up."

"It smells," Franklin said.

"I don't think it looks so bad," I said. "Nothing like what I was imagining."

"This your little boy?" Cyndi said. She was looking at him the way girls look at children and dogs, something cute for the future.

"Franklin, Marion, this is Cyndi." I looked over towards the bar where Fay was standing, frozen into a pillar of salt. "That's Fay."

"Nice to meet you both," Marion said. Franklin stayed quiet, stepped on his own toe and twisted. "It's been a long time since I met anybody who worked in this bar."

I hadn't thought about it, but it was true. Marion didn't come to the bar. Marion didn't even call the bar. "Have you been to your folks yet?" I said.

"Franklin wanted to stop here first thing," she said. "Wants to see his daddy."

"You'll go over with us?" Franklin said.

"Come on and have dinner," Marion said. "You know my mother wants you."

Franklin let go of his mother and clamped onto my waist. "Let me call Wallace and see if he can come in," I said. "It should be fine."

"I probably should have called you first," Marion said. "It's just that Franklin wanted it to be a surprise."

"One call," I said. "Everything's going to be fine."

Franklin and Marion sat down at a table and Cyndi went and got them each a Coke while I called Wallace. A good man, Wallace, a good sport, said he could come in, no problem. When I came back I saw that Fay was still standing there. "He looks really nice," she said in a small voice. "Good looking. Looks like you."

"He's a great boy," I said.

Cyndi came up to where we were standing. "You go on with them," she said, so pleased about meeting my family. "We'll be fine."

"I'll be back to close," I said. "It'll be an early night."

"Just have some fun," Cyndi said. She shook her head. "I never even knew you were married, much less had a kid."

Fay got pale, paler, and headed off to the kitchen. There was plenty of time to worry about her. I was making a science of it. For now I wanted to see my son.

When we got outside Marion told Franklin to ride over with me. He seemed happy to do it. "I'm going to be teaching you to drive before too long," I said as I unlocked his door.

"I don't want to spend any more time in that car," he said. "It's a long way from Miami."

"Do you like it there?"

"It's okay," he said, getting up on his knees and pressing himself against the window.

"Put your seat belt back on."

Franklin slid back into place and did as he was told. "I like Memphis better than Miami."

"That's because you're from Memphis. You always like the place you're from best." This wasn't true, really. I knew plenty of people who hated the place they were from. "Maybe you'll move back."

"That's what I want to do. I keep telling Mom."

"And what does your mother say?"

Franklin looked at his hands carefully for a minute and then took a deep bite out of one of his fingernails. "Stop that," I said.

"I think she wants to come back. She misses everybody. She says Miami is full of old people and hoods."

"Hoods?"

"Bad guys," he said casually. "Am I going to get to stay with you while we're here?"

"If it's okay with your mother," I said. "I sure think you should." And that's when it came back to me. I thought what a wreck my apartment was and then I thought about why it was a wreck and then I put it all together, that I wasn't just going to have dinner with Marion's parents, I was having dinner with Marion's family. With her sister. Marion was right behind us at the stop light.

"There's Mom," Franklin said, and he started waving like a madman.

Nine is maybe the last good age. Your children will still kiss you and let you pick them up every now and then. They still get in your bed at night when they're having dreams. They can still get excited over seeing somebody. I barely had the car stopped when Franklin tore up the walk to his grandparents' house and started banging on the door. Marion and I followed behind with the bags.

"Look at this!" Mr. Woodmoore said. "Who's this big boy?"

"What a sight," Mrs. Woodmoore said. "The three of you walking up together, just like a family." She was practically putting off light she was so happy. I couldn't remember a time the three of us walked anywhere looking like a family, but I was glad to see her so pleased.

"Aunt Ruth!" Franklin called.

And there she was, lipstick on, hair done right. "Everybody's home," she said, smiling. She kissed Marion on the cheek and picked Franklin up. "Lord, what do you feed this boy to make him so heavy?"

"Cement," Franklin said.

"Good to see you," she said to me, like I was a distant cousin who came around once a year at Christmastime, like it hadn't been just last night she was looking for her bra underneath my bed. She leaned over and gave me the lightest kiss on the cheek. It didn't even last a second.

"You've got lipstick on your face," Franklin said.

I reached up and wiped the spot away with my hand.

"Of course we didn't drive straight through," Marion was telling her father. "We spent the night outside Atlanta."

"So what do you think we're having for supper?" Mrs. Woodmoore said to Franklin.

The circus went in to eat.

"Everybody knew about this except me?"

Ruth smiled. "Not everybody," she said, taking a sip of beer. "I didn't know a thing about it. If I'd known Marion and Franklin were coming in" — she reached over and tickled him behind the knee which made him laugh hysterically — "I wouldn't have gone out last night. I would have stayed here and gotten ready."

"Well, we couldn't tell you," Mrs. Woodmoore said. "Marion told us that there wasn't to be a word to anybody. She wanted it all to be a surprise."

"I wasn't thinking about you not telling Ruth," she said.

"There you go," Ruth said, giving a deep nod to her sister.

"Well, you didn't send a list of who to tell and who not to tell so we just didn't tell anybody. It's not like there was any harm in it."

"No," Ruth said, looking at me. "No harm done."

Under normal circumstances, I think I would have excused

myself and gone into the bathroom to cut my throat, but there was Franklin. I couldn't stop looking at him, his long legs and clear eyes, the way he clapped his hands when he got excited. It didn't keep me from knowing I was in a room with two sisters I'd slept with, one who didn't know and the other who might be on the verge of telling, but it soothed my fears enough to keep me seated.

"Franklin," Mrs. Woodmoore said. "You pass your daddy the pot roast, and take some more for yourself. Both of you, thin as rails. Marion, you've got your work cut out for you, fattening this one up."

Only Ruth flinched. Me and Marion, we were used to hearing this stuff from her mother. We didn't even notice it anymore.

When it was time for me to get back to work Franklin wouldn't let me go. "I'll come over tomorrow," I told him.

"I want to go," he said, holding onto my waist. "You said I could sleep with you."

"I said if it was all right with your mother and tonight's not the night."

"Just let me go down to the bar for a little while," Franklin said. Suddenly, there were tears all over the place.

"Somebody's getting sleepy," Marion said.

"Stop the waterworks," Mrs. Woodmoore said. "You're going to have to stay here with me tonight. That's all there is to it."

I kissed him on the pink horseshoe scar near his eye. "I'll be back tomorrow," I said. "Count on that."

Franklin nodded. The storm had passed and he seemed just as happy to stay as to go. "Come on," he said to me, and took my hand to walk me out. Nobody in that house could say good night from their chair in the living room. They had to get up, all of them together and walk right out the door with me. Sometimes they would walk me to my car and lean into my rolled-down window and keep on talking until I was forced to let out the clutch so the car could inch away. That night they only went as far as the porch, what with Franklin so sleepy and the air still wet and heavy from the storm. They were all waving as I walked away, calling out good-byes like I was going to war, because that was the way they did things. Maybe people come back quicker if you make them feel like you can't bear to see them go. I looked back from the middle of the street and waved. Ruth and Marion were standing together at the door underneath the dim forty-watt glow of the front porch light. The hems of their skirts were touching. If you looked quickly there would be no saying which was which and since I wanted to kiss them both I kissed neither.

THAT WAS something," Wallace said. "What a surprise, them just showing up like that. It's not your birthday or anything?"

I shook my head. "Just a visit. I appreciate you coming down on such short notice. It's a big help."

"No problem."

"Good crowd," I said, and went under the bar to turn the music down. People were screaming at each other trying to make themselves heard.

"It's a different crowd," Wallace said.

"I was thinking that yesterday. It must be tourists. I don't seem to recognize anybody."

Carl came up to the bar looking a little out of it. "I heard your son was here," he said.

"That's right."

"Well, I'm sorry I missed him. I'd like to meet the little guy. I like kids."

"I'm sure he'll be around."

Wallace put down the box of beer he'd been unloading into

the refrigerator. "I'm going to take a break," he said. He wasn't asking for permission. As soon as he said it he was gone.

"What's with him?" Carl said.

"Probably hasn't gotten out all night. You stand behind a bar long enough, you go a little stir crazy."

Carl nodded and kept an eye on the door. "I appreciate you helping me with the punching last night."

"Well, you did fill in waiting tables. It seemed like the least I could do."

"It's a good thing to know." Carl looked over his shoulder and saw that there was somebody sitting at his table by the kitchen. "That's a friend of mine," he said. "I better go say hello to him."

"Sure," I said.

"But I mean it, I want to meet your kid. I bet you're a good dad."

"Doing my best."

Carl smiled and headed off for his spot.

I was feeling better about things already. It was like some part of myself had been gone and I'd gotten used to it being gone. But now that it was back I could see what I'd been missing. It had only been a couple of hours, but I was already thinking about all the things we were going to start doing now that he was home. I was thinking home for good. I couldn't help myself.

Fay wandered up to the bar looking like she'd come in lost and was planning to ask for directions. "Did you have a good time?"

"I'm glad that Franklin's home."

"Is he going to be here long?" She looked like she was straining to hold herself together, using everything she had to keep from crying.

"It's not for sure yet," I said. I wanted to do something, pat her hand or something, but I was worried that it might just make things worse. "Right now it's just for a visit."

"And that woman, his mother, she thinks she might stay too?"

"She might."

Fay nodded. Maybe she was going to say something else, but Wallace came back and she just sort of drifted off again. I thought maybe there'd be a chance to talk to her after closing, when things quieted down some.

Wallace was tapping two fingers on the edge of the bar sink. He looked like he was trying to figure out how it was the earth kept going around the sun. "What's up with you?" I said.

Wallace was a scary sight, big as he was. If you didn't know him, he could worry you. But I knew him.

"Come outside with me, chief," he said.

We went out the front door together. It was a nice night, finally, after all that rain. It wasn't even cold anymore.

"I don't like to be in the position of telling somebody else's business," he said. "I've been putting it off, thinking you'd notice yourself. But I see you getting fonder and fonder of this kid." He wasn't looking at me. He was keeping his eyes up, straight ahead of him. His voice was low like it always was and I had to lean in to him. There were people milling around all over the place. I could hear the band playing in the park and they didn't sound bad.

"Are we talking about Fay?"

He shook his head. "She's a good girl," he said. "I feel for her. But her brother is a scummy drug dealer."

A group of girls came up on the sidewalk and couldn't seem to decide if they wanted to pass us on the left or the right. Wallace and I stepped back, but they all started laughing and crossed the street.

"Carl?"

Of course it was possible. As soon as it was out of his mouth the pictures started going through my head. The new people at the bar, the way he sat at his little table and received them like the goddamned godfather while we all brought him Cokes and asked how it was going. The only part that didn't make sense was my not seeing it. It was true.

"The girl, she's the reason I hated to say anything. You know that it just winds up being hard on her. She's so good to that asshole."

"Jesus."

"The thing is, we're getting a reputation. I heard it when I was out last night and if I've heard it then it's only a matter of time before the cops hear it. It would be a real waste of time seeing everything go down over such a piece of white trash."

I felt a prickly rage crawling over my skin. "I don't know what I was thinking about."

"You're involved," Wallace said. "Takes ten times longer to see something once you're involved."

I was thinking about Franklin, about this place and Miami, about the whole rotten, dangerous world.

"Don't get into it with him," Wallace said. "You'll wind up killing him and that won't do anybody any good. You just want to get him out. I can get him out for you if you want."

I shook my head. "That would be my job," I said. I gave myself a minute. I breathed in the good air and looked down the street to Handy Park where I used to play. This was where I lived. Wallace and I went back inside.

There was somebody else at Carl's table, a white woman who had one of those faces you'd never remember. Could have been twenty and could have been thirty-five. She had her hands folded between her knees.

"You've never seen my office, Carl."

He looked up at me, maybe he was irritated or maybe I was just reading into it. "I'll come up in just a little while," he said.

"Time's up," I said. "You don't have a single second to spare." I leaned in between them. "If you get your butt out of this chair right now and your lady friend here makes a run for the door, then maybe I won't be so inclined to kill the both of you."

The woman was gone, tilting her chair over backwards and not stopping to pick it up. Just like I thought, the minute she wasn't in front of me anymore I couldn't remember a thing about her.

"You're being awfully rude," Carl said.

"Get up," I said. "Bring your jacket."

Carl got up and picked up his jacket. He looked over towards the door, but what he saw was Wallace so he got in front of me and headed for the kitchen.

"Hello, Carl," Rose said. "You two going upstairs?"

"We won't be a minute," I said. Carl kept quiet.

I took him into my office and closed the door. I didn't bother to lock it. The room was small and there were twenty different ways to stop him if he decided to make a run for it. "Empty out your pockets," I said.

"I'm not going to empty out anything."

"Carl, you've got to gauge the situation here. You've got to know that I'm an inch away from breaking your neck, and if I decide to do that there's not going to be a single goddamned thing you can do to stop me. You empty out your pockets and you're buying yourself some time. And I may still want to kill you anyway."

Carl looked sullen. He looked like a boy who'd just been told to turn down his stereo and pick up his room. He reached into the pockets of his jeans. There was a roll of Certs, three keys, less than half a buck in loose change.

"Jacket pockets."

"Would you like to watch me take my clothes off?"

"Empty out your fucking pockets."

Two balled up Kleenex, a movie stub, a folded up piece of paper. I was tired of waiting. I took the jacket and patted around until I found the pocket in the lining. There was a bottle of Quaaludes, three dime bags and a heavy paper wallet with pictures of butterflies on it. "This is pretty," I said.

"It's not your property."

"It sure the hell is." Carl had six hundred and fifty dollars in cash and eleven bits of glossy magazine paper, neatly cut and folded. Eleven little envelopes. "You're not very smart, carrying this much stuff on you. This is dealing. This isn't personal possession." I moved my hand over in a straight line and made it into a neat pile, the Certs and cocaine and change, all of it.

Carl put both of his hands out on my desk, those same little pink and white hands. "Look," he said quietly. "Things have gotten really bad. I needed to make a lot of money. It was for Fay, too, so we could get out of here. That's what she wants."

"Don't talk to me about your sister."

"You got to give it back to me. That stuff's not paid for. Don't you understand? I don't own that, I just borrow it. The people who own it, you don't want to mess with them."

"I will never be messing with them."

"I wouldn't have done this," he said, his voice getting higher. "My father died. Nothing's gone right since then. I didn't know what I was doing."

I turned and looked at him. His nose was running. His thin shoulders were bending forward. "Tell me what your father says now, Carl."

He stood up. "Fuck you," he said. The thin hand rolled itself into a fist, but he was way too slow. He hit right into my hand, which was up in front of my throat by the time he got there. I held his hand inside my hand.

172

"You're changing too much," I said. "You've got to pick a tune and stick with it. You've got to decide right from the first if you're going to play tough or pathetic and then you can't ever change. You go back and forth this way, you just look sloppy."

"What are you going to do?" I couldn't stand to look at him. He was a little rabbit in a trap.

"I'm going to do you a huge favor," I said. "I'm not going to turn your sorry ass in."

"But what are you going to do with all of that?"

"I'm keeping it," I said. "I'm keeping the goddamned Certs."

"You can't do that."

"Let's not go around about this. The drugs are gone. The money I'll decide about later."

Carl started to say something, but I squeezed his hand a little and made him stop. Whatever it was, I didn't want to hear it. "You're just going to make it worse," I said. "Believe me when I tell you it can get worse."

Fay comes in right on time. The digital clock clicks over to twelve and there's the door, open, shut, then quiet steps disappearing into the carpet. Taft can hear the difference between Fay coming in and Carl. Carl fumbles with his keys. He has to pull on the handle to get the lock to work. He whistles a little outside, hums inside. It's soft, but Taft hears it and in his mind he checks him off. With Fay it's all quiet. There's only the sound any door would make when opened. He wonders how long she's been on the front porch, saying good night to somebody or other. For a minute he wonders what she does, what she lets them do, but as soon as a picture comes into his head he stops it. She promised she would be in the house at twelve o'clock and so she is. The rest he doesn't need to know.

Taft rolls over on his side, folds his pillow in half and pushes his hand into the fold. There is light from the full moon coming in through the window and he can see his wife sleeping on her back. Every time she exhales her lips part and then close, like she's blowing something off her face. Taft watches her with real interest for a while, then he looks out the window and waits for Carl to get home so he can sleep.

Taft can't sleep until both of his children are home. It's the real reason why he won't let them stay out late on school nights. It makes it too hard for him to get up and go to work in the morning. On Friday and Saturday nights they can stay out until midnight. Taft is off guarding the lumber. His wife sets the alarm for twelve and gets herself up to look for them. She's a sound sleeper. The reason tonight is different is because yesterday was Lyle Sealy's wedding anniversary. Lyle guards the lumber on Thursday nights. He asked if Taft would switch with him so that he could take his wife to dinner in Oak Ridge. Taft agreed, even though it meant he'd work in the carpet factory all day Thursday, guard Thursday night, and make carpet again all day Friday. Taft is sympathetic to things like anniversaries. Lyle is a young man. He's right to take his wife to dinner. The truth is, Taft probably would have said yes if Lyle had told him he wanted to stay home to watch *Diamonds Are Forever* on late-night TV. Taft isn't very good at saying no.

This morning at breakfast, after ninety minutes of sleep between jobs, Taft tells Carl and Fay he'd like them not to go out tonight. "I need the sleep," he says. "It wouldn't kill us to all stay home together for once."

"Dad," Fay says, putting down her spoon beside her cereal bowl. "I can't cancel a date on Friday morning. It's rude."

"It's just one date," Taft says.

"He asked me two weeks ago." Fay starts to roll a piece of her hair between her fingers, the way she does when she gets agitated over something. "I can't break it off just because you're too tired to wait up."

"Fay," her mother says. "Just do what your father tells you."

But Fay doesn't even register the comment as part of the conversation. "Maybe you should just go to sleep for a change," she says.

"You'll never understand about things like this until you have children of your own," Taft says. He looks over at his son. "Carl? What about you, do you have plans?"

Until this minute Carl has been eating toast, what looks like half a loaf of toasted bread. He makes it in the oven because it takes too long to get the amount of toast he needs out of the two slice toaster. "What?"

"Are you going out tonight?"

"Sure I am," Carl says. He looks surprised. His shirt is covered in crumbs. "You told me I could take the car. The stock cars are in town this weekend."

Taft has forgotten this. Carl's only had his license a few months. This is the first time Taft had agreed to let him take the car out at night. It had been heavily discussed and planned. "All right," he says. "Maybe tonight's the night I'll learn to sleep with the two of you gone."

"That's just great," Fay says. "I say I have a date and you tell me to cancel. Carl says he's going to the stock car races and all of the sudden it's okay to be out."

"You got your way," Fay's mother tells her, keeping her eyes on her coffee cup. "Be happy about it."

Taft isn't worried, just tired. After the kids go out that night he falls asleep watching television, but as soon as he gets into bed his eyes spring open. All day he dreamed about sleep. On the line the carpet seemed to be coming at him in a flood. It moved like water. He had to keep stopping and blinking to get things settled down again. He's no kid anymore. He can't stay up like this. There was a time when Taft could stay up all night, sometimes two nights in a row, but that was before marriage and children. Now he wants to sleep, but he can't because he has to wait for the sound of Carl's key in the lock. Fay, now Carl. One, two. He listens for the door.

At quarter past twelve Taft thinks, Forget it, he'll be fine, but the more time that passes the less chance he has of getting to sleep. Twelve-thirty, one o'clock. Taft's wife stretches and rolls over. He pulls the blanket back over her shoulder and gets up. He finds his slippers beneath the bed in the dark. He walks down the hall in his pajamas to Fay's room and opens the door. Her single bed is pushed into the corner and he has to go in to really see her. Asleep, she is always a baby. Her knees pulled up, her face flushed pink. Taft can remember her in a crib, can see her at two and seven and twelve. Always, she slept on her stomach, her fists knotted beneath her chin. On the walls there are posters of boys Taft doesn't recognize. The boys are wearing jeans and leather jackets and no shirts. The autographs over their chests are signed in such elaborate hands that Taft can't make out their names. It used to be that only boys would hang up pictures of girls.

After he leaves Fay's room he goes to check Carl's. Maybe he fell asleep for a minute. Maybe he didn't hear him come in. The floor is covered with clothes, weight disks, open magazines, empty cassette tape boxes. Carl's bed is unmade, but he hasn't been sleeping in it. The room is so torn up it looks like a crime scene, a kidnapping, and Taft hardly notices it. One-fifteen. Taft goes outside.

There's no harm in walking around in your pajamas late at night in your neighborhood in Coalfield. No one is up. It's pleasant outside, not too warm. Taft thinks in the summer maybe everyone should stay up at night and sleep during the day so as to enjoy the more comfortable temperatures. Every house on the street is dark. People here are careful not to leave the lights burning. Taft walks to the end of the driveway. He looks down the street. He steps into the street to get a better look. He comes back, opens up his mailbox for no reason and checks inside. Every day when the mail comes Taft is hopeful for a minute that it might be good news.

More time passes. Taft is so awake he can hardly blink his eyes. He decides that at two-thirty he's going to call the police. His mind is playing tricks on him, like it was that afternoon in the factory. He starts to think of Carl dead. He is thinking of his funeral, of his crying wife and daughter. He is thinking of drunk drivers reeling over the highways in pickup trucks, games of chicken, fake stock car races, late-night swims at the quarry ending up in drowning. He sees dark blue suits and newspaper notices, the wrestling team taking up two pews in the church, their crew cut heads bowed in prayer. Taft thinks how he will tell this story for the rest of his life. He'll say, I told him he couldn't go out that night and then I changed my mind. He is sitting in the kitchen, trying to remember what Carl was wearing when he left so he can describe him to the police. Then he hears a car in the driveway. A door slams shut and the car drives away. Taft meets Carl at the door.

"Dad," Carl says.

There he is, wearing a red T-shirt, not the blue one Taft had been thinking of. Taft feels like he's choking. He doesn't feel the pain in his chest, but he remembers it suddenly. His hand goes up towards Carl and then drops back before he's touched him. "You all right?"

Carl nods.

"Where the hell have you been so late?"

"I had an accident."

Carl is looking down at the floor. Taft looks behind him, through the open front door. No car. "Anybody hurt? You hurt?"

Carl shakes his head.

And just as he's about to question him, just as he's about to find out where the car is and why he didn't call, Taft is overwhelmed by the knowledge that this is Carl, here, alive. All fears mean nothing. He was wrong. Here stands his whole son, not a mark on him. He puts his hands on Carl's shoulders. He can feel them shaking. "But you're okay?"

"I wrecked the car."

They only have the one car. Taft's wife drives him to work and picks him up later. The children take the bus to school. It's a gold Buick LeSabre. It isn't a new car. It was going to need tires this year. No matter how badly it's wrecked, they'll get it fixed. The money. The deductible is five hundred dollars and that money does not exist anyplace, period. Even if they found five hundred there would be the insurance costs, which would go up and up. Carl wouldn't be allowed to drive anymore. There'd be no way to cover him. There will be a lot to think about tomorrow, a lot to figure out. He'll have to be stern with Carl then. There will have to be punishment. But it's late now and they're there together. Whatever is true tonight will still be true in the morning after they sleep.

"Go on and get to bed," Taft says. "It's late."

"Don't you want to hear about it?"

"Tomorrow. You get some sleep." He smiles at him, just the smallest bit, but it makes everything clear. What matters is you, Taft is telling him. You, alive and well, not the car.

Carl nods and heads down the hallway to his room. Taft goes back to bed, to his wife. There's a lot to figure out, money, but he's dead tired. He's sure the second his head hits the pillow he'll be asleep, but once he lies down he can't even make his eyes close. The fear, which he knows now is groundless, stays with him. Even with Carl safe in bed, Taft feels like he still isn't home.

"Dad? You awake?"

I was just holding the phone, not talking into it. The clock said six-thirty. I hadn't been awake at six-thirty since Franklin left for Florida, which could only mean that it was Franklin on the phone. "I'm awake."

"Nobody here is up," Franklin said.

"I'm up," Mrs. Woodmoore called from somewhere behind him.

"Oh," he said. "Gramma's up."

"Did you sleep okay?" I said, still sleeping myself.

"I slept fine. I slept on the sofa. Aunt Ruth is sleeping in the room she used to share with Mom and Mom is in Uncle Buddy's room. Gramma said Mom and Aunt Ruth should share their old room like they used to, but they didn't want to."

I nodded into my pillow, thankful at least for the fact that I didn't have to picture them sleeping in the same room.

"Are you coming over?"

"Not this early."

"But you're coming over?"

"Have your mother call me when she wakes up. Then we'll decide what the plan for the day is."

"Putt-Putt golf," Franklin said.

"We'll see. Wait till she gets up. And don't wake her up. Do you hear me?"

"Yessir."

"I'm glad you're back."

"I'm glad I'm back," he said to me.

I knew he was going to wake up Marion. Even if he didn't actually go into her room and shake her, he would stomp back and forth in the hall and pretend to trip and fall into her door. I didn't have much choice but to get up and shower.

There I was, getting ready to spend the day with my son, thinking about where I was going to take him to eat and when we'd go down to the river, and as happy as I was I couldn't help but feel Carl like a dark shadow in the room. Fay had told me at the start, it was just that he was trying to find a way to deal with his pain. I hadn't thrown him out when I knew he was using drugs. I hadn't gone to his family or talked to him about getting help. I was plenty understanding of his problems then. But when he was dealing in the bar, that was that. I didn't want to reconcile with him, try to bring him back. What I wanted, really, was never to have known him. Looking at Carl was like looking down a well. There was not time or love or money enough in the world to fill that hole, and even knowing that, the need and soreness of him followed me around. Fay would be working that night, and I wondered if for once he'd give her the car to drive herself home, or if he'd just park across the street somewhere when she was due to get off and wait for her.

I took my shower and set about cleaning up the apartment. I needed to do the laundry. I was thinking about it when the phone rang again.

"I'm up," Marion said.

"Sorry to hear that."

She yawned, such a long yawn that she finally put her hand over the receiver. "You'd think I'd be used to this."

"I hear once they get a little older they sleep all the time."

"I'm not counting on it," she said. "Come on over and take us to breakfast. You don't have to be at work for a while."

"No hurry."

"Good. I'm hungry. I'm starving."

"You're always hungry when you wake up," I said. "I used to think I should leave a bowl of food on the bedside table so you could just roll over in the morning and feed yourself."

Marion laughed. "If you'd done that," she said, "things might have worked out differently for us."

I took them to the Shoney's. Ruth was still asleep when I picked them up, or she was staying in her room. Carl and Fay and Ruth. I felt like I needed to make myself a schedule so that there'd be time to smooth things out with all of them. Funny that there was comfort in being with Marion, the person who always headed up the list of people to be soothed.

"You getting waffles?" she asked Franklin.

"Waffles," he said.

The waitress showed up and she smiled at Franklin. "You on vacation already?" she said to him. She was a tall black girl with a head full of shiny curls. She looked so cheerful, so completely free of personal problems standing there in her brown and orange striped polyester uniform. I was wondering why I couldn't find myself such a happy waitress.

"I left early," Franklin said.

"Now that's smart thinking," the waitress said, pen waiting in the air just above her order pad. "Hang out with your mom and dad. What'll you folks be having this morning?"

We gave our orders and she brought us our own pot of coffee. She filled our cups and left the rest on the table.

"Stop staring at that girl," Marion said when she left. She was laughing. "You're getting too old for that."

"It's not what you're thinking," I said.

"You don't know what I'm thinking," she said, trying to make herself sound bad and laughing again. She stretched like she was still in bed and then stared out the window at a clear day and a lot full of parked cars. "Memphis looks good. You wouldn't believe how tired you can get of all that sunshine and those pink buildings."

"Everything's pink," Franklin said.

"I imagine that would wear on you."

Marion nodded, smiled again. "I'm going over to the hospital this afternoon, say hello, see if I still have any friends in this town."

"See if you still have a job?" I asked.

Marion gave Franklin a light push on the shoulder. "Go wash your hands. The food's going to be here in a minute."

"My hands are clean."

"I saw you petting that dog outside. Go on." She shoved him a little so that he slid out of the booth seat. He nodded and headed off.

She watched him walk towards the cash register and stop at a pile of comic books featuring the Shoney's Big Boy. "Don't talk about this in front of him," she said to me. "I don't want to get his hopes up about anything. I haven't made up my mind. I just got here last night."

"But you're going to see about a job?"

"I'm going to say hello to my friends," she said. "Maybe I'll see what's going on." She looked at me like for a minute she was worried. She patted my hand, something she must have picked up in Miami, as I don't remember Marion being much of a hand patter. "Now I'm getting your hopes up."

"I'd rather see the two of you in Memphis," I said. "I don't make any secret about that. I have to tell you though, for someone who doesn't like Miami, you sure seem happier than I've seen you in a long time."

Marion spooned a packet of sugar into her coffee. One sugar, no milk. I could have done it for her. "I wanted to get away from Memphis for a long time," she said. "I had to get away. But I did that. Now it doesn't seem like coming back would be such a bad thing."

I knew this woman. She had once thrown a plate of macaroni and cheese at me. Macaroni and cheese with cut up chunks of stewed tomatoes in it, the way I like it.

"Clean hands," Franklin said.

"Let me see." Marion took his hands. She looked at both sides, like she was a nurse checking for something more serious than dog hair, then she kissed them, palms up.

We ate our breakfast and I paid the check. Once we got outside I told Marion to go on to the hospital, that I'd take Franklin around and bring him back before it was time to go to the bar. "Does he need anything?" I said. "I could take him shopping, clothes or school supplies?"

"I could think of some things," Franklin said.

Marion stared at him. "He's spoiled rotten," she said. "His grandmother had a whole year's worth of clothes waiting on him. Don't buy him a thing." She kissed Franklin in the parking lot. "Be good," she said. "I'll catch up with you later on. You be good, too," she said to me, and then she got in her car.

Boys with their fathers who don't belong to their fathers, I can spot them anywhere. They're taking tours of the pyramid, playing Putt-Putt golf at ten o'clock on a Saturday morning. They're filling up the zoo, carrying cotton candy and a bag of carmeled corn, balloons and a thirty-five dollar stuffed yak from the gift shop. Custody day, I used to think to myself when I passed them. Court-appointed visitation day. And I'd be prideful knowing that wasn't the way it was with my boy. I saw him every day, whether his mother was living with me or not. I bought his shoes and helped him with his math homework. I stood behind him in the bathroom when he brushed his teeth because if I didn't he never brushed the back ones. The dentist told me that. I held his head when he threw up in the toilet after catching the flu. I pulled up socks, fixed belts, took him to church when I didn't have the slightest interest in going myself. Nobody who saw me with my son would think that I was only some weekend father. But that was all before Miami. Now here I was, pulling off the interstate into Big Mountain Golf Land, already thinking about the chili dog stand we could go to for lunch. It wasn't until just that minute that I had feelings for every father who had tried to endear himself in the few hours he had, every father who wanted his kid to go home and tell his mother about how great the day had been. The kid's life is screwed up and I'm the one who did it. That's what us custody fathers think. If I can make it look like Disneyland for a while, then more power to me.

"It's still early," Franklin said. "I want to go through one more round."

So we did. Then there were chili dogs, ice cream, a trip to the mall where I bought him a pair of sneakers that were big and puffy as marshmallows. He loosened up the shoelaces and wore them out of the store.

"Don't you want to tie those?" I said.

Franklin just looked at me like I was crazy.

By the time I got him back to the Woodmoores' it was nearly three o'clock and I needed to be getting over to the bar.

"You'll call me later?" Franklin said.

"You bet."

"Do you want to come in and say hi to Mom?"

I looked at my watch again. I wasn't thinking about Marion so much as I was Ruth. "I better get going," I said. "We'll have a lot of time tomorrow."

"Okay," he said. He picked up his shoebox which had his old

shoes inside and put them under one arm. Then he leaned over and kissed me. Mrs. Woodmoore opened the front door and waved to us. He was all ready to go, but he didn't, he sat there with his hand on the door and watched her, like he was trying to decide which one of us he'd rather stay with.

"Go on, now," I said. "I'm coming right back."

W<small>HEN</small> I got to work that afternoon, Fay was waiting for me. "What did you say to Carl last night?" she wanted to know. Was it possible that she was getting smaller? I wondered how fast a girl that age could lose weight. She looked like she was wearing somebody else's clothes, the clothes of somebody a whole lot bigger than she was.

"Nothing."

"You said something to him." She came around to the other side of the bar so she could keep her voice low. Cyndi wasn't far away, and she was watching. "When he came back to get me last night he was calling you every name in the book. He said you stole from him."

"What do you think?"

"Of course I don't think you stole from him, but something happened."

"If Carl has something he wants to tell you, then he's the one to tell you. I don't want to get into this thing."

"But Carl's not telling me." Her voice was going up. She

stopped herself and put a hand up on the bar. "You think he knows about us?"

Us. Now there was a question. If Carl knew about us then he was one up on me. "I don't talk about you with your brother."

"Maybe he figured it out." The color was rising in her face just thinking about it. "Carl wouldn't understand about that. He'd take it the wrong way."

I leaned over to her. "Nothing happened," I said. "There's nothing to know. I don't think that's what Carl's problem is."

"Then what's his problem?" she said, hurt.

"You know his problem. You know all of them. Carl's got to start taking some responsibility for himself."

"You folks not serving drinks here anymore?"

I was all set to say something smart, but when I looked up it was Ruth sitting there, perched up on a barstool for God knows how long.

"Look at this," Ruth said. "It's the girl with the dry hair. You know, you should pin that hair back. Get it out of your eyes. You've got pretty eyes."

Just like that those eyes filled up and spilled over and Fay covered them with her hand.

"It was a compliment, girlfriend," Ruth said. "You shouldn't take a compliment so hard."

Fay went off to the kitchen with her head down.

All I could think was that Ruth must have taken a lot off of white girls when she was young to make her hate them so much now. Either that or she just had a bigger mean streak than I had given her credit for. "Why in the hell are you picking on her?"

"You doing her too?" Ruth smiled.

"Jesus."

"That's not a no," she said, looking over in the direction of the kitchen doors through which Fay had disappeared.

"She's got enough troubles. Just leave her alone."

"That's just like you, going around picking up wounded birds. I bet you used to hold bird funerals when you were a kid. Did you? Get little boxes for coffins and call all your friends over. Tie two sticks together for a cross."

"Ruth."

"Give me a beer," she said. "No, give me a glass of wine. Give me something nice 'cause I'm not planning on paying for it."

I looked around under the counter till I found a bottle of burgundy that shouldn't have even been in a bar like that. I opened it up and poured her a glass.

"You should be a fly on the wall where I live," she said, taking a sip of the wine. "That's good," she said. "It should probably sit here for a minute. Isn't that what wine needs to do? Hang out?" She smiled at me. "I'm losing my point. You're a regular topic of conversation. How good you look. How good you are with Franklin. How lonely you look. Doesn't he look lonely to you, Ruth? It's hard for me to say anything. I don't think you look so lonely. I think you look like a man who has more company than he can handle."

"I know this is hard for you," I said.

"Hard for me? Why's that? Because you're not crawling up the side of the house to get into my bedroom at night? It's not hard for me. It's hard for you."

We looked at each other until I looked away. Ruth used to love having staring contests when she was a kid. She always won.

"Let me see that bottle," she said.

I handed her the bottle and she read the label. "Look at that. It's from France."

"What do you want me to do, Ruth?"

She put the bottle down on the bar. "I sure don't want to see you winding up with my sister again."

"Is that what you think is going to happen?"

"That's what Marion thinks is going to happen."

That was speculation on her part. I knew Marion well enough to know that if she had such thoughts she'd keep them to herself, and I didn't believe she had them to begin with. And I didn't want Marion back. I didn't even think about it. Maybe for a second it crossed my mind in the Shoney's, right after she told me not to look at the waitress. I thought about it and then just that quick I stopped. Don't beat a dead horse. That was my father's favorite expression. I believe it was his only piece of advice to me. When I was young I had this picture of a man standing in a field next to a dead horse and a turned over plow and he was beating it with everything he had, kicking it and beating it with his fists. It was cruelty I thought my father was warning me against. That it was important not to be cruel to something, even if that something was dead.

"If you're worried about this, then I'll tell you truthfully you don't have anything to worry about. If what you're saying is I can't see Marion, that you'll be able to prevent that, then come on out with it."

And Ruth, who made a point of never being hurt, looked hurt for just a second. "It wasn't my intention to blackmail you, if that's what you're worried about." She shook her head and took a healthy sip of her wine. "You are the stupidest man I ever met in my life," she said to her glass.

"I'm sure that's true."

"You coming over for dinner tonight?"

"Tomorrow night," I said.

"Tomorrow. Well then, I guess I'll see you tomorrow. Tell that little waitress of yours that her Aunt Ruth said not to be so sensitive."

"I'll tell her."

She downed the rest of the wine and picked up her purse.

"You take care of yourself," I said.

"Count on that," Ruth said.

As I was watching Ruth walk away I couldn't help but think I'd gotten up too early. That was my problem. Every time I tried to think about Franklin, the other things started crowding him out. What I needed was a simpler life. I'd have settled for the one I had a week before.

"Cyndi," I said. "Go back in the kitchen and get me some olives. We're about out."

"You know where the kitchen is," she said and kept right on walking. News of what I'd done, or some version of what I'd done, seemed to be traveling fast. I wasn't much when it came to a code of honor, but there was no sense in trying to explain this one to anybody. Maybe that was me feeling bad about Carl, trying to at least give him the dignity of telling whatever lies he was telling. People have short memories. Just look at Marion. They'd all be mad for a while and then they wouldn't be. The thing to do was keep quiet, pour drinks and wipe down the bar. That's exactly what I did until five o'clock when Wallace came in. He hadn't asked me any questions the night before and I hadn't said anything, but I had to admit there was some comfort in having him there.

"How's it been going?" he said, stepping behind the bar and tying an apron around his waist. Most men won't wear aprons, but most men aren't Wallace.

"It's been a real joy."

He pressed his lips together and nodded. "I figured as much. That one giving you trouble too?" He pointed at Cyndi.

"That one always gives me trouble."

"I've been wondering about her relationship to the defendant," he said. "Not that it's any of my business."

"This is a business," I said. "It's all our business."

"Tonight's the night you show me about the money. I figure with your family in town" — he stopped for a minute — "and everything, that it might do you good to spend a little less time here in the evenings."

"I wonder who's working for who these days."

"I'm not telling you how to run the store, chief, I'm just offering."

Good man, Wallace. "I appreciate that, and about last night —"

Wallace put up his hand. "As long as the problem is gone then you don't need to say anything else about it."

"It's gone." But it was always possible to speak too soon. The phone was ringing even as the words were coming out of my mouth and since I was standing closest to the phone, I was the one who picked it up.

"Let me talk to Fay," Carl said.

Fay was still spending her time hiding out in the kitchen. "Fay," I hollered through the door. "Telephone."

She followed me out into the bar, not too close. "You want to take it up in the office?"

"I can get it here," she said.

She picked up the phone behind the bar and it seemed like an awfully long time before she said anything, and when she did all she said was "Christ."

"All right," she said. "All right. I'm coming." After she hung up the phone she stood there and looked at it like she was waiting for it to start ringing again. Wallace and I tried to make ourselves busy.

"Carl's in jail," she said, like it was an old secret and she was just the last one to find out. "I'm going to need you to drive me down there, I guess. I could take a cab, but I want to be able to leave right away."

"In jail?" Wallace said.

She nodded.

There was a part of me saying no, no rides to jail. It was the same old tired part of me that had said no to everything concerning Fay and her brother right from the word go. I was sorry that it didn't ever seem to be the part that won out.

"You're going to be busy," I said to Wallace. "Just you and Cyndi here."

"I'll give Arlene a call," he said. He took it all in stride. Life didn't seem to surprise Wallace the way it did me.

"I guess we're going to jail then. What's his bail?" I asked Fay.

"No bail," she said. "He's a minor. I'm going to see if I can get them to release him to me." She ran her hand over her hair, smoothing it down. At that moment she barely looked seventeen and I couldn't see the police releasing anybody to Fay.

Down on Beale there's a police museum. It's free and open as late as any bar. People like to go there when they're drunk. It makes them feel like they're doing something wild, like they're turning themselves in. There isn't much to see, really. Framed pictures of famous policemen and dead policemen, glass cases full of badges and old guns and tin whistles, station log books saying who was brought in on what charge. You don't have to go back too far to find plenty of people brought in for the crime of being uppity, not getting off the sidewalk quick enough, having the wrong tone in their voice. Anyone who says that Memphis is

192

bad only needs to drop by the police museum to see when Memphis was worse. I'd been there plenty of times on plenty of different occasions. It was only two blocks from where I worked. But it gave me a bad taste for police stations. If I wasn't given to the fake one, I didn't see that the real one would suit me any better.

Fay got into the car. Old home week.

"Which jail?" I said.

"Shit." She leaned over and put her head against the dashboard.

"It isn't something a person would think to ask, really. It says something good about you. Your not knowing." I was trying to be funny, but that was a washout. "We'll go to the big one," I said, not entirely sure which one was biggest. "If he isn't there, they'll be able to find him for us."

"I'd appreciate it," she said.

I started over to the station on Poplar since it was closest and, I figured, our best bet. I'd lived in Memphis all my life. A man can know where the police are without ever having gotten into too much trouble. The traffic was thick with people wanting to get home. She would have gotten there quicker if she'd walked.

"That's what last night was about, wasn't it?"

What was I going to tell her? "More or less."

She was tired. "I guess I figured as much. Whenever I talked to him about it he'd say it used to be a problem but now it wasn't anymore. You want to believe somebody, you know, your brother."

"Sure you do."

"I wasn't doing him any favors, letting him slide. You, you're the one who was trying to help him."

"I wasn't helping Carl," I said. "I just wanted him out of the bar. I wish I could tell you different."

She shook her head. "You just don't see it. I've read articles about these things. If you really want to help somebody, you have to be tough with them." Fay pulled her legs up onto the seat and hugged her knees to her chest. "Listen, if it's all right with you, I'd like to tell them Carl works at the restaurant, that he washes dishes there or something. I think it would make things look more solid if we could tell them you're his boss too."

"I make a point of not lying to the police."

"It's not such a lie, really. He's there all the time. He's worked for you before, a couple of times anyway. You could just tell them that, if it came up."

Fay knew I was going to do what she wanted and I guess I knew it too, but I didn't say anything. I figured we could all wait and see.

The sergeant working the desk was a black guy with a name-plate that said Lowe and for the first time I thought my being along might do some good. There was a little waiting room where a couple of people who looked like they were just a step away from being on the other side of the bars were sitting in red plastic chairs. They reminded me of the people I'd seen in the bus station, the last time Fay and I were out looking for Carl.

"Excuse me," Fay said, and the sergeant looked up at her and then at me. I nodded. "We're here to see about Carl Taft."

"Prisoner?"

Fay pulled back. "He's my brother," she said. "You're holding him." Like he was a dress she'd put on layaway months ago and finally had the money to claim.

"Taft," the sergeant said, typing it into a computer in front of him. "He's here."

"May I have him, please?" Her voice was respectful, serious and kind. She wasn't being too sweet. She wasn't leaning into his desk or acting tough. There were lots of different ways to talk to cops. Everybody I'd seen in my life had struck some sort of pose, but Fay, I would have to say, was a natural.

The sergeant looked at his screen. "He's a minor," he said. "We'll have to release him to the parents."

"Our father is dead," she said, "and our mother is out of town until next week. I'm his sister. I'm all he's got here."

"So who is this?" he said, pointing the eraser end of a pencil at me.

My mouth opened up to speak, but Fay was already going. "I work for him. He drove me down here. Carl, my brother, he works for him too."

"Sort of a family thing," Sergeant Lowe said, and not in a nice way.

But Fay took it as the description she'd been looking for. "Yes," she said. "All of us at Muddy's are close. It's a small place. It is like family."

I was wondering what bar she was thinking of.

"Muddy's? You work at Muddy's," he said to me.

"I run the place."

"Does Guy Chalfont still own Muddy's? Is Guy still alive?"

"He's in Florida now. I get a postcard every once in a while. He sold out, probably ten years ago now. A doctor bought the place."

"A doctor." Sergeant Lowe shook his head. "Christ, I'm sorry to hear that."

"It's fine," I said. "He never comes by. The place is running same as always." I started to say, You should come by sometime, but I didn't want to look like I was offering anything. I wouldn't offer anything to get Carl out of jail.

"I should get down there. Twenty years ago I had a beat on Beale. I got so sick of the place." He stopped himself and looked up at Fay. "You know this kid had cocaine. That's no small thing. You get into coke, you're talking about a felony. That's bad. You don't want a felony. Tell your brother he'd be a lot better off with pot if he was looking to get into trouble."

"Yessir," Fay said.

"You'd have to be eighteen before we could even think about releasing him to you. I'd rather have his mother. I don't like turning kids over to kids. Are you sure your mother isn't home?"

"Not until next week," Fay said.

"No other family?"

"We just moved here from east Tennessee a few months ago. Coalfield," she offered.

"Coalfield. Jesus Christ. Who thinks the names of these places up?" He tapped a couple of keys on the computer, but the screen was facing away from us. "This boy has no priors. Nothing in Coalfield, right?"

"No, sir."

"Of course not, nice boy like this. And you, you're eighteen?"

Fay nodded.

"I'd have to see some identification before I believed that."

This was where things were going to start to unravel. I didn't see any way around it. Fay reached into her purse and pulled out her wallet. I wondered how much trouble I would have saved myself if I had asked to see some ID on the day she came in looking for a job, saying she was twenty.

The sergeant took her whole wallet and looked at her driver's license. "Well, happy birthday, Elizabeth Fay Taft."

"Thank you," she said.

I stared at her, at the side of her face, the line of her nose. Eighteen. Elizabeth. A birthday spent in a bar and a police station without anybody knowing it.

"You're cutting this one pretty close, you know." He shook his head. "That brother of yours got it all figured out, doesn't he. Hell of a kid, bringing his sister down here on her birthday."

"May I have him, then?"

He looked at us for a minute. He knew there was something dead wrong with the picture, but a line was starting to form behind us. A pregnant woman with a baby, a man who looked to be about ninety-five. You wouldn't want to keep either of them standing too long.

"It costs a lot of money to keep a kid," he said. "Kids have all sorts of rights, you wouldn't believe it. Even kids like this one. I don't see any way to hold him until Mama comes home." He took out a piece of paper and fed it through the typewriter. "What this says is young Carl Taft is cited back. That means he comes back here next week with his mother and talks to the investigator. I don't care if that means you have to drive up to Coaltown and get her yourself. Next week it's Mama, not you. Understand?"

"Yessir."

"And you," he said to me. "I still haven't figured out where you fit into all of this. But you would be well advised to keep these children out of here."

"I'll do my best," I said, though all I could think of was washing my hands of the whole thing.

The sergeant picked up the phone. "Bring down Carl Taft," he said. "Tell him his sister's here." He looked back at us. "You two have a seat," he said, pointing over towards the plastic chairs with his pencil.

Fay and I sat down to wait while the pregnant woman moved up to the desk to tell her story.

Where they were keeping Carl that it took so long to find

him, I could only guess. We sat there for an hour, each of us with plenty to say and neither of us willing to say a word of it there. Police stations can make some people feel like they're in church. Everything has to be silent and respectful.

Maybe I expected Carl to look different, thinner, if that was possible, a little messed up. But they hadn't held him long enough. As soon as I saw him come through the doors carrying the manila envelope full of his possessions, I knew we'd made a mistake by not leaving him in overnight. He hadn't been there long enough to get scared. He'd only been there long enough to get mad.

The first words out of his mouth were for me. "What's he doing here?"

"Keep your voice down," Fay said. The sergeant looked up and she waved to him.

"Don't forget what I told you," Sergeant Lowe said.

She nodded and pushed Carl ahead of her out the door.

"You come back to see if you can't steal something else from me?"

We got in the car. Fay in the front seat, Carl in back.

"Where'd you leave your car?" I said to him while I backed out of the space.

"You want the car now?"

I hit the brakes and they both lurched forward on their seats. I looked at him. I just looked. That was plenty.

"What happened?" Fay said.

"It was bullshit," Carl said. "Total bullshit violation of my civil rights." His voice was softer now. "I was just standing there and this cop shook me down and said he found coke on me."

"Back up," Fay said.

"I was standing there."

"Where?"

"The zoo," he said. "The car's at the zoo. One of those faggy bicycle cops goes by."

"And you said something?"

"I didn't say anything. Maybe I said, nice bike or something. I can't even remember. Well, the next thing I know this guy is right up in my face. What's your problem, he says. I don't like your face, he says. So I said something back. I'm not going to stand there and take it from some cop who doesn't even get his own car, for Christ's sake."

"Jesus," I said.

"So this cop, and I know this has got to be against the law, he slams me up against the wall with all sorts of people around and he starts going through my pockets. Everybody is so interested in what I have in my pockets these days. He finds a pack of cigarettes that some guy had given me and he rips them open and there's a little bit of tin foil in the bottom of the pack with some blow. I don't know if he put it there himself or what, but it wasn't mine."

"It wasn't yours?" Fay said.

"Some guy gave me those cigarettes. I asked to bum one and he said I could keep the pack. I didn't look in the pack. You think I take apart every pack of cigarettes I get to make sure there's no coke laying around in the bottom? How was I supposed to know?"

"And you told this to the cop?" I said.

"Sure that's what I told him. It was the truth."

I felt truly ashamed for Carl just then, more for how stupid he was becoming than any bad thing he had ever done. I didn't say anything else. I just drove.

"That's my car, up there," he said, pointing.

I pulled up next to the gold LeSabre with the bashed-in front. I wanted to think of him getting in and driving away, doing all the idiotic things he was destined to do someplace far from here, and then maybe coming back, years later, when he could be the person his father had known.

"You should thank him," Fay said. "If it wasn't for him they wouldn't have let you out."

"They had to let me out," Carl said. "I'm a minor." He slammed the door and then stuck his head inside Fay's window. "Come on."

"I'm going back to work," she said, and rolled the window up.

I watched him standing there in my rearview mirror, cursing to himself. He wouldn't be thinking about what he had done to his sister or what he would tell his mother. He would be worrying about having lost the coke he had left. He would be worrying about dealers who didn't like stories. Carl's luck was going bad and if I'd been in possession of any sympathy just then I would have been worried about him myself. He was playing in a league that flossed their teeth with skinny boys like him.

Fay and I drove along for a while without saying anything. The traffic hadn't gotten any better, so half the time we were just sitting there, not even moving. We were both worn out, exhausted. Carl had that effect on people.

"It's not that he's a bad person," Fay said, touching the space between her breasts. "Inside. I know that's a stupid thing to say. Oh, he's acting like a complete idiot, but on the inside. But with Carl, it's true. I knew him before all this. You can still see how it is with Carl, can't you?"

"Sure," I said, and really, it was true. I've met bad people and I've met people who just fell off the track. Carl fell, which means you can get mad at him and tired of him, but you don't so much blame him.

"He'll come around," she said. "I believe that absolutely. The question is how much trouble will he be in when he finally does."

I pulled the car into the alley behind Muddy's and we sat there for a minute. Us alone in a car together had good reason to make me nervous.

"It didn't take all that long," she said, looking at the back of the bar.

"Not too bad."

"I'm kinda hungry. Could we get something to eat? Something fast?"

It wasn't about being hungry, since Rose's food was free and plenty good. She just wanted to stay out a little while longer. Then I remembered it was her birthday. "A person ought to get taken out to eat on her birthday."

Fay looked up and smiled. She had forgotten too, if only for that minute. "I'd like that," she said.

I took her across the street to Doe's Place, which is big and open and bright. All the chairs were desk chairs, secretary chairs. We sat down at a table that was such a bright, fake blue it made me think of the blue paper people put behind fish tanks to make the water look like an ocean. Olie, the cook, waved at me from the open grill.

"What does it take to get you to cross the street and come see me?" he called out.

"I haven't seen you over there drinking much lately."

He laughed, the big loud laugh of a cook who kept a bottle of beer going for the whole day. "I'll be over," he said. "I got to find out what's going on between you and that pretty girl." He pointed a spatula at Fay.

Fay blushed and, with that, became a pretty girl.

"Get yourself a steak," I said to her. "Anything you want. It's your birthday dinner." All the steaks in that place were bigger than her head, but I could get Olie to cut one down for me.

"Are you getting a steak?"

"I'm at Doe's," I said. All of the sudden I was glad to be there, glad to be back at Doe's after a long time away, glad to be with Fay. "You told me your birthday was next week."

"I didn't want to tell you what day. I didn't want you to think you had to get me a present. But this is a present. You're taking me out to dinner. I walk by this place all the time. I've always wanted to go in."

"You've never been here? Olie," I said. "She's never been to Doe's. Give us two tenderloins, and make one of them a size that won't scare her."

"I can do that," he said.

The waiter, who had been cut out of the whole transaction, came over to see what we wanted to drink.

"Nobody could have told me an hour ago that this could have turned out to be a nice day. Carl's home, safe for now. Of course, he's going to have to tell Mom, go back next week."

I put up my hand. "Enough about Carl."

She raised the Coke that the waiter had brought to her and touched it to my beer. "Enough about Carl." She took a sip of her drink. "So, you having fun with your boy?"

"Sure," I said. "I haven't seen him much yet, but we're going to have a lot of fun."

She nodded. "You thinking you might get remarried to his mother?" she said, cutting to the chase.

"That seems to be the question of the day. I was never married to his mother, and I don't expect I ever will be."

"Do you want to be?"

"I'm way past that."

"Good," she said.

Olie brought the steaks over himself. "A little one for the pretty one," he said, giving a plate to Fay. "Tell me, are they getting younger or are we getting older?"

"I think it's both," I said to him. "Olie, this is Fay. She's a waitress over at Muddy's and today's her birthday."

"Birthday!" Olie said. "You should have told me. I would have put a candle in your steak. How old are you today, pretty girl?"

"Eighteen," Fay said. So much blood had risen to her face that her skin looked nearly burnt.

"Eighteen," Olie said, putting a hand on my shoulder. "Perfectly legal and completely marriageable. That's what I like to see my boys running with. Now you enjoy your dinners, both of you. He treats you bad, you come tell me," he said to Fay.

She nodded, too embarrassed to say anything. Olie laughed and left the table.

"You've got a friend for life," I said. "You could probably get a job over here if you ever needed one."

"You shouldn't have told him it was my birthday." But she said it happy.

"He's glad to know." I started to cut into my steak. A hot knife through butter, I swear.

"So what do you think?" she said.

"What do I think about what?"

"About marrying me," Fay said, "now that I'm eighteen."

My knife hung right over the steak. I had to stop and take the sentence apart in my head to make sure I'd gotten it right. This one I never saw coming.

"I know you think I'm crazy, but I'm not. Listen," she said, putting down her fork. "I can go anywhere now. We could leave. We could go out west, California, Nevada, it wouldn't matter. Don't look like that. We could stay here, too. I really wouldn't mind. It would be all right, being in Memphis if I was married to you. We could keep everything the same as it is now. You work in the bar and I work in the bar. I like it there." She put her hand over my hand. My hand still had a knife in it. "I love you," she said. "I'm not making this up. I don't mean to scare you to death or anything here, but I think this is a good idea and maybe you just haven't thought about it before."

"No," I said. "I hadn't thought about it."

"That doesn't mean it's a bad idea." Fay took a bite of her steak. "This is awfully good."

I took a bite of mine. Not because I wanted it, but because I liked the idea of having my mouth full. Then both of us were eating, cutting and chewing and saying how good everything was and not saying anything else.

"Like that?" Olie called from the grill.

"It's great!" Fay shouted back.

"I can't marry you," I said.

"I know you'd have to say that," she said, taking a sip of her Coke. "All I'm asking is that you think about it. To me, it makes such sense. You could take some time on this, not say no right away."

"I don't see how it could change."

"But you don't know for sure," she said.

She seemed pretty cheerful about the whole thing. No woman had ever asked me to marry her before, if you discounted drunk girls in bars when I was playing. Even Marion hadn't asked me, even when she wanted to.

"You don't think there would maybe be a few, well, obstacles to us?" I could think of fifty without even taxing myself.

Fay looked at me square and gave herself a minute. "No," she said. "Think about it. Don't say anything. Just think for a while."

We finished up our dinner. I was trying to think about it, but my mind couldn't even get near it. "We need to get back," I said, looking at my watch and not seeing what time it was.

"You kids have fun," Olie said.

We waved to him and walked out onto Beale like we were together. With all the streetlights going it was hardly like night.

Fay turned into an alley. "Oh my God," she said. "Look at this."

I followed in behind her to see and when I did she grabbed both of my hands and lifted up on her toes to kiss me. She pressed her whole self into me. I felt her through the clothes.

"Wait a second," I said.

She looped one of her ankles between my legs and pulled me in closer. She kissed me.

"Fay." I pushed her shoulders back and she nearly lost her balance, standing on one foot.

"Kiss me," she said.

"This isn't the time. A man needs to think, all right?"

She stepped back from me, just a little, and she nodded. "You're right," she said. "Absolutely right. I don't mean to be in such a rush."

I was relieved. I didn't want to hurt her feelings. It had been a hard enough day, her birthday.

"You're not mad at me?" she said.

"No."

She took my arm and held on to it. "That's all I need to hear."

How could I get mad at a girl who kissed me that way?

THE TOW was thirty. Taft let the AAA lapse last year to save a little money. Don Holland went to high school with Taft. He's done well. Used to be he did auto body out of his back yard, but it got to where he had so many cars they were parked all over the neighborhood and he had to get a regular shop. Now he's open on Saturdays, too. He answered the phone himself when Taft called this morning asking if he could go out and get the car off the road before the police found it. Taft came down to Don's place as soon as they'd brought the car in.

"Radiator came through it okay," Don says. "And the battery's fine."

Taft nods. The car is right in front of him. The left front end is smashed, the headlight gone, the tire ripped and pointing in, the metal is crumpled in the front and actually ripped along the side, just waiting to rust. The front grille is hanging down on the grass. A heavyset dog with a white face and a feathery tail comes and sniffs at the grille and then walks away. There are more than a dozen cars parked outside of Don Holland's shop, not counting the Chevy truck and the Pontiac that belong to Don. They've killed all the grass. There are also four white chickens that the dog doesn't seem to mind at all. They're scratching in the dirt, wandering underneath the cars. "What are we talking about here?" Taft asks.

Don takes out a little calculator from his pocket and punches in some numbers. Then he takes a hard look at the car and starts punching again. "Insurance pays twenty-three hundred dollars. You pay seventeen hundred."

Taft sits down on the hood of a Mazda that's behind him.

"The best thing is that he didn't hit another car." Don stops and thinks about this. "Well, the best thing is that nobody was hurt. He hit a guardrail and not a tree. That's good. That's metal. See the way that looks in here?" He points to the whole bashed in left front of the car. "We could say it was a hit-and-run and that way Carl doesn't become completely uninsurable."

"At least that's something," Taft says.

The way Don is biting his lips Taft knows there's more coming. "The problem is your blue book. I looked it up. In top condition the car is worth twelve hundred, which means the insurance company is going to total it. Five hundred for the deductible and you get seven hundred."

"I pay four hundred in premiums."

"That's them figuring you're going to hit somebody in a Jaguar. That's not them replacing your car."

Taft nods and pulls down the brim of his Caterpillar hat. He tries to look like he's thinking things over, but there's nothing to think about. They have to have a car and seven hundred dollars doesn't cut it. There is not seventeen hundred to fix it.

Don Holland likes Taft. He liked him when they were in school. He knows you've got to be careful about doing people favors. It winds up being bad business and bad friendship. "I'll tell you what," he says. "I make it drivable. Not good looking, but drivable. I'll realign the front end, straighten out the frame and put on your spare for four hundred dollars, and that's just between you and me. No insurance."

"I don't want to be cheating you."

Don holds up his hands. "I'm telling you, the car looks just like that. We can maybe rig up some sort of headlight for the front so you don't get pulled over. It's going to drive, but you won't be winning any beauty contests in it. I can do that much, if that's what you're interested in."

This is exactly what Taft is interested in. "I don't care about anything else," he says.

Don squats down next to the spot where the metal is ripped. When he touches it Taft holds his breath, thinking that he's going to find something else. Mechanics can be like doctors in this way. "I can show you sometime about pounding out some of those dents," Don says, "maybe trying to find a secondhand fender. Even a little Bondo would work." He puts his finger through a round hole in the metal. "The truth is, you don't have to do it all at once. Little at a time, you can put it together."

Of course, do it piece by piece. Taft feels the panic starting to move away from him. Sure, he can do it this way.

Don looks around the yard. "How'd you get over here?"

"Walked."

Don stands up and brushes off his hands against his jeans. "Let me run you back. I'm supposed to pick up some things for my wife anyway. I might as well drop you off."

"It's nice enough out."

"Come on," he says. "It's frying hot. I'm going and I won't feel good about driving past you on the road. I'll take you by the place we picked up the car."

Taft was going to say no, but now he agrees. He hasn't gone

208

out to River Road where Carl had the accident and he wants to see. Don tells his two mechanics that he's going out. Then they get in the pickup together and go.

Taft is thinking on the ride over that he has to find a way to move his family in from the edge. It can't keep being like this. Every time something happens they're scrambling around like a bunch of headless chickens to get back on their feet. There has to be a cushion, a little something there to fall back on. In his mind he starts to look for ways to cut back, things to save. His wife was right, he shouldn't have started that deck, but the wood was already paid for and he got it all at a good discount anyway. He could open a savings account, put in everything he made at the lumberyard. That was the whole point of taking the job in the first place. But as soon as a little more money was there, a little more money was needed. It would have to be something else. He would have to figure that out.

"It's up here," Don says, and pulls the truck off to the shoulder of the road. They get out and walk over to see what might have happened.

"Those guardrails," Don says. "They can take a hell of a lot."

The guardrail looks nearly as bad as the car. It's stretched and bent. You can see the shape of the fender, little flecks of gold paint where Carl had brought the car to rest. What's bad though, really bad, is looking over the other side. Taft feels like he's going to be sick. It's nearly a straight drop down fifteen feet. It is a beautiful drop. The grass is dark green and thick and at the bottom there is a wide creek that's full of water from last week's rain. Turns out he hadn't been so crazy after all, thinking about Carl being dead that night.

"Sweet Jesus," Taft says, leaning over and then pulling himself back.

"Do you know how it happened?" Don says.

"It's those damn stock car races. Two boys were in the car with Carl and two other boys were in another car and they started racing. At least that's what Carl told me this morning. They came around that curve" — Taft points up the hill — "and Carl couldn't hold it. He hasn't been driving very long. I never should have let him go to those races. It puts too many ideas in a boy's head. For all I know, they were driving side by side. If a car had come around there I guess they'd all be dead." Taft looks over the edge again.

"It makes you think," Don says. He gives the guardrail a kick and the metal doesn't so much as shudder. "I'm glad my kids aren't driving yet."

"Don't ever let them," Taft says.

Don takes Taft back to his house. "I appreciate the lift and everything," he says. "I'll have that money for you."

Don nods. "No hurry. I'll see if I can't get things workable by Tuesday."

Taft gets out and slams the door. He wonders if he should ask Don in for a beer, but he isn't sure what they'd talk about other than the accident and Taft doesn't want to talk about that anymore.

Taft calls out hello, hello, but there isn't any answer. Everybody's gone. Taft isn't sure how this is possible, seeing as how it's Saturday afternoon and there's no car. He walks through the quiet house and looks for his family in each of the rooms. At least they bought the house. Not that they were anywhere close to owning it, but at least they weren't paying rent anymore. That was something. It's just after noon, but since Taft wondered if he should ask Don in for a beer he's starting to want one himself. He's not a drinker, not by any stretch, but seeing that guardrail bent has rattled him and he thinks that sitting down with a beer might make him feel better. If somebody comes in, he can get rid of it fast. Taft tries never to take a drink in front of his kids.

Taft finds a can of Budweiser in the back of the refrigerator. There are two left. He cracks one open and takes a sip. It's not so bad, the quiet, the beer. He feels like he's doing something racy and it pleases him. He twists the stick on the Venetian blinds in the living room to make things dim, then he goes and flips on the television. He finds a program on public television about trout fishing in Montana and he sits down to watch it. Drinking and watching TV in the middle of the day. Why the hell not?

The men on the TV are tying complicated flies made out of thread and bits of colored feathers. "Cutthroat, grayling, white-fish, rainbow," they're saying. Taft is drifting, thinking about standing in a river with those men someplace far from where he is, nothing better to do with his time than fish and get paid for it. They're standing hip-deep in water, swinging their long poles back and forth over their heads. That's when the doorbell rings.

Taft is startled for a second, realizing that he was almost asleep. He gets up to answer the door and takes the can of beer with him without thinking about it. Then he thinks he has to get rid of it. He looks around and the doorbell rings again. He runs and puts it back in the refrigerator.

When he opens up the door there's a little black boy standing there. He's wearing red shorts and dirty tennis shoes and a T-shirt that says BOYS CLUBS OF AMERICA on it. There's a cardboard box next to him on the front porch.

"Hello," Taft says.

"Hello," the boy says, staring just above Taft's belt, which is how high up he comes on him. "I'm selling chocolate bars for my school. They're a dollar fifty cents. You want one?"

"For your school?" Taft says, a little confused. "Not for Boys Club?"

The boy looks down at his T-shirt. "This was my brother's," he says. "They don't have Boys Club anymore."

Taft is going to say yes, maybe because it seems like a shame the kid doesn't have a Boys Club to go to, even though he isn't exactly sure what one is, or maybe it's because he always says yes to these things. Then he remembers about the money, about cutting back. "I don't need any chocolate right now."

The boy looks up at him then. Taft isn't so tall. "You sure?" the boy asks again. "Whoever sells the most gets a bike."

"That's pretty good," Taft says. He feels sorry for the kid because he knows already that he isn't going to win, at least not in this neighborhood. He looks behind him, down the street for any sign of a parent. It's not safe to let your kids go door to door by themselves. It's safe around here, but who knows where the boy is heading next. "You by yourself?"

At this the boy takes a big automatic step backwards. "My dad dropped me off and he's picking me back up again."

Taft had no intention of making the boy all nervous. It's awful the way kids have to be so scared of everybody these days. "Who's your dad?" he says, trying to sound nice, not that he would know his dad in a million years.

"Tommy Lawson," the boy says.

At this Taft smiles, big and open. For reasons he can't exactly name, this is the best news he's heard all day. He squats down and makes himself shorter than the boy. "Tommy Lawson at Royal Hill Carpet?"

"Yeah," the boy says suspiciously. He is a good looking boy, Taft sees that now. Pretty skin and big, round eyes. He can see how he looks like Lawson.

"Well, I know him. I work with him. Me and your dad are friends." Taft hasn't seen nearly as much of Tommy since he came back to work after losing those two fingers in the accident. He was mostly doing cleanup now, nothing with machinery. He was lucky, really, that he got to keep his job.

"You make carpet?" the boy says.

"Sure do. What's your name?"

"Tommy," the boy says. "Who are you?"

"Levon Taft," he says. "Ask your dad. He knows me."

"Taft," the boy says.

"You want to come in and have a Coke, Tommy?"

The boy looks torn now. It's hot enough outside to make a person sick at his stomach and by the nearly full box of candy Taft can tell he hasn't been having much luck with sales. "I'm not supposed to go inside anywhere."

Taft nods. There's no point in trying to talk him into it. It's a good rule. If Tommy Lawson was teaching his kids not to go inside with strangers then he shouldn't be trying to undo it. "I'll tell you what. I'll get you one and you can drink it out here if you want."

Tommy likes this idea. Taft thinks it must be his day for compromise. "Okay," Tommy says.

Taft goes back into the kitchen and gets out a bottle of Coke and his half a Budweiser. It's one thing not to drink in front of your own kids, but it didn't make much difference if they were somebody else's. He brings the drinks outside and sits down on the porch next to Tommy. "You want me to get that? Here," Taft says, and pulls off the crown cap for him.

"It's hot," Tommy says.

"It sure is that." It's only the first of June, but it's hotter today than it is in August. They sit there and drink their drinks for a while. Taft wonders what the neighbors would think if they came walking by right now, what his wife and his kids would think, and he laughs a little.

"What's funny?" Tommy says.

"Not a thing. How sales been going?"

"Slow," he says, and kicks the box lightly with the toe of his shoe.

"What's the money for?"

"Skeleton," he says. "The science teacher thinks we need to have a skeleton."

That seems pretty advanced to Taft, a bunch of little kids looking at a skeleton.

"You want a skeleton?" Taft asks.

"I want a bicycle."

Taft nods. There probably wasn't much chance of a bicycle for Tommy since his father's problems at the plant. "How's your dad doing?"

Tommy looks up at him and squints. "I thought you knew him."

"I do, I just haven't seen him in a while."

"He's okay. He had an accident, you know. He lost two fingers." Tommy holds up his left hand with the index finger and middle finger bent back so you can't see them. Taft thinks there might be nicer ways of talking about your father's problems, but who knew what kids were thinking about.

"Hell of a thing," Taft says.

"Hell of a thing," Tommy says back to him. "You got all your fingers?"

Taft puts down his beer can and holds up his hands. "Ten of them."

"My dad says that it happens to people who work in the factory all the time and so I shouldn't mind it."

"Well, he's right," Taft says. "It just hasn't happened to me yet. I expect it will sooner or later."

"I'm not going to make carpet when I grow up because I'm going to play basketball like Michael Jordan." Tommy brings his hands up and shoots a free throw from the line. "Got to have all your fingers to be a basketball player."

Taft is thinking about the black boy at the wrestling meet in Memphis, the boy who beat Carl. Taft is thinking how much he hated that boy, how much the very sight of him on the mat had made Taft hate him, but this boy, little Tommy Lawson, Taft likes fine. He wouldn't have any objections to having this boy around, so polite, so nice. And he's smaller. Taft likes them better when they're smaller.

"I oughta go," Tommy says, tilting back his Coke bottle to get to what's left in the bottom. "The chocolate's getting mushy. Thanks for the Coke." He stands up and goes for his box.

"Wait a minute," Taft says. "I've got to buy some."

"You said you didn't want to."

"That's before I got to know you. I didn't know you were Tommy Lawson's son."

"You want one?"

"I want four. There are four of us who live here. Me and my wife and my boy and girl."

"Four!" Tommy says, like every problem he had in the world has been solved. "I haven't sold four all day."

"Well, you have now. Do you know how much four cost?" He's just testing him, seeing how good he is in math.

"Six dollars."

Taft opens up his wallet, but he only has a five. Sometimes there's some change in the drawer next to the stove. Taft goes inside and sifts around through some junk until he comes up with eighty cents. Then he goes into Fay's room and takes two dimes out of the jar of change she keeps on her dresser. "I got it," he calls out, and comes back into the kitchen.

But Tommy's right behind him. "It's nice in here," he says.

"I thought you didn't come inside." Taft thinks the boy should have asked, not just come right in. If you say you don't come inside then you don't.

"I figured if you were buying four candy bars you were okay."

Taft hands him the five and the pile of change and the boy lays four soft candy bars side by side on the kitchen table. It's a lot of money to pay for candy. They're extra big, but you can get candy bars that size for seventy-five cents apiece at the Kroger. He walks Tommy to the door. It would have been plenty to buy one. Taft could kick himself. This is where the money goes.

But once they're back outside and he feels how hot it is and thinks about how rotten it's going to be going up and down the street, he starts to feel sorry for Tommy all over again. "Look," Taft says. "You need to be more specific. Don't say you're selling them for your school. Tell people that you're raising the money to buy a skeleton for your science class. Tell them that you want to be a doctor when you grow up and so you need to have a skeleton in your school. People like to know where their money's going."

"But I don't want to be a doctor. I want to play basketball."

"Doesn't matter. I'm not telling you to lie, I'm just saying people want to make some sort of connection. They want to think that if they buy the candy bar and you get the skeleton then maybe you'll be a doctor. It makes them understand better."

"What about me winning the bike?"

"The only thing you have to worry about is selling the most candy bars. You sell the most then you win the bike."

Tommy thinks it over for a minute and nods. "I'll give it a try," he says. "I'm not doing so good the other way."

"There you go," Taft says.

"See you later," Tommy says.

"You tell your dad I said to say hi."

216

He isn't to the end of the driveway when Marjorie from next door pulls in and lets out Taft's wife and Carl, who are both carrying a load of groceries.

Taft's wife puzzles over the picture for a minute and then she smiles. "How are you?" she says to Tommy in an overly friendly voice. It isn't every day there's a little black boy in her yard.

"You want to buy some chocolate for a skeleton?" Tommy asks her.

"They're with me," Taft says, coming forward to take a sack of groceries. "And you don't say 'Chocolate for a skeleton.' It sounds like the skeleton is eating the chocolate. It's creepy. Say 'Chocolate so we can buy a skeleton for science class.' "

"Okay," Tommy says. Carl is walking forward in such a way that he looks like he's going to walk directly through Tommy, so Tommy takes a big step to the side to let him pass. He watches Marjorie pull out of their driveway and back into her own. "Is she your family?"

"No."

"Then it's okay if I sell her a candy bar?"

"Sure," Taft says. "Give it a try."

Taft and his wife and Carl head in the front door. "You've been drinking with that boy?" his wife says.

"He had the Coke," Taft says.

She stoops down and picks up the bottle and the beer can.

"That was Tommy Lawson's son. Tommy Lawson from Royal Hill. He's the one who lost two fingers on the line."

"I remember that," she says.

"I bought some candy bars from him."

Taft's wife looks at the four candy bars lined up across the table. "Four?" she says. "Isn't that a little much?"

"One for each of us, I figured." Taft is starting to feel embarrassed about the whole thing. Now that she sees them, he thinks she's right. He shouldn't have bought so many.

All this time Carl stays quiet. He doesn't look at Taft or his mother. He doesn't say a word about little Tommy Lawson. He just puts down the bag of groceries and starts back to his room.

"Carl?" Taft says. "Don't you want to hear about the car?"

Carl stops, turns around and comes back. He's not moving any too fast. "Sure," he says.

"Don Holland says he can make it drivable for four hundred dollars. That's no body work and it won't go on the insurance."

"Four hundred?" his wife says.

"What we're going to do is put that on Visa, then Carl, you can pay it off a little at a time. I think that's fair. You can see if there isn't some kind of job at the lumberyard that you could have until wrestling season starts up again."

For just a second something goes over Carl's face and he looks like he's going to say no. It's so quick that neither of his parents see it, and when it passes he's just Carl again. "Sure," he says.

"You think that's fair?" Taft asks him.

"Sure."

"I went out to River Road with Don," Taft says. "You should just be glad it was dark last night so you couldn't see where you almost ended up."

They all stand there for a minute, looking at each other like somebody's going to say something. "Is that all?" Carl says.

Taft nods, even though he thought there would be more. "That's all."

Carl slinks off towards his bedroom.

"I don't want another four hundred dollars on the Visa card," Taft's wife says. "We made a promise, you remember? No more of that. Not for anything. You know good and well we can get it from Lily and Cal."

"No," Taft says.

"I know you don't like that." She puts a jar of peanut butter in the cabinet over, the sink. "But it's not going to be the end of the world. They'd be perfectly happy to help us."

"I don't want to owe them anything," Taft says.

"It's not owing," his wife says. "It's family. Sometimes a person takes help from their family."

"It's not my family," he says. He goes back into the living room because he doesn't want to talk about it anymore. He wonders if the fishing program is still on.

At ten o'clock Taft gets dressed in his security uniform to go to the lumberyard. Carl has stayed in and Taft is glad. He didn't want to ground him on top of everything else. When he leaves for work Carl is lying on the floor of the living room watching television. "Maybe we'll get that deck finished up tomorrow," Taft says. They haven't worked on it for a while now. There's really not much left to do.

Carl shrugs. "Sure," he says, not looking up. They were going to do it today, but with everything else that was going on neither one of them had felt like it.

Taft says good night to his wife and tells her to call him if she needs him, just like he does whenever he goes out at night. Fay is already gone. She left with her date at eight o'clock and promised to be home by midnight. Her date had waited in the car for her and honked.

As soon as Taft gets to the lumberyard he's tired. He hasn't had more than a half dozen hours of sleep over the last three nights and now that he's alone it hits him hard. He would have called in sick tonight, something he's never done, but he knows how badly he needs the money. All he has to do is walk around, whistle, turn on some lights. It isn't a difficult job.

Time goes slower than he's ever remembered it. Slower than

it had last night when he was waiting on Carl. He tries not to look at his watch and when he finally does only five minutes have passed. He goes back to the office and turns on the little black-and-white TV. Then he turns it off and puts his head down on the desk and goes to sleep. The sleep is easy. It comes, deep and fast.

The minute Taft hears something his head jerks up. It isn't a dream. He stops to make sure he's really awake. He hears something. Voices, footsteps, something, a car door? Security guards who carry guns make seven dollars an hour and have to take a special training class. Taft would have been happy to take the class if it meant an extra two dollars an hour, but the lumber-yard said they didn't need anybody with a gun. Just a person, a warm body walking around, that'll be enough to keep people away.

"What if somebody does break in?" Taft asked them. "Somebody who has a gun, then what do I do?"

"Just like you'd do at home," they said. "Call the police."

Taft looks at the phone, but he doesn't call. It could be nothing. It is almost definitely nothing. He doesn't hear anything now. Who knows? He was asleep. He shouldn't have been asleep. There's probably nothing there at all.

Taft rebuttons the button underneath his tie and puts on his cap. He walks out of the office and down through a row of soft pine two-by-fours that are stacked up over his head. There are so many corners. So many places for people to wait for him. Taft feels himself starting to sweat. He knows it's just because he's tired. If he wasn't so tired this wouldn't be bothering him at all.

"Daddy?" He hears a woman's voice. He stops and listens. "Daddy?" The voice sings the word. It stretches it out into a high-pitched question and Taft answers.

"Fay?"

"Daddy?"

They call back and forth to one another, working their way through the maze of lumber in the dark, in and out of the occasional bursts of floodlights. Then suddenly Taft makes a turn and there she is, standing in a bright circle of light wearing a pale pink dress. A pink moth, that's the first thought that comes to his mind.

"You sure are hard to find," Fay says.

Taft just looks at her for another minute. He hadn't ever remembered her looking so pretty. He gestures to someplace behind him. "I was all the way in the back," he says.

"I bet you were sleeping," Fay says, and laughs because she doesn't mean it at all. As far as she knows, her father never sleeps.

"Maybe I was," he says, walking towards her. "What are you doing down here?"

"I was just down here," she said. "I'm out with Chip. Do you know Chip? We were driving right past here and I said, 'That's where my dad works,' and as soon as I said it I thought I should come over and say hi."

"Where's Chip?"

Fay walks over to him. "I left him in the car," she whispers. "Chip is really boring."

"Will he be all right?"

"He's got a radio," Fay says. And as soon as she says it Taft thinks he can hear music, just the slightest bits of some kind of music he wouldn't like at all if it were closer.

"It's late," he says. "You should be home. Your mother's going to be worried about you." But when Taft looks at his watch it's only eleven o'clock.

Fay laughs again. "You were asleep."

"I just thought it was later."

She looks around. It seems funny to see someone all dressed up in a lumberyard in the middle of the night. Her flat white shoes are nestled in sawdust. Her hair, which is nearly brown, looks gold in the bright light. "I've never been here before," Fay says. Her voice is full of reverence, like the place she is in is not a lumberyard at all.

"Do you want to see it?" Taft says. "Shouldn't you be getting back to your date?"

She waves her hand in front of her. "Let him wait," she says. "It's good for him." Taft is surprised that she would even think of such a thing. "I'm here to see you."

"Well," Taft says, taking her arm and walking her down the first row. "This is the soft pine. These are two-by-fours."

"Two-by-fours," Fay says.

"And these ones, over here, these are four-by-sixes."

"Bigger," she says.

"Exactly."

"It's like a garden," Fay says. "Except all the trees are laying down."

Taft is so happy she's here. With someone else it's easier to stay awake. He doesn't spend enough time with Fay, he thinks. That's because he doesn't understand her. The dresses and the lipstick confuse him. He can't keep the names of all the boys straight. Carl is easier for him. The weights and the wrestling make sense. Fay is smarter than her brother. Taft only realizes it just this minute. He should be paying more attention to her.

"I felt bad about the car," Fay says. "I know you're worried."

"These are the hard woods," Taft says. "All of this is special order, some rich guy building a house outside of town. These are the expensive ones. That's maple." He puts his hand on the wood. "Feel it."

Fay pets the wood like a sleeping cat. "Carl is stupid," she says. "I don't know, maybe he's not stupid. I feel kind of sorry for him too. He just doesn't think."

"That's why we have to keep an eye on him. Make sure he's thinking."

"That's a big job," Fay says, and laughs. It's a beautiful sound. "What's that wood there?"

"Walnut."

"That's awfully nice. How did you get to be so smart about wood?"

"That's what I do here all night," Taft says. "I walk through the stacks and I think about wood."

Fay looks around, down each of the dark alleys of lumber. "I've never thought about it before, what you do when you're here."

He wishes she could stay all night. When she's here, right in front of him, he knows she's safe. Somewhere from far away there's the lightest beeping sound. A car horn.

"That's Chip," she says.

"You ought to get back. And go right home. Just because you've checked in with me doesn't mean you don't need to go home."

"I'm plenty ready," she says. "I've had enough of Chip."

Taft walks her back to the car. Fay leads the way, taking the turns like she's been through a hundred times before. Taft sees an old red GTO sitting on the other side of the fence. There's a tear in the wire where Fay walked in. Taft makes a note to report that.

"Okay," she says.

"You get home safe."

Fay hugs him. Puts her arms around his neck and goes up on her toes to be closer to him. She hugs him like she does on

Christmas. She holds him there where Chip could see if he were looking and Taft puts his hands against her narrow back and presses her to him.

"Don't worry," Fay says, and then she lets go.

Taft smiles at her. "What makes you think I'm worried?"

WHEN I saw Marion the next day I had half a mind to tell her that Fay had asked me to marry her in Doe's. I wanted to tell her like it was a story, something that happened a long time before or to someone else. "You'll never believe what one of my waitresses said to me last night," I'd say. I wanted to see her not believe me, open up her mouth dumbstruck for a minute and finally say, "Get out of here." And then I would tell her it was true, every word of it. Marion and I had struck up a weird sort of friendship over the years, after we had loved each other and then hated each other. We were used to telling things. That was the way we fought. We didn't hold anything back.

And what would Marion say, after she had laughed and acted shocked? What she would say after everything settled down would be, "Well? Are you thinking about it?"

That's what I kept hearing over and over in my head.

Of course I wasn't thinking about it. There was nothing to think about. Where did I even start with the reasons? She was way too young and I had hardly known her for any time at all. She was looking for somebody to be her dead father and those weren't grounds to be happy. I had Franklin and she had Carl and neither of them would be so pleased about it. I was black and she wasn't and while that wouldn't have been enough to stop me if there was nothing else on the list, it deserved mention. I like black women, always have. I could see myself showing up at clubs with my eighteen-year-old white wife and all the boys nodding their heads at me when we came in the room, saying to each other, Well, would you look at that? Nickel's gone and got himself a piece of candy.

There were other reasons, hundreds of them, that made me so sure that all I was wondering was why I hadn't been more firm with her in the restaurant. I won't deny caring for her. I won't deny that the sight of her little hands folded over each other on the tabletop while she spoke thrilled me in a way I couldn't fully account for. But thoughts like that were not the kind that led a man to marriage. I was sure. I was flattered, but there was no doubt in my mind.

Yet as much as I tried I couldn't stop Marion's voice from playing in my head. Over and over again she was leaning back and looking at me and saying, "Well, are you thinking about it?"

"What're you chewing on this morning?" Marion said. "You've been quiet ever since you got here."

I was sitting at the Woodmoores' breakfast table and Marion was pouring some coffee. "I'm just not getting enough sleep," I said. "I forgot what it was like to work all night and have Franklin in the morning."

"Wears you down," she said and took a chair across from me at the table.

"Might be more fair if we split the load. Sometimes I get up too early, sometimes you get up too early."

She grinned at me. "Stop this," she said. "You're being terrible.

I never should have told you I was even thinking about coming back."

"Just stating my case," I said. I took a sip of the coffee. Marion always did a good job with the coffee. When I made it, it was too weak or thick enough to stand a spoon up in. "How'd things go over at the hospital?"

"It's still there. I was sorry to see they'd been getting along so well without me."

"But they missed you."

She tilted her head and looked at me out of the corner of her eye. "They missed me enough, I guess. I've still got friends there. I talked to the head nurse, saw a couple of the doctors. The doctors here are nicer than they are in Florida. I don't know why that is. In Florida all the doctors think they're movie stars."

Just then Franklin came in, and when he saw me he came over and locked his arms around my neck and stood there.

"There's the doctor now," Marion said.

I twisted around to look at him, but he stayed behind me. "You going to be a doctor?"

"Drummer," he said quietly into the back of my neck. It gave me a chill the way he said it.

"A drummer?" I reached back and got him by the waist and pulled him onto my lap. He was getting too big, but that didn't stop me. "Since when are you going to be a drummer?"

"I don't want to hear about this," Marion said.

"When did you decide you were going to be a drummer?"

"Since always," Franklin said.

"He's just started talking about this," Marion said. "It's just a phase. I'm praying to God every night he grows out of it soon."

"I just told you about it," Franklin said to his mother. "I knew before."

"He's making all this up to get in good with you," Marion said. "I think maybe he's been talking to his aunt Ruth too much." She was making it sound like it was all a joke, but I was holding him in my lap. I was looking at his arms all of the sudden, his hands. I was thinking about the way he walked. My heart was beating faster.

"Who's the best drummer?" I said to him. His face wasn't four inches away from mine. Even if Marion was joking, Franklin could see my face. He knew I was serious.

"You are."

"You never saw me play."

"Sure I did," Franklin said. He moved his face in. Marion wasn't even in the room anymore. I could smell the Cheerios on his breath. "I saw you all the time. You used to practice at home. You used to play with the headphones on."

"You were just a baby then."

"I remember. I sat on the floor. I saw you play at Muddy's when you were practicing. I sat with the waitress."

"What's he talking about?" Marion said.

"Nothing." But I remembered, even though I had forgotten. I used to bring Franklin with me to practice sometimes when he was little, three or four years old. I'd get in a hurry and there wouldn't be time to take him back over to the Woodmoores'. Marion was in school then. It was easy to keep things from Marion when she was in school.

"I was going to be a drummer even before then." Franklin backed off my lap and went and opened up the silverware drawer. He picked out two spoons for himself and started tapping a beat against the edge of the sink. Not a wild beat, not thrashing around like a kid that age would do if he was talking about drumming. This was measured and even, perfect time.

"He's been doing that lately," Marion said.

"Why didn't anybody tell me about this?"

"Tell you he's hitting spoons on the table? I didn't think there was any reason to tell you."

"Who's the greatest blues drummer of all time?" I said to Franklin. A kid who could beat with a set of spoons had been listening to somebody.

"You are."

"Who else?"

"Art Blakey," Franklin said, looking at me over his shoulder. "I want us to play sometime," he said.

Art Blakey, exactly right. "Sure." My drums took up one big walk-in closet in my apartment. I didn't go in there much.

"Your father doesn't play anymore," Marion said. The whole business made her nervous.

"Yes he does," Franklin said. "Don't you?"

"Sure I do." When I quit playing it had been to please Marion, to try and win her back. But that wasn't something I had to do anymore.

I told them tomorrow I'd be able to take the whole day off. "I'm finally going to teach Wallace how to do the money tonight," I said. "I've been talking him through it, but tonight's the big night. After that, it'll be a lot easier to get away."

"Can you take me down to Muddy's?" Franklin said. "We'll play."

Marion was staring at me hard. "Let's talk to your mother about that later," I said.

Even after I got to the bar I couldn't stop thinking about it. I knew I was going to be a drummer by the time I was Franklin's age. Besides, even if he was just saying it as a way of trying to please me, that was something in itself. I was going to get out my old records, make some tapes for him to listen to. I could put my drum set together, too. That was what he wanted, to be able to fool around on a real set, give up the spoons for a while.

"It seems to me it would be against the law to just kick a person out of a bar that you didn't even own in the first place without any reason," Cyndi said. She had a bad habit of sneaking up on me when I was thinking about other things. And she always seemed to start in the middle of the conversation. With Cyndi there was no beginning.

"We're talking about Carl now?"

"You kicked out anybody else lately?"

Cyndi was leaning on the bar rail, all of her weight shifted over to one side so that there was something tilted about her. "Listen," I said. "I figure you know why I got rid of Carl. I bet if you gave it any thought at all you'd see that I was a nice guy for not turning him in. Maybe even for not turning you in." I gave her a long look. My looks didn't work on Cyndi the way they did with other people. This girl wasn't afraid of anything. She held her wrists out in front of her.

"Arrest me if you think you're so goddamned holy."

"Go away, Cyndi," I said. "Go stand on the other side of the room. You're a good waitress when you feel like working and I know you need the job, and since I'm about thirty seconds from firing you I think it would be better for all of us if you just stayed away from me tonight."

"Last time we talked about my job you were saying that I was going to get more responsibility. Now I hear Wallace is closing. When did that happen?"

"I'm serious," I said. "Get away from me."

Cyndi gave me a long, ugly look, one that made it clear how small and stupid she thought I was. "Nothing would please me better," she said, turned on her heel, and walked across the room.

Wallace and Arlene came in first, then Fay and the new boy

named Teddy I'd just hired. The weather was getting warmer, business would be picking up. The band that was coming in that night had a good draw. Things would be busy.

"How's it going?" Fay said, coming up behind me.

"Pretty good."

"You been thinking?"

"Now, Fay," I said.

But she put up her hand to stop me and it stopped me. I remembered that she'd done that the first day she came in. "You're going to say that you've been thinking and you've decided it isn't possible. I withdraw the question so you can have a little more time."

I had to smile at her. "That's a sharp way of putting things off."

"We're not talking about it," she said.

"How's Carl doing? Has he told your mother yet?"

"Carl is sulking mostly," she said. "He's staying in his room. He's mad at me too now. I'm not sure why. I think he's just mad in general. The truth is, it's a little easier this way. I don't have to feel as sorry for him."

"He's going to have to make his date at the police station," I said. "You don't want to blow those people off."

"See," she said. "Now you've got it too. I call it Carl fever. You want to stop worrying about him, but you just can't."

It would have been difficult not to think about Carl that night. It seemed like every time I turned around there was some stranger asking after him.

"I'm looking for a friend of mine," a businessman said to me. He must have been forty years old. He was wearing an expensive suit and sunglasses to keep out the darkness. "Carl. Have you seen him around?"

I wondered what the chances were of this man ever being

friends with Carl. I wondered about them eating a meal together. When you call your dealer your friend the word is getting misused. "Carl's gone to prison," I said. "Busted for dealing. I hear he's talking a lot, too. They're planning on taking everybody down."

And out goes the businessman.

I must have told the story a dozen times. Wallace was pushing his own version, too. Every time I told it, it got a little better. Carl had an address book. He had written down every sale. Carl liked to make sketches of people, didn't he ever show them to you? He was awfully good. They got everything. The police got him at home. We were losing customers left and right, but as the crowd started thinning out I could see the people I knew. Things weren't so different after all.

The band was good. They were locals. Most of the boys I'd known for twenty years. I knew them all in different circumstances, in different bands, but they sounded good together. When it got late they started playing a song that was so slow and sad that I had to stop what I was doing to listen. You run a bar for long enough, there's almost no song that can make you listen. Even Rose poked her head out from the kitchen door and stood there. The music had made her dreamy and for a minute she looked like what she was, a lonesome soul. Then from across the room I saw Cyndi put down her tray and walk up on stage, dead in the center of things. No one in the band seemed to mind her. Nobody said anything. Cyndi started to dance her hula dance. It was slower, sadder than the song, and this time I didn't think about stopping her. Everybody in the bar quieted down to watch. She closed her eyes as her hands went out to the side and waved, one long, slow wave starting up in her neck and moving down her arms and out through her fingers. She was wearing jeans and a T-shirt that said ELVIS in big red letters. She took the clip out of her hair like she was in a dream. Cyndi had beautiful hair, I admired it to myself every day that I saw her. It was heavy and black all the way to her waist. Her hips moved up and down in a slow response to her hands, and every now and then she turned a circle without hardly moving her feet at all. In those kinds of dances everything is supposed to mean something, and I wondered what Cyndi was saying with her hips. Maybe she was dancing for Carl. Maybe Wallace was right and there had been something between them. This could have been the dance the girl dances when the boy is thrown into the volcano. There was no way of knowing. The band kept playing, probably glad to have things so quiet for a change. They must have written the song, or maybe they were making it up as they went along. When they were finished they all clapped for Cyndi. She bowed her head a little and then walked off, picking up her tray and going to see who was running low on beer.

The night went on and on, same as always. We had a hard time getting all the customers to leave. I flicked the lights and said last call, then drained out what was left of the small, wet ice cubes from the cooler. Once everyone was gone and things had been cleaned up, once all the chairs were upside down, Fay stopped by to say good night.

"I'm not coming in tomorrow," I told her.

"Maybe you'll come by," she said. "Bring your little boy. I'd like to see him again. I'm getting used to the idea." I started to say something, but she shushed me. "I'm going home," she said.

"How are you getting there?"

"Carl's at the Rum Boogie. I'll just go up the street and meet him there."

I wondered if Carl was planning on moving shop to the Rum Boogie. I knew the people up there, they were friends of mine. Sometimes it seemed like dirt never got cleaned up, it just got moved from one place to the next. "Get Teddy to walk you." I flagged the new boy down. I hadn't thought about him all night. "Hey Teddy," I said. "Walk Fay up to the Rum Boogie. I've got to close."

"Sure thing," he said.

Teddy put on his jacket and waited for Fay by the door. He was a couple of years older than her, a skinny college kid. He was probably pretty damned pleased I'd asked him to do this for me. "Good night, then," she said.

I told her good night.

I watched the two of them head up the street. Wallace watched me watch them. I turned around and put a heavy hand on his shoulder. "This is a big night for me. You learning to do the money. Pretty soon we might be making you a manager or something."

"I wouldn't mind that," Wallace said. "I've been in the market for a career."

"A smart man like you, Wallace. You can come up with a better career than this."

I took the drawer out of the cash register and we went through the kitchen to the office. I had him count all the money. He was quick. You could tell just by the way he was counting. He made neat piles out of everything, rolled the change. I counted along behind him. Everything was coming out right.

I opened up the desk drawer and took out the deposit slips and the cash sheets I filled out for my own record. Carl's paper wallet was still in the desk. I hadn't decided what to do about it yet. I'd disposed of all the drugs that night, but the money puzzled me. I figured on giving it to Fay. It was more hers than anybody's as far as I could tell.

"Now what?" Wallace asked.

"You have to write everything down here, ones, fives, tens,

twenties, all the way across, then total it up. That goes back in the desk. Then you do it again on the deposit and put that in the bag with the money."

"Easy enough."

"It kills me to think of all the years you were wasted being a bouncer," I said. "I could've had you running things."

Wallace was just about to answer when we heard something downstairs. All the time there were noises, drunks banging on the door trying to get in for a last drink, somebody who forgot their jacket or purse and didn't want to wait until morning. "Let's go see," I said. "When you close, this is part of the job."

We went downstairs and I was trying to remember if I'd locked the door. If it was a drunk it was a whole lot easier to tell them through the window that they couldn't come in for another shot. I was worried that it would be Fay, that Carl hadn't come for her. The Rum Boogie would be closed up too by now.

"Hello?" Wallace said. When nobody answered he flipped on the lights. Nothing. Clean and quiet.

"Whoever it was went on," I said. I checked the front door. It was locked. "This happens. You should be sure to lock the door."

"It didn't sound outside," Wallace said. "It sounded inside."

"I know," I said. "It used to make me nervous as a cat up there with all that money. But it never does turn out to be anything. There're a lot of cops around here. They come down at closing time to check things out."

But as soon as I said it I heard it again and Wallace was right, it was an inside sound. Somebody was trying to get out the kitchen door. The lock on the door had been broken for a month. It didn't work from the inside anymore. Rose unlocked it when she came in in the morning and she locked it back up at night when she left.

"Rose?"

"It's not Rose," Wallace said. His voice was quiet and steady and he went and picked up a chair off the top of a table.

I had taken a step forward when Carl came out of the kitchen. When I saw him the first thing I felt was relieved. "Jesus Carl, why didn't you say something? I didn't know it was you. I could have shot you."

Wallace hadn't moved. He was still holding the chair. The legs were out, like Carl was a lion he was taming.

"You couldn't have shot me," Carl said. "I have the gun." Carl wagged a black gun in the air in front of his face. Though there was no way of telling for sure, it appeared to be the same gun I'd been pushing from side to side in my desk all these years. Carl looked like he'd been underwater for a month and had just come up, damp and white and puckered. I wasn't four feet away from him. I could smell his nervous sweat. Then I saw he had the night deposit bag under his arm.

"This is what you're doing? You're robbing the bar?"

"I'm not robbing," he said. "I'm reclaiming. You were the one who was robbing. I want to know what you did with my property."

"I flushed it down the toilet."

Carl's hands were shaking. It seemed to be all he could do to even hold on to the gun. "You sure as hell better be lying. Liar like you, I don't expect that would be so hard."

There was Carl, his nose running and his hair soaked through with sweat. I had picked this boy up off the street, carried him in my arms to his bed. I had gone and gotten him out of jail. I had let him sit in my bar night after night and treated him fairly and now I was mad: the tone of his voice, the way his eyes were red and wet. I wasn't going to stand there and listen to him carry on about what was his. "Put down the goddamned bag, you sorry little prick."

"You don't get to talk to me like that anymore," Carl said.

"I'll talk to you any way I damn well please."

"Quiet," Wallace said.

I turned to look at Wallace and that's when Carl shot me.

There was a lot going on at once and most of it was sound. The sound of the gun, the sound of me sitting down hard on the floor, the sound of somebody pounding on the glass window in the front of the bar and hollering, the sound of Wallace's chair being thrown on the floor and then the steady banging sound of Carl's wrist hitting the brass rail of the bar, over and over again until there was a crack that was nearly as loud as the gunshot. At first I thought Wallace was trying to make Carl let go of the gun, but he did that the first time his wrist hit the rail. It took Wallace three more tries to break it. Carl was wailing, making animal sounds.

I stood up and saw that there was a world of blood on the floor.

"Sit down," Wallace said, like there was still danger, but there wasn't any danger and I could see it was Fay who was pounding on the door. Sure enough, they'd thrown her out of the Rum Boogie.

By the time I got there I was starting to get lightheaded. I was beginning to feel a pure white pain from my shoulders to the top of my head. I saw that there was blood on the glass when I turned the lock. Blood on the lock and my hands. Fay seemed to almost come through the glass and when she was inside she put her hands around my neck, one in front and one in back. I thought she was like Marion's mother, trying to strangle me. I thought she'd come in late and only seen the part where Carl's wrist got broken, that she'd missed the part where he'd shot me.

"It's okay," I said to her, but it was a strain to talk she was choking me so hard. I tried to push her off, but she was fixed to me.

"Hold him," Wallace said. He was standing beside her. There was blood all over Fay. It was on her face and smeared across the front of her blouse. I thought maybe there had been two bullets, one I hadn't heard. I thought she'd been shot too.

"Fay," I said, and touched her cheek with my hand. "Where're you hurt? Tell me."

She was crying some but not sobbing. "Get me a towel," she said to Wallace. "Get me something from the bar."

Where had Carl gone? He was quiet all of the sudden. "Carl doesn't still have that gun, does he?"

"I took it from him," Wallace said.

"Fay's been shot," I said, still trying to see where. "Sit her down."

"I'm not shot."

Then Wallace was back with the towels. When he went to give one to Fay she took her hands away and in that second I could see the blood, my blood, come shooting out onto her. I bent my head and it poured like a river into her hair. "Jesus Christ," I said, feeling sicker than I had before. I'd been shot in the neck. It didn't seem like a good place to get shot. Wallace and Fay tied me up with towels and then Fay put her hands back in place. They felt better once I knew what they were there for.

"We've got to get to the emergency room," Fay said. "We have to go right now."

I was all ready when Wallace turned around to Carl. For a minute I had forgotten about Carl. I could see him then. He was heaped underneath the bar, pressed against it. Some stools had been knocked away. "The second we show up at that hospital they'll be coming for you, Carl."

He didn't act like he heard. "The hospital will come for him?" I asked.

"The police will come for him. Gunshot wound and they have to call the police."

Gunshot. Gun and someone shooting. I knew it was Carl who had shot me, but even knowing it I felt myself forgetting. I was all the way to the door when I remembered and turned around. I'll tell you what turns a person to salt: it's pity, the awful sin of taking pity on someone who doesn't deserve it and never asked for it. Carl was nothing like a man. He'd wadded himself up, made himself smaller than I would have thought anyone could. I knew how it would go once the police got a hold of him. In that minute I saw the rest of Carl's life. There was salt in my mouth. "Shit," I said. I wanted to go over there and kick him, but I didn't have the energy.

"Come on," Wallace said.

I wished I had a day or an hour even. An hour could be enough time to think. I wanted a lot of things. "We can't go to the hospital," I said. The words made a sick sound. It was a little hard to talk, but I couldn't tell if that was because of Fay or the hole in my neck. "That's armed robbery, attempted."

"Right," Wallace said.

Fay was looking at me. She knew what I meant. Punishment, terrible punishment, but not ten years in prison. That would be the end of it for him. As much as he had it coming I couldn't end a boy's life. "They can have him," she said quietly.

I started to shake my head, but that was a huge mistake on my part. I almost blacked out from the pain. Wallace slipped a hand under my arm. "Take me to Marion," I said. "Marion can fix this."

"We're going to the hospital," Wallace said.

"No."

"Damnit, you can't let him off for this."

"Don't fight with me now," I said. "I don't feel like fighting."

Wallace looked around for a split second. He was a football player. He had to make his decisions quick and get behind them. "Fay," he said. "Wipe your face up and take Carl to the hospital. I broke his arm. I'll take John to Marion's."

"Carl can take himself to the hospital," she said. "I'm coming with you."

There wasn't time for this. We were going to stand there bickering until I bled to death. Wallace disappeared and came back with Carl underneath one arm and the blue bag in the other. I could see the butt of the gun sticking out of his belt. Carl made some sort of sound, but it wasn't a word. He was limp and dangling under one of Wallace's arms. He was too small to hurt anything, to be anything. The four of us went out into the clear night. Wallace was good enough to carry Carl across the street and down a ways before he dropped him on a grassy slope near the sidewalk. That way he didn't look so much like he was tied to our bar.

"I'm going to get my car," Wallace shouted. "You stay right there." He took off running. Even with those bad knees he could still move faster than any man I knew.

"You want to check Carl?" I said, but I didn't care if she did or didn't. I was bored with Carl. I had forgotten about him.

"Not a word," she said. She didn't look over at him. She kept the pressure on my neck steady and even. "You've done enough for Carl. Does it hurt bad?"

It hurt bad, so much that at some point it stopped being pain and started being something else, something more complicated and complete. "Yes," I said.

I had told Wallace there were cops around there, but I guess I was lying. A gunshot and any amount of screaming and still we were the only ones on the street. Wallace's car came down the alley doing seventy-five and he leaned over and opened the door for us. We eased into the car. Fay had to practically sit in my lap in order to keep her hands around my neck. I could have held on to it myself, but I didn't think she'd let me. She touched my chest just as lightly as she could with her chest.

I gave Wallace the Woodmoores' address. I started to tell him the best way to go, but he stopped me.

"I know," he said.

"We all have to be quiet when we get there," I told them. "I don't want to wake up my boy."

"I should be taking you to the hospital," Wallace said, and he hit the steering wheel with his open hand. "I don't know what the hell I'm thinking about."

Wallace kept rattling on, but the lights were leaving trails and so I didn't listen to him. Every car we passed, every streetlight, had a tail a block long and they were weaving themselves together into ropes. Then we passed Marion, waiting at a bus stop and I wanted to stop but I didn't say anything about it.

"Marion can fix this," I said. I believed that, too. She was smart, smarter than all of us. She was sitting at the kitchen table, studying so hard for her examinations, getting good grades in every class. I sent her through nursing school. I sent her for just this reason.

Wallace got on the interstate. It wasn't the way I would have gone. I watched the green exit signs pass over our heads: Eastmoreland, Linden, Lamar. Getting off at Lamar you still had a ways to go. Even with there being no traffic and Wallace driving like a madman, we weren't getting anyplace. I wondered if I was bleeding much. My chest was damp and cold and I started to shake. Then I realized it wasn't me, it was Fay. Her hands were shaking. She was shaking up against me.

"Hey," I said, and bounced my knee a little. "You okay there?"

"Maybe I need to go home now," she whispered.

"Now?" Wallace said.

"In Coalfield nothing like this happens. It wouldn't have happened."

"She doesn't mean go home," I said to Wallace.

"Maybe it would be better if I was closer to my father," Fay said, her voice gone all dreamy. "I've got a piece of hair stuck in the corner of my eye. Can you get it out for me?"

I reached up and brushed her hair away from her face. I tucked her hair behind her ear. Pretty little seashell ear.

"If he was alive, he wouldn't have known what to make out of all this. He could never have believed what's happened. But I think he understands more now that he's dead. He's smart and he's so patient with me. He protects us. He protects all of us. I think he forgives us."

Wallace was looking over at Fay. I could see him out of the corner of my eye. Don't worry about him, baby, you go ahead and talk. A night like this, the girl deserves to say anything that might make her feel better.

"You're so cold," she said, and touched her cheek to my cheek. "You're turning all gray."

"All of this is going to be fine," I told her. "You'll see."

Fay moved in closer until her mouth was against my ear. I will tell you this, the person who is holding your neck to keep you from bleeding to death is closer to you than anyone has ever been in your life. "Promise me," she said.

And out of nowhere came the Woodmoores' house. They always kept their front light burning. Something about Mr. Woodmoore growing up in Mississippi and looking out after your own.

Wallace got out and knocked on the door. He was gone for so long I forgot about him altogether and went to sleep. Then Ruth started crawling around in the bed. She got up on top of me. She was licking my face. I was going to tell her I was tired and that it wasn't the time for things like that, but she saw Fay there in my lap before I had a chance to say anything. The two of them were frozen there, staring.

"Jesus," Ruth said. She reached into the car and put her hand on my face.

"Go get the baby off the couch," Wallace said.

"Okay," Ruth said. "Okay." She ran her thumb over my forehead and then hurried back inside.

"It'll just be another minute now," Fay whispered.

When I looked up again Ruth had split into Ruth and Marion. They were holding hands, but it was only so Ruth could pull Marion and make her go faster. They never wanted to stand next to each other. They wouldn't let their mother cut their dresses from the same cloth. If one got up to dance, the other would sit out.

Marion rubbed her free hand across her face. She had a hard time waking up. Franklin is crying in the next room and it's all she can do to make herself get out of bed. "Nickel?"

"I'm here," I said.

"Why isn't he in the hospital?" Marion turned on Wallace, like everything was his fault. Poor Wallace, standing there on the sidewalk, taking it.

"He won't go."

"Get out of the car," Marion said. "Can you walk?"

"Sure," I said. The truth was, walking was getting a little bit harder. Everything was getting harder. My feet caught on the curb and Wallace had to help me. I noticed my left shoulder was pulling down. Fay came with me, holding on to my neck. It was a stretch for her. She was walking up on her toes.

"Who's she?" Marion said.

"That's the waitress from the bar," Ruth told her.

The party went into the Woodmoores' house, all of us pressed together. I didn't want to raise a lot of commotion. I didn't want anybody else waking up, but as soon as we were in the door here came Marion's parents down the stairs in their bathrobes and slippers. Mrs. Woodmoore took one look at me standing there and she started to let out a yell. It was all Ruth could do to stop her. "Quiet," she said sharply. "Don't wake up Franklin."

"What?" Mr. Woodmoore said, taking off his glasses. "What?"

"He's been shot," Ruth said.

The light inside woke all of us up. I could see how bad we looked. Wallace's shirt had blood all over it and Fay was a horror show. It showed up more on her. Standing between me and Wallace she looked like a child not much older than Franklin. She looked like she'd just gotten swept up with us somehow and that we'd best take her back to wherever she came from. I wondered what I looked like. A person only has so much blood. After a while you can't bleed like that anymore.

Marion led me into the kitchen and the whole pack followed.

"Who did this to you?" Mrs. Woodmoore said. She had a look in her eyes I knew, like she was ready to kill somebody. "Where are the police?"

I was starting to panic. It was a little room and my feet were cold as stones. There were Woodmoores all around us.

"I want everybody out except him," Marion said, pointing at Wallace. "I've got to take a look at this."

I closed my eyes and when I opened them again it was just like she said, everyone gone but Wallace. Except Fay was there too, but she didn't count. She had attached herself to me.

Marion shuddered like it was the first time she'd seen me. "Jesus," she said. She opened up a drawer in the kitchen and took out a stack of dishtowels. The kitchen was too yellow, yellow cabinets and yellow curtains. A yellow refrigerator. "I'm going to take a look at this now." She gently worked loose Fay's hands. "You did a good job," she said to her. "You saved his life." I was glad to see Marion talking sweet to Fay. Fay wasn't holding up so well. She smiled at me when she stepped back. She stretched out her fingers, then rubbed them together like they hurt. Marion started to roll back the bar towel, which felt thick and crusted, but the second she pulled it loose the blood came rushing out of my neck and covered up Marion like a sheet. Fay grabbed right back on.

"Shit," Marion yelled, wiping her eyes. "What're you thinking about bringing that over here? You're going to die. The second that girl lets go of you, you're going to die."

If that was the case I figured on living forever.

"We're going to the hospital. I mean right this second. God-damn you coming over here all shot up like this."

"For Christ's sake, Marion. You can fix this," I said. She never would do a thing to help me.

"With what? You want me to get my mother's sewing kit? Listen to you. Get up and get in the car."

"No," I said.

"Why?" She looked to be on the verge of shooting me herself, finishing me off.

"He won't go," Wallace said. I was glad to have him talking for me. It wore on me, trying to talk. "He knows who shot him. He's just a kid. He doesn't want the kid to go to prison. You take him to the hospital, there'll be cops."

"Let the kid rot in prison for all you care," she said to me.

Fay kept quiet. She was concentrating on her job. I didn't say anything either. I was looking at the blood on Marion's chin.

"He won't argue with you," Wallace said. "Think of something else."

Marion stood there and I could see she was trying to do exactly that. She was serious when she was thinking. "I know some-body," she said finally. "I'll see if I can't get him to come down to his office. You'd see a doctor, wouldn't you? If he wasn't in the hospital?"

I nodded, which is to say I started to nod, but the pain that came up was like a knife working around in the hole and it brought tears to my eyes. The pain made everything in the room bright. I knew everything again. I was there.

"Hold yourself still," Marion said, her voice a little softer now. "I'll find somebody. The bullet went all the way through, out the back. At least that's something." She slipped her thumb into my mouth and pulled up my lip. I seem to remember her fingers in my mouth from a long time ago. "You're getting shocky," she said. "Your gums look like hell." Then she left the room to make the call.

I was glad to hear the bullet was gone. I'd been wondering about that. Wallace went to the sink and started washing his hands. "I'll tell you what," he said. "And Fay, I'm sorry, I don't mean any offense to you, but if you die over this, trying to keep him out of jail for what he's done, then I'm going to kill him. You think about that. If you die, then you're not saving Carl's life at all."

"I'm not going to die."

"Well, if you do, then you know. Fay, you want me to spell you for a minute? Are your arms getting tired?"

"I'm okay," she said. She looked up and gave him the weakest sort of smile.

When Marion came back she was wearing a light blue run-ning suit and carrying a folded blanket of the exact same color. "He'll do it," she said. "As a favor to me. He's not happy about this."

"Nobody's happy," Wallace said.

"Help me cover him." The second she said it the cold in my feet spread everywhere and I was freezing. She knew it was coming. Marion handed one end to Wallace and they wrapped me up, working the blanket in between me and Fay.

"You have to stay here," Marion said to Fay.

"No," Fay said.

"We can't be bringing over too many people. The doctor is nervous as it is, and I have to go because I'm a nurse and Wallace has to go because he's the only one who can pick Nickel up if he faints. You've done a good job." She put her hands over Fay's to let her know she meant what she said. Fay understood her. Fay only wanted what was best. She worked her hands out from underneath. Marion was holding my neck.

Fay had been so close to me all night I could hardly see her, but when she stepped back I saw everything, me shot and her brother lying in the grass with a broken wrist, Taft dead and her here in Memphis. "Can I wait here until you come back?" she said to Marion.

"Sure."

We went out past Ruth and the Woodmoores. "How do you feel?" Mrs. Woodmoore asked me.

I felt shot. "Okay," I said.

Marion finally seemed to be in a hurry to get somewhere and she took me out the front door. She was careful on the steps going down. Wallace came along beside us and held my arm. Fay stopped at the porch with Ruth and the Woodmoores. They stood there together under the porch light. I couldn't turn to see them, but the Woodmoores would wave. We had forgotten to tell them Fay was staying.

"Fay," Taft says, "go call your brother. Dinner's on the table."

• • •

247

God help anyone who's trying to find their way through the city of doctors' offices in the triangle made by Baptist, Methodist and the V.A. hospitals. Ail the buildings are brick, most of them are low and painted light colors with big letters on the front, like they were apartment buildings in those giant complexes out by the airport. All the parking was for doctors. I was always lost when I came down there, but Marion directed Wallace through the turns like she'd never left Memphis. "Pull over here," she said.

The building we stopped in front of didn't look any different from the others. Marion led us up the walk, holding me by the neck. The door she went to was open, and the three of us got into an elevator. It let us off in a dark hall, but even in the dark she knew exactly where she was and we walked along until we got to the right door and then we went inside.

The lights in the office were on. We'd come into a small waiting room, two couches, four chairs, stacks of magazines on the table, a fish tank going, but I didn't see any fish. "Doctor Bowles?" Marion called.

"There's no fish," I said.

She told me to hush.

The man who came through the door didn't look enough like a doctor to suit me. He was big, big-boned and tall and his hair was sticking out all over his head like he'd been sleeping on it wrong, which he probably had been. He was wearing blue jeans and a sweatshirt that said VANDERBILT. He looked like a cowboy who'd been sleeping outside on the ground.

"Thanks for getting over here so fast," Marion said.

He shook his head. "I was going to go dove hunting in the morning. I was going to be up in three hours. This is why they have emergency rooms." He looked at me hard, like he was trying to decide if he shouldn't just go home and get back in bed. "Come on," he said, and we followed him.

The four of us went down another hall and the doctor flipped on the lights in a room lined with glass cabinets. There was a long steel table in the middle and a couple of big lights hanging down. It was bright in there. Bright and clean.

"You know this is against the law," he said, "not reporting gunshot wounds to the police. I don't know who shot you or who you shot, but we've got a system for dealing with these things. Lie down on the table."

"He didn't shoot anybody," Wallace said in a cold voice. "It was a robbery. He knew the kid who was doing it."

"Says the man with the gun in his belt," the doctor said.

Wallace looked down at the gun and started to say something. The doctor put up his hand. "Stop it there. I don't want to know. The less I know about all of this, the better. I like your wife," he said to me. "She's a hard worker. Best nurse we ever had at Baptist. I'm doing this as a favor to her. That's all that needs to be said."

"Fine with me," I said.

I got up on the table and Marion helped me put down my head, which I appreciated. Any sort of movement made it crazy. I was looking straight up into a bright light. Sometimes Marion or the doctor would look down at me. Marion would smile. It was good to lie down. I could have gone to sleep for a week. Not for one minute of my life had I been as tired as I was just then.

"You," the doctor said. "Come here and hold his neck for a minute."

Then there was Wallace's face. "Hey there, chief," he said.

"Marion, get some gloves and a packet of towels." She walked away. There was the sound of drawers opening and I wondered how she would know where to look for things. I could hear paper being torn and hands working themselves into rubber. Everything was so bright.

"Okay now," the doctor said. "You take the towel away, then you and the towel go stand on the other side of the room, or leave the room if you want to."

I felt Wallace's hands peel off the heavy towel, some towel from the yellow kitchen. I bet it was ruined now. "You hang in there," he said to me, and then I heard the sound of a door opening and shutting. I didn't blame him. I wouldn't have wanted to stay either.

"Keep the pressure on," the doctor said, "here. I think this is venous bleeding, so it means it has to be the interior or the exterior jugular. If that's the case, then this is your lucky day. Bet you didn't know you were lucky, did you, brother? Bullet hits the carotid and you'd have a hell of a time finding somebody who'd be able to hold your neck tight enough. Even if you didn't bleed to death you'd have a stroke later on. Messy business. Bad if it kills you and worse if it doesn't. I'm going to get some Xylocaine. Keep holding it, just like that."

Then the doctor's face was gone and I could hear the sound of glass bottles clinking together. Marion's face blocked the light for a minute. "You're doing fine," she said.

"Franklin didn't?"

"Never woke up," she said. "You know how he sleeps."

The doctor's voice came from somewhere else. "You know," it said. "A person isn't supposed to operate on a member of her own family. Marion shouldn't even be doing this." Suddenly his face was back over mine. "What would you say to eight cc's?" he said. "That'll make things a little more pleasant."

I didn't know why in the hell he was bothering to tell me all of this, considering that I didn't know what he was talking about. Maybe it was for Marion's benefit. Maybe he was just trying to keep himself awake by chattering. Everything he said was noise, a conversation at the table next to yours that you don't care about but can't stop hearing. I felt a stick and a deep burning sting.

"I'm going to try and wash this out a little. It's a mess. Bullets make such a goddamned mess."

He was moving around, but it was starting to feel like less. Then there was more paper tearing and he put a piece of cloth over my chest and on my face so I couldn't see anymore. Then somebody covered me up. I was sure I'd be asleep by now. "I'm going to be awake for this?" I said from underneath the cloth.

"General anesthesia is a luxury afforded to those who go to the emergency room. I can't do everything myself. You let me know if it starts hurting and we'll give you a little more juice. I'm going to turn your head now. You're not going to like this."

Things turned bright again, everything was wiped clean. I sucked in the air underneath the towel and tried not to make noise.

"It's all that swelling," he said. "Blood in the muscle, nothing we can do about that. I'm going to open you up now."

I hadn't thought there would be any cutting. I thought the hole in my neck was plenty big enough for anyone to work through. I guess you never ask the right questions before things start. I could feel him sliding a knife through my neck, but it felt far away. It felt dead, like touching your leg when it's asleep.

"My, my," he said, clucking his tongue. "That looks like hell. See that? The belly of it there. There's the spinal accessory nerve."

I could only imagine he was talking to Marion. He seemed to forget about me as soon as he covered me up.

"There's the jugular. Ripped to shreds. Give me a real operating room and I might be able to do something about fixing it, that would be a real piece of work. But seeing as how some people don't like hospitals, I'm just going to tie it off."

I was wondering if that wasn't something I might be needing later on. Suddenly there was a sharp pain that laid all the others to rest. It hurt so much I could hear it and I jumped. "Christ," I said from beneath my towels.

"That hurt?"

"Damn right it hurts."

"I'll give you a little more juice," he said. "But if you don't hold still I'll see to it you never walk again."

He stepped away and when he came back there was the stick again and then the burning, numbing pain.

"Have you ever seen this done? Here, watch this, just in case the next time he gets shot in the neck you have to do it yourself."

"He wanted me to do it this time," Marion's voice said.

The doctor laughed, a good long laugh that I thought was disrespectful to Marion, but she didn't say anything. "Two-o silk," he said. "Put the suture through the vein. See that? That's why you need the round needle. Now make a knot on the side, wrap it around to the other side and make another knot there. That way it doesn't slip off. Hell of a thing if it slips off. Now we do it again here." He was quiet for a minute. "And we cut the vein in the middle. Put a hemostat on that. Good. Now hold it there. Because I like your wife I'm going to do something here called a double ligature, brother. That means you get another set of knots. Backup knots. Marion, you want to do one of these?"

"No, sir."

"She doesn't want to do one. Well, that must mean she loves you after all." He started humming then. I tried to remember the song. Something about Paris. "See, that takes care of our bleeding. You can take the hemostat off now. Get me some Vicryl sutures to sew the muscle."

I could feel some tugging in my neck, but things were good and numb now. The muscle took some time.

"Four-o nylon to close. We'll make these stitches nice and small. I did a rotation in plastics, you know. I was good at it too. Could have gone in for plastic, the real money. Spend my life making bigger breasts and smaller noses. Nobody calls you at three o'clock in the morning because they don't like their breasts. But no, I had to go head and neck. Strep throats and gunshots. Look at this. Look how pretty that is. There won't even be such a scar."

Franklin's Coke bottle scar.

"Let me just debride the wound and we'll be through. I'm just going to cut away what's loose. You got some pieces of muscle and tissue hanging off here that aren't so attractive. This one stays open. Gunshot wounds are dirty things no matter how you clean them up." There were sloshing sounds, the feeling of someone working around inside of me. Then I felt something cold running down the back of my neck. It made a pool on the table underneath me. I had the worst feeling that he had poured it in at the top and it had run all the way through. "Get me some iodoform gauze," he said, and Marion went off. Why did I keep thinking he was talking to me? "I want you to take these stitches out when they're ready. Seven to ten days, whenever it looks good. You'll know."

"Yessir," she said.

He pulled back the sheets and the light came flooding in from everywhere. "Sit up, brother. You lived after all."

Marion was taping pads to my neck and then winding the thing up with gauze. The doctor was writing out notes.

"Go pick these up tonight," he said. "Five hundred milligrams of Cipro twice a day and some Demerol fifty for the pain. Don't slide on the antibiotics. You are an infection waiting to happen."

"When do we come back?" I said, bringing my hand up to touch my neck.

He pushed my hand back down. "You don't ever come back," he said. "I've done my good deed for this year. You have any problems, you go to the hospital. Nobody will bother you about a gunshot wound that's fixed up so nicely."

"I really appreciate this," Marion said.

He put his arm around her shoulder. "I wish you'd come back to Memphis. Nurses good as you are hard to find. Keep an eye on him. Keep him down until he feels like getting up. Change the dressing every day. And you," he said to me. "I'm sending you a bill. A huge bill."

"Right." I put my hands behind me on the table. I was feeling a little lightheaded and I didn't think it would be a good time to fall.

"Call the big guy," the doctor sad. "Get him out of here. He looks like he's going to faint."

Wallace came back and stuck his head in the open car window. "I, um, I don't have enough money. Either of you have any money?"

"How much is it?" Marion asked.

"One hundred twenty-three dollars and some change. That's with the tax and everything."

"A hundred twenty-three?" What was I taking, uranium?

"It's the Cipro," Marion said, reaching into her purse. "That stuff costs a fortune. I should have thought about that."

"It's okay," Wallace said. "I just don't — "

I was trying to reach into my pocket with my left hand, but I couldn't quite get my shoulder to join in. "Reach back there and get my wallet," I said to Marion. She slipped her hand beneath me and went into my pocket. "Give him the credit card."

Marion handed Wallace my whole wallet out through the window. "Come back and tell us if they give you any trouble."

The all-night pharmacy wasn't close to anything. It was out by the fairgrounds where they held the farmers' markets in the summer. The store was huge and bright and there were almost no cars parked out front. The windows were full of banners, sales on notebooks and pantyhose and diet pills. No sale on antibiotics.

"I should have sent him in there with money," Marion said. She was sitting in the back seat. "I don't know what I was thinking of."

"There's plenty else to think about," I said. I wished the headrest was higher up. I closed my eyes.

Wallace came back and put my wallet and the sack on the dashboard. He backed out the car and headed towards the Woodmoores'. Was it four in the morning? Five? We were all quiet. There wasn't anything left to say. We felt sad. I'd been shot, Wallace had seen it happen, Marion had been saddled with fixing it. The two of them had looked inside my neck while I lay there.

When we got to the house the front door was unlocked and the lights in the living room were on. Mrs. Woodmoore was asleep sitting up on the couch, her head back and mouth open. Fay was sleeping with her head in Mrs. Woodmoore's lap, her legs stretched out. Ruth and Mr. Woodmoore had gone upstairs to bed, I guess. It was late.

Wallace and I stood by the door and looked away. I didn't like coming up on people when they were asleep. Marion leaned over Fay and shook her mother's shoulder. "Mama," she said quietly. "We're home."

But it was Fay whose eyes opened first. She sat up quickly and looked embarrassed. Fay moving is what woke Mrs. Woodmoore.

"You're all right," Fay said.

Mrs. Woodmoore shook her head and pushed her glasses back into place, then she wrapped an arm around Fay. "See there? Didn't I tell you he was coming back? Didn't I say he'd be fine? This girl has been so worried about you." Marion's mother got up and put a light hand on either side of my face. "How you feeling, baby?"

"He's tired," Marion said. "He's had a hell of a night."

And I was tired. Too tired to feel like talking about it. Fay stood up from the couch and swayed a little, trying to get used to her own weight. She'd been cleaned up. Her hair had been washed and was still a little damp. She was wearing her jeans and a white undershirt that looked to be one of Mr. Woodmoore's. I could see Mrs. Woodmoore leaning her over the sink and washing her hair, working the blood stains out of her clothes.

"Wallace," I said, my voice feeling sore. "Any chance I could get you to drive me and Fay home?" The way it sounded we were going together. I hadn't meant that.

"You can drive her home," Marion said, "but he's staying here. Somebody has to keep an eye on you for a day or two, make sure you don't start bleeding, make sure you take your pills."

"Isn't it nice having a nurse right here?" Mrs. Woodmoore said to me.

"I think I should get home," I said, but I could have cared less where I slept.

"You don't have to think," Marion said. "I let you out of going to the hospital, but we're not even going to talk about this one."

It would have been good if there'd been a minute to talk to Fay, see how she was doing, but it wasn't going to be possible with everybody standing there. She was looking at her feet. There was still some blood on her tennis shoes.

"Thank you for letting me wait here," Fay said.

"Any time, sweetheart." Mrs. Woodmoore put her arm back around Fay. "I've got half a mind to just keep this girl with me."

Fay dipped her head down and touched it to Mrs. Woodmoore's shoulder, then just as quick she straightened up again.

"I'd appreciate it if you could carry me home," she said to Wallace.

"Sure," he said, and he opened up the door for her.

"I'll see you tomorrow," I said. Poor Fay, I was thinking, but then I forgot. My neck was still numb and it gave my head the feeling of floating off someplace by itself.

"I'm so glad," she said, standing in the doorway. "I'm happy that you're okay." Mrs. Woodmoore gave her one more kiss and then Fay turned around and left. Wallace nodded and followed her out.

"Who was she again?" Marion said.

I started to answer, but her mother jumped in. "That's Fay Taft," she said, watching her from the window. "She works for John in the bar."

Mrs. Woodmoore told us good night and we all headed upstairs. Franklin was sleeping in Buddy's room with Ruth, which left Marion and me in the twin beds she and Ruth had slept in as girls. When Marion flipped the wall switch two ruffled lamps on two matching bedside tables lit up. Ruth had been right about the room. The frilly curtains and the rose covered wallpaper made me think of a clipped poodle. The more I looked at it, the fuzzier it got. Marion picked up a stuffed tiger off one of the beds and threw it on the floor to pull back the spread. "This one's you," she said.

I'd been in that room before.

She took the two bottles out of their paper sack and handed me a couple of pills, then she went to the bathroom and got me a glass of water. "Take these. They'll be a little hard to swallow."

"I don't have any pain."

"Trust me, it's coming."

I took the antibiotic and it went down like a baseball. As soon as it was past my tongue I knew I'd made a mistake. I started to cough and coughing made everything worse. Then I sat down on the edge of the bed, shaking, worn out from a pill. "I'm going to wait on this other one awhile," I said.

Marion helped me out of my clothes like a nurse. "Put your arms out," she said, but my left arm didn't go out too well.

"This going to be a problem?"

"For a while is all. It's going to take some time for everything to come back." She kneeled on the floor and untied my shoes. I didn't like her doing that, but when I leaned over I felt a throbbing that made me straighten up again. "Just let me," she said.

When I was sitting there in my underwear she put her hand behind my head and helped me lie down. "I'm going to be right here," she said, getting into the little bed next to mine. I didn't know if she was taking her clothes off or not. I couldn't turn my head to the side.

Taft sleeps past one in the afternoon on Sunday. His wife has hung blankets over the curtains to keep the room extra dark. She unplugged both the phones and told the children, "No noise. Nothing." He hadn't gotten in from the lumberyard until after five in the morning. It seems as if it's been weeks since he's had any sort of real sleep. Even when he wakes up and looks at the clock and feels ashamed for having stayed in bed for so long, he's still tired. He could easily roll over and go back to sleep for another couple of hours, but he told Carl they'd get the deck finished today. A person can't spend his whole day in bed. Taft gets up and feels for his bathrobe in the dark.

"What're you doing?" Taft's wife says when she sees him in the hall.

"You shouldn't have let me sleep so late."

"You've got to get some more rest," she says.

"I want to get to work on that deck."

259

"Oh, who cares about the deck. Take it easy for a change." She reaches up and runs her hand over his head. "Your hair's all funny."

"Hair's not meant to be slept on for so long," he says. He puts his arm around her and squeezes her until she gives out a little yelp.

"Stop that now," she says, laughing. "I'm on my way to church. I want to be sure they'll let me in."

"Church?"

"They're having a rummage sale. I was going to take the kids over so the house would be quiet."

"Well, you better leave Carl. I want him to help me with the deck." Then Taft remembers Fay down at the lumberyard. He should think of a project to do with her now so the two of them can start spending more time together. That would be fair. Something with Carl, something with Fay.

"All right," she says. "If you don't want to rest, I can't make you." She calls for Fay, who comes down the hall towards them. She's wearing denim shorts and a little sleeveless shirt that she's tied up at her waist. "Do you want to run over to church with Marjorie and me for a while and look at the rummage sale?"

Normally she'd say no. Fay doesn't like going places with her mother, but she likes church. Her friends are there. "Sure."

"How'd your date end up?" Taft says.

"Boring till the very end. But I got home early, didn't I?" she says to her mother.

"She did."

"I've been thinking that there has to be a better way for me to spend Saturday nights," Fay says. "Maybe I should try to get a job at the lumberyard, see if I can't learn something about wood."

"What are you talking about?" Taft's wife asks.

But Fay just smiles. She likes having secrets from her mother.

She likes the fact that this is something just between the two of them. "See you later, Daddy," she says.

"You girls have fun."

And then they're gone, off to find Marjorie.

Taft checks Carl's room and when he doesn't find him there he goes to look in the garage. Carl's on his weight bench doing butterflies. It's the first time in sixteen years that Carl has gotten up before Taft.

"You want to finish up that deck?" Taft says.

Carl exhales, raises, inhales, lowers. "Sure thing," he says.

"I'll just get cleaned up a little," Taft says.

"I'm going to be done here in a minute." He's covered in sweat. Every muscle looks like it's straining. Taft wonders how much more he could do. Carl pushes his weights up again.

"Take your time," Taft says. Taft walks down to the bathroom to shave. He turns on the water in the sink and brushes his teeth while he waits for it to get hot. He wishes he felt better. He doesn't have enough free time to not feel well for a day.

Something was wrong when I woke up. I was lying in a river of sweat and the pain that was in my neck was pulling all the air out of the room. I was being shot over and over again. Every time my heart beat the gun went off. I heard it. I could feel myself shaking.

"Marion?" I said, but it was hard to make the word. "Marion?"

"I'm right here." She got out of her twin bed and came and knelt next to mine. She put her hand on my chest. It was so cool. It made me think of water. "You want that pill now?"

It is something like indigestion, but he hasn't eaten anything since supper last night. Taft stands in front of the mirror, look-

261

ing for what's wrong. He thinks the dark blue bathrobe makes him look pale. He opens the medicine chest and takes out a bottle of Rolaids. He has just gotten the lid off when it comes. The first wave hits him in the chest and knocks him back against the bathtub. He is lying on the rose colored bath mat, trying to catch his breath. It is being crushed out of him by something. Something is sitting on his chest. There is that pain he remembers, the one in his left arm that is going all the way up to his jaw. He feels it in his shoulder and neck. He waits for it to stop, but it isn't stopping. He slides over onto his side and lies on the floor. Everything is clear now, what he's done, what he should have done. He is more afraid than he could have thought possible. He calls out, not a name but a low, long sound. He calls until he can't anymore. There shouldn't be this much pain. Not for anything.

Carl hears something. He has just come in from the garage.

"Dad?"

He can see him from the kitchen. That's the way the house is, everything in one straight line. The bathroom is at the end of the hall. Carl sees Taft lying on the white tile floor, the bath mat pushed under one shoulder.

"Dad?"

Carl is running down the hall. He's only got on his gym shorts and tennis shoes now. He took off his shirt in the garage.

I am there when he gets there. I am standing in the bathtub behind them.

"Dad?"

Carl takes Taft's head and shoulders and pulls them up into his lap. Taft is white and sweating. He is holding his left arm in his right.

"Are you all right?" I say. "Are you all right?"

"I'm going to call the hospital," Carl says. There is so much fear. He is petting his father's head wildly, over and over again.

"Stay with me," Taft says.

"I'll just be gone for one second."

"Stay," Taft says. He is sure of it now. He is afraid to be alone.

"I'll stay with him," I say. "Go on and call. Run!"

But Carl stays. He listens to his father. Taft is slipping.

"Pinch his nose and open his mouth," I tell Carl from the bathtub. "Blow two deep breaths into his lungs. Give him oxygen."

Carl is petting his father. He pulls the bath mat over Taft's chest. Carl's bare back is narrow and smooth as he leans over.

"Straddle his chest. Put the heel of your hand two finger widths above the breastbone. Cover your hand with your other hand and push down fifteen times. Listen to me. I took a class. The doctor who owns the bar made me take a class before I could have the job. Two breaths, push fifteen times, two breaths, fifteen times. Do this, Carl. Listen."

"Dad?"

Taft's eyes are open. He is looking at Carl. He almost sees him. The blankets over the windows make the room too dark. It is impossible to get up now.

"I'm going to call," Carl says. "I'll only be a second. I have to have some help."

"Blow in his mouth," I say. I crouch down in the tub to be closer to them. I could reach out. I could touch his hair.

"One second," Carl says. Taft doesn't answer and Carl slides his shoulders back onto the floor. He is holding his father's head in his hand, but he can't seem to put it down on the floor. The floor would be cold. His arms are weak from so much lifting. They tremble. He grabs a towel off the rack and rolls it into a sort of pillow which he puts under Taft's head. Then he runs to his parents' bedroom and dials 911 and waits and waits, but the phone is dead. He slams it down and runs into the kitchen. But that one is gone too. He doesn't think they might just be un-plugged, that his mother unplugged them just this morning so his father could have a little rest. Carl runs back into the bath-room. Nothing has changed. "I'll just be a second," he says loudly, and he runs out the door to find somebody who can help.

But Taft is dead. I know. I am there with him when it hap-pens. The last thing he thought of was pain and it stays with him on his face. His eyes are open. He is looking for Carl to come back. I slide down into the bathtub and press my cheek against the cold white enamel. Outside I hear Carl yelling. It sounds like he's running around the house in circles. It sounds like he will never find anyone to bring him back inside.

When I woke up, Marion was dressed and her bed was made. She was sitting on the made bed, reading a book. "Are you still alive?" she said.

"I am."

"It might be hard to talk for a while. Don't strain yourself." Marion looked like she got less sleep than I did. There was a black thumbprint under each of her eyes. "All night I was think-ing about the neck," she told me. "Do you know what the chances are of somebody getting shot in the neck and coming out of it as well as you? Everything's in the neck. All the veins and nerves, the spinal cord and the spine. Christ, the spine. I can't believe you're even here."

"I'm here."

Marion put down her book and came and sat on the edge of my bed. She wiped my forehead off with a damp towel. "You had a bad night."

"I know."

"Reminded me of when Franklin was little and he'd get those

awful flus. Remember that? Every time I'd think he was going to die. His fevers ran a hundred and three, a hundred and four."

"I remember."

"I think that's when I decided to go to nursing school. I thought a person couldn't have a child without knowing how to save his life all the time." She put her hand on my head and smiled at me. It was a comfort having her there. I'd known Marion for a long time.

"You tell Franklin?"

"I told him you had an accident. That you were upstairs sleeping. He wants to come up and see you, but I'm going to wait until that fever is down some. Better he sees you when you're more yourself." She picked up my glass of water from the bedside table and took a long drink. "One of these days you're going to have to tell me what all this was about," she said. "One day when you can talk and we have plenty of time. I want to know what happened."

"Sure."

"And that girl. You'll tell me about her too. I'd say it was none of my business, but the way you showed up here last night I figure I'm entitled."

"Sure."

She slid a pill out of each of the bottles. "I'm going to dope you up again," she said. "See if we can't get a jump on the pain this time." She wasn't asking me. She put her strong arm underneath my back and pulled me up so I could swallow. She held me there, propped up, while I took the pill. "They never teach you how to do these things in school. This is on-the-job stuff you're seeing here." She settled me back against the headboard so I was sitting up. "You're going to feel better soon, tomorrow, the day after. You'll be surprised. You get shot and it'll turn out to be nothing at all. When it's all over you'll be sitting in the bar saying, Hell, I take bullets as a pastime. When I see a bullet coming I jump in front of it." She took a paper sack off the dresser and took out some scissors and tape and gauze. "I'm going to change this dressing while I've got you sitting up. I've got some four-by-fours in here somewhere. Here we go." She held up a package for me to see. "You'd think that a man who had a child might not want to get shot. You'd think he might step to the side."

"Listen."

"I'm not listening because I don't want you talking. Just hold still. This shouldn't hurt."

I felt the cool scissors slide inside the bandage and then I heard her snipping. All that hurt me was to see such pain on Marion's face.

"You've got a hole in your neck," she said. She crumpled up the old bandages and put them in the bag. "I'm going to see if I can't clean this up a little. Just keep your head up, eyes straight ahead." I could feel her swabbing at me. She was trying her best not to let it hurt me and I was trying not to show her that it did. "Just a little bit of infection. It's not so bad. But you've got some blood here."

"Don't tell me," I said. I'd wanted to say that last night at the doctor's.

She smiled. "I don't blame you." She taped on a new set of pads and then wound gauze around my neck. "You look real sporty now. Like you're wearing an ascot." She picked up the trash and put it all back inside the bag. "It's something having you so quiet. If I said so, you'd have to sit there all day and listen to me. I would have shot you myself years ago if I knew that's what it would take to get you to listen to me."

I started to laugh, but it hurt like hell.

"Calm yourself or I'm going to get you a bigger pill."

Mrs. Woodmoore came in carrying a tray. However sorry she

was about my being hurt, you could tell she liked having someone sick in bed that she could take care of. "How's John Nickel
this morning?"

"Getting better," Marion said.

"I made you a lunch of nothing you'd like," Mrs. Woodmoore
said, putting the tray down on Marion's bed. "That's what she
told me to do, Jell-O and broth, apple juice."

"I'll give it to him," Marion said.

"You get yourself downstairs and see your son. He wants to
know what's going on up here. I'll make sure this one eats. We
don't spend near enough time together, me and John. Everybody
wants to know what's going on. Your father and your sister have
been asking questions all morning. That nice young man Wallace came by with flowers. He says everybody at work is going to
want to know."

"All right, all right, I'll go downstairs." Marion sighed and
pushed herself up. When she got to the door she turned around
and looked at me. This Marion wasn't so different from the old
one, not when she was standing in her little girl's bedroom being
nice. "Don't keep him up forever," she said. "Let that Demerol
knock him out."

"Just as long as it takes him to eat broth."

It was nice outside. I could see out the window. The lilac bush
had grown rangy and tall and was pressed up against the second-
story glass. Mrs. Woodmoore never let her husband trim the lilac and now it had turned into a sort of tree. I had spent a lot of
time in that back yard over the years. I knew those lilacs as well as
I knew anything.

Mrs. Woodmoore went and shut the door. "I've got to talk
to you," she said. She put the tray in my lap and handed me the
spoon. I couldn't look down very well, so she moved my hand so
that it was right over the bowl. "That girl, Fay, she wanted me

to tell you she wouldn't be coming over. She was afraid you'd think she didn't care about how you were doing. I told her you wouldn't think that."

Fay not coming over? "Course not."

"Quiet," she said, looking at the door. "Eat the soup. I don't want Marion knowing about this. Fay told me things last night. Poor baby, she was so upset. You could imagine she would be. She told me about it being her brother and about her being in love with you."

I was trying to make sense of this, trying to picture Fay pouring out her heart to Marion's mother.

"What you have to understand is that now her mother and her uncle and aunt, they're all going to know, about Carl's problems and her working in the bar. As soon as they found Carl it was all going to come out. Fay said she figured her uncle and aunt were probably looking for her last night. And I think it's only right that those people know what's going on with those children. It's too much of a burden for a young girl to be keeping so many secrets."

I couldn't make sense of these names coming out of Mrs. Woodmoore's mouth.

"Everything's got to be different now. It wasn't what she wanted, but people have to start thinking about what's best. She was thinking about what was best for you and your family, too. That shows real maturity in a girl her age. And I'll say it, she's right. Intended or not, she's brought you a lot of trouble. Just look at you here." She took the spoon from me and fed me some broth. I hadn't been eating at all. "You've got other things to take care of, much as you might like that girl. You're too smart a man to get caught up in something like that. Take a little of the Jell-O now, just so Marion can see you tried some."

I opened my mouth and she slipped it inside. If you don't see the color there's no telling what flavor it's supposed to be. Fay was in the dining room now. They were all sitting around that big table. Carl's arm was in a cast and his head was down. The uncle was talking. I could see it from the window, but I couldn't make out what he was saying.

"You go to sleep," Mrs. Woodmoore said, and picked up the tray. "We can talk about this some other time. I just wanted to let you know. It was so important to her that you didn't think she just never showed up. She was a sweet girl. I could sure see how a person would want to help her."

I eased myself down into the bed and closed my eyes. There were her little hands and the curve of her neck. She was walking away from the bar in a knit cap. She was standing in the light at Shiloh and everything was behind her, the monument and the tombstones and the Tennessee River.

I couldn't keep track of time. When I woke up I didn't know if I'd been asleep fifteen minutes or three hours. It was a sleep so heavy and dreamless that my mouth felt thick with it. I wondered if Marion had put something in that last pill. My neck was stiff but maybe not quite so sore and when I pulled up my hand to touch it I brushed somebody next to me, sleeping in the single bed. I hoisted myself over on my side, but I already knew. There was only one person small enough to fit in that little bed without waking me. Franklin's head fell back over the top of the pillow and his mouth was open. I could see all of his teeth. Not a single filling. Franklin didn't mess around with sleeping. He did it fast and hard. He must have gotten into bed with me to see how I was doing and then conked out himself while he was waiting for me to wake up. Franklin never could watch anybody else sleep. That's how we used to get him to bed when he was little, me and Marion would sit in our chairs and let our eyes close, fake soft snores and drop our chins. Franklin would go out in no time.

But he was a big boy now, he'd caught on to those baby tricks. Asleep in that little bed that had been his mother's, he didn't look too old. Big, bigger than maybe I would have liked, but he wasn't gone from me yet. His blue and red striped T-shirt had ridden way up past his stomach and I ran my hand over his warm skin before pulling it down. There was never anything so smooth. I took hold of his wrist. I could feel the little bones. I could smell his warm breath.

Without waking up, Franklin rolled in towards me. He pressed himself against my arm. He crossed a leg over my leg. Then we were quiet for a while. We stayed there, just like that. When he was with me there was nothing bad that could happen. That was the only way to make sure someone was going to stay safe, you had to keep them with you, close, where you could keep an eye on things. It wasn't possible for me to look after all of them, not every day, every minute, the way they needed looking after. The thing was, you had to choose. Pick one job and do it right. I was picking Franklin.

I had had enough of sleeping for a while, but that didn't mean I was going anywhere. It hadn't been bad not going to the hospital. I'd tell that to Marion when she came back in. Where was I going to find a hospital room like this? A good view and my boy right up in the bed with me.

Taft pulls a green sweater over Carl's head. He's always afraid he's going to tear his ears off, the neck fits so close. Taft's wife never seems to mind the ears. She doesn't worry about things the way he does. Taft is watching the children while she makes the trip to the big grocery in Oak Ridge. "Put your arms out," he says. Carl raises one arm and Taft threads it through the sleeve. "Other arm now," Taft tells him.

Fay has gotten her own sweater, a cardigan. She has buttoned it up by herself. Fay likes to do things herself now, she's at that age. Taft calls her a big girl and big sister and she likes that.

It's a Saturday, the last part of February. For just less than a month, both of Taft's children are four years old. Carl turned four the first of February and Fay will be five next week. She has been telling people she was five since Christmas. Taft puts on a denim shirt over his T-shirt and rolls up the sleeves, checks the laces on Carl's shoes.

"I'm going outside," Carl says.

"In a minute," Taft tells him.

"In a minute," Fay says.

He doesn't like Fay saying she's five. He's still wondering how he got to be twenty-six and he thinks it's partly his own fault. He rushed himself, saying he was older when he was sixteen so he could go get a beer with his friends, saying he was older to the draft board who turned him down anyway on account of a hernia, getting married right away, before there was any thought of other girls or other ways things could work out, but that was fine. Look at these babies. Even if he did rush himself, it isn't a bad place he's rushed to.

Taft sits back on his heels, hands Fay a Kleenex. Everybody's ready. It's cool outside. In March there's no telling. One day it's seventy-five and the next day there's snow. He takes the kids out the back door, watches them down the steps, though they can do that fine. They rent a two-bedroom house at the end of the street and the street borders on a field. The edge of the field takes a sharp slope down to a creek. Fay and Carl love the creek. They'd stay down there all the time if Taft would let them, but there are strict rules, not going without a grown-up, no putting your feet in when the water was high, which it was now from the snow melting off in the mountains. The creek makes Taft and his wife nervous, the way it gets deep in the middle, gets fast once it starts to turn. There are always other people's kids playing down there alone and Taft wonders what those parents are thinking.

"I can get there first," Fay says, and takes off past the end of the gravel and into the grass. Carl runs after her on automatic, doesn't even think, just runs. Taft lets them go. It's a long field, let them run themselves out a little, he thinks, then they'll be easier to rein in. His children are blond, the way Taft had been as a child, though he isn't now. They are running, running, gaining on the water.

Taft watches them, but he's thinking about the washer he's been meaning to change in the bathroom sink, wondering if there's one in his toolbox that will fit. He's thinking about work and wishing he had been able to get some overtime this weekend, but he doesn't have enough seniority for overtime. When he looks up again the kids are farther away than he'd like. "Fay," he calls, "mind your brother. Wait till I get there before you go down."

Fay stops and turns and smiles. Just the sound of his voice brings her around. She waves while Carl shoots past her.

"Carl." Taft tries to make himself sound stern. He moves a little faster, into a kind of horse trot. He isn't afraid of anything. As close as he is, from here to there, nothing can happen. He is twenty-six. His hair hasn't started to thin and his hearing hasn't been damaged by the noise of the machines in the carpet factory and he hasn't had that partial bridge yet. He is still fast enough to outrun any sort of trouble and there is no trouble because Fay has stopped in the middle of the field and Carl has stopped at the edge before the slope down to the water and they are both waiting for their father. They are doing exactly what they've been told.

Carl raises both of his arms over his head and his green sweater pulls up, showing a sliver of stomach. Taft passes Fay and is almost to Carl. He isn't running because he doesn't need to. From where he is now he could practically catch him if he were to fall.

"Hey," Carl yells. "Watch me."